Not a Penny More,
Not a Penny Less

Not a Penny More,
Not a Penny Less

Jeffrey Archer

BOOK CLUB ASSOCIATES LONDON

Printed in Great Britain by
Richard Clay (The Chaucer Press), Ltd,
Bungay, Suffolk

To Mary
and the fat men

ACKNOWLEDGEMENTS

I acknowledge all the help I received from so many people in writing this book and wish to thank them: David Niven, Jr., who made me do it, Sir Noel and Lady Hall who made it possible, Adrian Metcalfe, Anthony Rentoul, Colin Emson, Ted Francis, Godfrey Barker, Willy West, Madame Tellegen, David Stein, Christian Neffe, Dr John Vance, Dr David Weeden, the Rev. Leslie Styler, Robert Gasser, Professor Jim Bolton, and Jamie Clark; Gail and Jo for putting it together; and my wife, Mary, for the hours spent correcting and editing.

Not a Penny More,
Not a Penny Less

PROLOGUE

'Jörg, expect $7 million from Crédit Parisien in the no. 2 account by 6 p.m. tonight, Central European time, and place it overnight with first-class banks and triple "A" commercial names. Otherwise, invest it in the overnight Euro-dollar market. Understood?'

'Yes, Harvey.'

'Place $1 million in the Banco do Minas Gerais, Rio de Janeiro, in the names of Silverman and Elliott and cancel the call loan at Barclays Bank, Lombard Street. Understood?'

'Yes, Harvey.'

'Buy gold on my commodity account until you reach $10 million and then hold until you receive further instructions. Try and buy in the troughs and don't rush—be patient. Understood?'

'Yes, Harvey.'

Harvey Metcalfe realized the last instruction was unnecessary. Jörg Birrer was one of the most conservative bankers in Zürich and, more important to Harvey, had over the past twenty-five years proved to be one of the shrewdest.

'Can you join me at Wimbledon on Tuesday, June 25th at 2 p.m., Centre Court, my usual debenture seat?'

'Yes, Harvey.'

The telephone clicked into place. Harvey never said goodbye. He did not understand the niceties of life and it was too late to start learning now. He picked up the phone, dialled the seven digits which would give him the Lincoln Trust in Boston, and asked for his secretary.

'Miss Fish?'

'Yes, sir.'

'Look out the file on Prospecta Oil and destroy it. Destroy any correspondence connected with it and leave absolutely no trace. Understood?'

'Yes, sir.'

The telephone clicked again. Harvey Metcalfe had given similar

9

orders three times in the last twenty-five years and by now Miss Fish had learnt not to question him.

Harvey breathed deeply, almost a sigh, a quiet exhalation of triumph. He was now worth at least $25 million and nothing could stop him. He opened a bottle of Krug champagne 1964, imported by Hedges & Butler of London. He sipped it slowly and lit a Romeo y Julieta Churchill, which an Italian immigrant smuggled in for him in boxes of two hundred and fifty once a month from Cuba. He settled back for a mild celebration. In Boston, Massachusetts, it was 12.20 p.m.—nearly time for lunch.

In Harley Street, Bond Street, the King's Road and Magdalen College, Oxford, it was 6.20 p.m. Four men, unknown to each other, checked the market price of Prospecta Oil in the final edition of the London *Evening Standard*. It was $9.10. All four of them were rich men, looking forward to consolidating their already successful careers. Tomorrow they would be penniless.

ONE

Making a million legally has always been difficult. Making a million illegally has always been a little easier. Keeping a million when you have made it is perhaps the most difficult of all. Henryk Metelski was one of those rare men who managed all three. Even if the million he had made legally came after the million he had made illegally, what put him a yard ahead of the others was that he managed to keep it all.

Henryk Metelski was born on the Lower East Side of New York on May 17th, 1909, and lived through the Depression in his most formative years. His parents were Polish and had emigrated to America at the turn of the century. Henryk's father was a baker by profession and had easily found a job in New York, where the immigrant Poles specialized in baking black rye bread and running small restaurants. Both parents would have liked Henryk to have been an academic success, but he was not gifted in that direction and never became an outstanding pupil at his High School. He was a sly, smart little boy, unloved by the school authorities for his indifference to stirring tales of the War of Independence and the Liberty Bell, and for his control of the underground school market in soft drugs and liquor. Little Henryk did not consider that the best things in life were free, and the pursuit of money and power came to him as naturally as does the pursuit of a mouse to a cat.

When Henryk was a pimply and flourishing fourteen-year-old his father died of what we now know as cancer. His mother survived her husband's death by no more than a few months, leaving their only child to bring himself up. Henryk should have gone into the district orphanage for destitute children, but in the mid-1920s it was not hard for a boy to disappear in New York—though it was harder to survive. Henryk became a master of survival, a schooling which was to prove very useful in later life.

He knocked around the East Side of New York with his belt tightened and his eyes open, shining shoes here, washing dishes there, looking always for an entrance to the maze at the heart of which

11

lay wealth and prestige. He discovered one when his room-mate, Jan Pelnik, a messenger boy on the New York Stock Exchange, put himself temporarily out of action with a sausage garnished with salmonella. Henryk, deputed to report this mishap to the Chief Messenger, upgraded food-poisoning to tuberculosis, and talked himself into the ensuing job vacancy. Then he changed his room, donned his new uniform and started work.

Most of the messages he delivered during the early 'twenties read 'Buy'. Many of them were quickly acted upon, for this was a boom era. Henryk saw men of little ability make fortunes while he was nothing but an observer. His instincts directed him towards those individuals who made more money in a week on the Exchange than he would in a lifetime on his salary.

He set about learning to understand how the Stock Exchange operated, he listened to conversations, read messages and found out which newspapers to study. By the age of eighteen he had had four years' experience on Wall Street: four years which to most messenger boys would have been nothing more than walking across floors handing over bits of paper; four years which to Henryk Metelski were the equivalent of a Master's Degree from Harvard Business School (not that he knew then that one day he would lecture to that august body).

In July 1927 he took a mid-morning message to Halgarten & Co., a well-established broking firm, making his usual detour via the wash-room. He had perfected a system whereby he would lock himself into a cubicle, read the message he was carrying, decide whether it was of any value to him and if it was, telephone Witold Gronowich, an older Pole who ran a small insurance brokerage for his fellow countrymen. Henryk reckoned to pick up $20 to $25 a week extra with the information he supplied. Gronowich, being unable to place large sums on the market, never led any leaks back to his young informant.

Sitting in the washroom, Henryk began to realize that he was reading a message of some considerable significance. The Governor of Texas was going to grant the Standard Oil Company permission to complete a pipeline from Chicago to Mexico, all other public bodies involved having already agreed to the proposal. The market was aware that the company had been trying to obtain this final permission for nearly a year. The message was to be passed direct to John D. Rockefeller's broker, Tucker Anthony, immediately. The granting of this pipeline would open up the entire North to a ready

12

access of oil, and that would mean increased profits. It was obvious to Henryk that Standard Oil shares would rise steadily on the market once the news had broken, especially as Standard Oil already controlled 90 per cent of the oil refineries in America.

In normal circumstances Henryk would have sent this information immediately to Mr Gronowich, and was about to do so when he noticed a rather overweight man (who had obviously had too many Wall Street lunches) also leaving the washroom, drop a piece of paper. As there was no one else about at the time Henryk picked it up and retreated once again to his private cubicle thinking at best it would be another piece of information. In fact, it was a cheque for $50,000 made out to cash from a Mrs Rose Rennick.

Henryk thought quickly. He left the washroom at speed and was soon standing on Wall Street itself. He made his way to a small coffee-shop on Rector Street where he carefully worked out his plan and then he acted on it immediately.

First, he cashed the cheque at a branch of the Morgan Bank on the south-west side of Wall Street, knowing that as he was wearing the smart uniform of a messenger at the Exchange it would be assumed that he was no more than a carrier for some distinguished firm. He then returned to the Exchange and acquired from a floor broker 2,500 Standard Oil shares at $19.85, leaving himself $126.61 change after brokerage charges. He placed the $126.61 in a Deposit Account at the Morgan Bank. Then, sweating in tense anticipation of an announcement from the Governor's office, he put himself through the motions of a normal day's work, too preoccupied with Standard Oil even to make a detour via the washroom with the messages he carried.

No announcement came. Henryk was not to know that it was being held up until the Exchange had officially closed at 4 p.m. because the Governor himself was buying shares anywhere and everywhere he could lay his grubby hands on them, pushing the price up to $20.05 by the close of business without any official announcement. Henryk went home that night petrified that he had made a disastrous mistake. He had visions of going to jail, losing his job and everything he had built up over the past four years.

He was unable to sleep that night and became steadily more restless in his small room. At 1 a.m. he could stand it no longer, so he rose, shaved, dressed and took a train to Grand Central Station. From there he walked to Times Square where with trembling hands he bought the first edition of the *Wall Street Journal*. And there it was shrieking across the headlines:

GOVERNOR GRANTS OIL PIPELINE RIGHTS TO ROCKEFELLER

and a secondary headline:

STANDARD OIL SHARES, HEAVY TRADING EXPECTED

Dazed, Henryk walked to the nearest all-night café, on East 42nd Street, where he ordered a large hamburger and French fries, which he devoured like a man eating his last breakfast before facing the electric chair, rather than his first on the way to fortune. He read the full details on page one, which spread over to page fourteen, and by 4 a.m. he had bought the first three editions of the *New York Times* and the first two editions of the *Herald Tribune*. Henryk hurried home, giddy and elated, and threw on his uniform. He arrived at the Stock Exchange at 8 a.m. and imitated a day's work, thinking only of the second part of his plan.

When the Stock Exchange opened officially, Henryk went over to the Morgan Bank to borrow $50,000 against the 2,500 Standard Oil shares, which had opened that morning at $21.30. He placed the $50,000 in his deposit account and instructed the bank to give him a draft for $50,000 to be made out to Mrs Rose Rennick. He left the building and looked up the address and telephone number of his unknowing benefactor.

Mrs Rennick, a widow who lived off the investments left by her late husband, rented a small apartment on Park Avenue, one of the most fashionable parts of New York. She was somewhat surprised to receive a call from a Henryk Metelski, asking to see her on an urgent private matter. A final mention of Halgarten & Co. gave her a little more confidence and she agreed to a meeting at the Waldorf-Astoria at 4 p.m.

Henryk had never been to the Waldorf-Astoria, but after four years on the Stock Exchange there were few hotels or restaurants he had not heard mentioned in other people's conversations. He knew that Mrs Rennick was more likely to have tea with him there than agree to see a man with a name like Henryk Metelski in her own apartment, especially as his Polish accent was more pronounced over the telephone than on meeting him face to face.

As Henryk stood in the soft carpeted foyer of the Waldorf-Astoria,

14

he blushed for his sartorial naivety. He imagined everybody to be staring at him and he buried his short, amply-covered frame in the large leather chair. Some of the other patrons of the Waldorf-Astoria were amply covered too, though Henryk felt it was more likely to have been *Pommes de Terre Maître d'Hôtel* that had caused their obesity than French fries. It was too late for him to wish he had put a little less grease on his black, wavy hair and to regret that his shoes were so down-at-heel. He scratched at an irritating pustule on the side of his mouth. His suit, in which he felt so assured and prosperous among his friends, was shiny, skimpy, cheap and loud. He did not match up to the decor, still less to the patrons of the hotel, and, feeling inadequate for the first time in his life, he edged gingerly into the Jefferson Room, stationed himself behind a copy of the *New Yorker*, and prayed for his guest to arrive quickly. Waiters fluttered deferentially around the well-provendered tables, ignoring Henryk with instinctive superciliousness. One did nothing but circle the tearoom delicately proffering lump sugar from silver tongs in a white-gloved hand: Henryk was enormously impressed.

Rose Rennick arrived a few minutes later with two small dogs and an outrageous hat. Henryk thought she looked over sixty, overweight, over-made-up and overdressed, but she had a warm smile and seemed to know everyone, moving from table to table, chatting to the regular Waldorf-Astoria tea set. She eventually reached what she had rightly guessed to be Henryk's table, and was rather startled by him, not just because he was strangely dressed, but because he looked even younger than his eighteen years.

Mrs Rennick ordered tea while Henryk told his story of how there had been an unfortunate mistake with her cheque, which had been wrongly made over to his firm at the Stock Exchange the day before. His firm had instructed him to return the cheque immediately and to say how sorry they were. Henryk then passed over the draft for $50,000 and told her he would lose his job if she decided to take the matter any further, as he had been entirely responsible for the mistake. Mrs Rennick had, in fact, only been informed of the missing cheque that morning and did not realize that it had been cashed, as it would have taken a few days to go through her account. Henryk's perfectly genuine anxiety as he stumbled through his tale would have convinced a more critical observer of human nature than Mrs Rennick. Readily she agreed to let the matter drop, only too pleased to have her money back, and as it was in the form of a draft from the

15

Morgan Bank she had lost nothing. Henryk breathed a sigh of relief and for the first time began to relax and enjoy himself. He even called for the man with the sugar and silver tongs.

After a respectable period of time had passed, Henryk explained that he must return to work, thanked Mrs Rennick, paid the bill and left. Outside in the street he whistled with relief. His new shirt was soaked in sweat (Mrs Rennick would have called it perspiration) but he was out in the open and could breathe again. His first major operation had been a success.

He stood in Park Avenue, amused that the venue for his confrontation with Mrs Rennick had been the Waldorf-Astoria, as it was the very hotel where John D. Rockefeller (the President of Standard Oil) had a suite. Henryk had arrived on foot and used the main entrance, while Mr Rockefeller had earlier arrived by subway and taken his private lift to the Waldorf Towers. Few New Yorkers were aware that Rockefeller had his own private station built 50 ft below the Waldorf-Astoria so that he did not have to travel eight blocks to Grand Central Station, there being no stop between there and 125th Street. (The station remains to this day, but no Rockefellers live at the Waldorf-Astoria and the train never stops there.) While Henryk was discussing his $50,000 with Mrs Rennick, Rockefeller debated an investment of $5,000,000 with President Coolidge's Secretary of the Treasury, Andrew W. Mellon.

The next day Henryk returned to work as normal. He knew he must cash the shares before the end of five days to clear his debt with the Morgan Bank and the stockbroker—the account on the New York Stock Exchange runs for five business days or seven calendar days. On the last day of the account the shares were standing at $23.30. He sold at $23.15, clearing his overdraft of $49,625 and, after expenses, realized a profit of $7,490 which he left deposited with the Morgan Bank.

Over the next three years, Henryk stopped ringing Mr Gronowich, and started dealing for himself, in small amounts to begin with. Times were still good, and while he didn't always make a profit, he had learnt to master the occasional bear market as well as the more common boom. His system in the bear market was to sell short—not a practice for the ethical in business, but he soon mastered the art of selling shares he didn't own in expectation of a subsequent fall in price. His instinct for the market trends refined as rapidly as his taste in clothes, and the guile learnt in the back streets of the Lower East

16

Side stood him in good stead. Henryk had discovered that the whole world was a jungle—sometimes the lions and tigers wore suits.

When the market collapsed in 1929 he had turned his $7,490 into $51,000 in liquid assets, having sold on every share he possessed. He had moved to a smart flat in Brooklyn and was driving a rather ostentatious Stutz. Henryk had realized at an early age that he had entered upon life with three main disadvantages—his name, background and impecunity. The money problem was solving itself, so he decided to expunge the others. Firstly, he made application to change his name by court order to Harvey David Metcalfe. Secondly, he cut off all contact with his friends from the Polish Community, and so in May 1930 he came of age with a new name and a new background.

It was later that year that he met Roger Sharpley, a young man from Boston who had inherited his father's import and export company, which specialized in the import of whisky and the export of furs. Educated at Choate and later at Dartmouth College, Sharpley had the assurance and charm of the Boston set, so often envied by the rest of America. He was tall and fair and looked as if he had come from Viking stock, and with his air of the gifted amateur, he found most things came easily to him, especially women. He was in total contrast to Harvey. It was that contrast which brought them together.

Roger's only ambition was to join the Navy, but after graduating from Dartmouth he had had to return to the family firm because of his father's ill-health. He had only been with the firm a few months when his father died. Roger would have liked to have sold Sharpley & Son to the first bidder, but his father, Henry, had made a codicil to his will to the effect that if the firm were sold before Roger's fortieth birthday (that being the last day one can enlist for the U.S. Navy), the money was to be divided between his relatives.

Harvey gave Roger's problem some considerable thought, and after two lengthy sessions with a skilful New York lawyer, suggested the following course of action to Roger: Harvey would buy 49 per cent of Sharpley & Son for $100,000 and the first $20,000 profit each year. At the age of forty Roger would relinquish the remaining 51 per cent for a further $100,000. There would be three Board members—Harvey, Roger and one nominated by Harvey, giving him overall control. As far as Harvey was concerned, Roger could join the Navy and come to the annual shareholders' meeting.

Roger could not believe his luck. He did not consult anyone at Sharpley & Son, realizing only too well that they would try to talk him out of it. Harvey had counted on this and had assessed his quarry accurately. Roger only gave the proposition a few days' consideration before he allowed the legal papers to be drawn up in New York, far enough away from Boston to be sure the firm did not learn what was going on. Meanwhile, Harvey returned to the Morgan Bank, where he was now looked upon as a reliable customer. The manager agreed to help him in his new enterprise with a loan of $50,000 to add to his own $50,000, enabling Harvey to acquire 49 per cent of Sharpley & Son, and become its fifth President. The legal documents were signed in New York on October 14th, 1930.

Roger left speedily for Newport, Rhode Island, to commence his Officer's Training Course in the U.S. Navy. Harvey left for Grand Central Station to catch the train for Boston. His days as a messenger boy on the New York Stock Exchange were over. He was twenty-one years of age and the President of his own company.

What looked like disaster to most, Harvey could always manage to turn into triumph. The American people were still suffering from Prohibition, and although Harvey could export furs, he could not import whisky. This had caused the fall in the company profits over the past few years. But Harvey found that with a little bribery, involving the Mayor of Boston, the Chief of Police and the Customs officials on the Canadian border, plus a payment to the Mafia to ensure his products reached the restaurants and speak-easys, somehow the whisky imports went up rather than down. Sharpley & Son lost its more respectable and long-serving staff, and replaced them with the animals that suited Harvey Metcalfe's particular jungle.

From 1930 to 1933 Harvey went from strength to strength, but when Prohibition was finally lifted by President Roosevelt after overwhelming public demand, the excitement went with it, and Harvey allowed the company to continue to deal in whisky and furs while he branched out into new fields. In 1933 Sharpley & Son celebrated a hundred years in business. In three years Harvey had lost 97 years of goodwill and doubled the profits. After a further twelve years he had amassed several million dollars and was becoming bored. He decided it was time to part with Sharpley & Son. He had in fifteen years built up the profits from $30,000 to $910,000. He sold the company for $7,100,000, paying $100,000 to the widow of Captain Roger Sharpley of the U.S. Navy and keeping $7,000,000 for himself.

Harvey celebrated his thirty-sixth birthday by buying at a cost of

$4 million a small, ailing bank in Boston called the Lincoln Trust. At the time it had an income of approximately $500,000 a year, a prestigious building in the centre of Boston and an unblemished reputation. Harvey enjoyed being the President of a bank, but it did nothing for his honesty. Every strange deal in the Boston area seemed to go through the Lincoln Trust, and although Harvey increased the profits to $2 million per annum in a matter of five years, his personal reputation could not have fallen lower.

The next turning-point in Harvey's life came when he met Arlene Hunter in the spring of 1949. She was the only daughter of the President of the First City Bank of Boston. Harvey had never taken any real interest in women. His driving force had been making money, and although he considered the opposite sex a useful relaxation in his free time, on balance he found them an inconvenience. But having now reached middle age and having no heir to leave his fortune to, he calculated that it was time to get married and have a son. As with everything else he had done in his life, he considered the problem very carefully.

Harvey met Arlene when she was thirty-one. She could not have been a greater contrast to Harvey. She was nearly six foot, slim and although not unattractive, she lacked confidence and was beginning to feel marriage had passed her by. Most of her school friends were now on their second divorce and felt rather sorry for her. Arlene enjoyed Harvey's extravagant ways after her father's prudish discipline; she often thought that her father was to blame for her never feeling at ease with men of her own age. She had only had one affair, and that had been a disastrous failure because of her total innocence. Arlene's father did not approve of Harvey, which only made him more attractive to her. Not that her father had approved of any of the men she had associated with, but on this occasion he was right. Harvey on the other hand realized that to marry the First City Bank of Boston with the Lincoln Trust could only benefit him, and with that in mind he set out, as he always did, to win.

Arlene and Harvey were married in 1951. They settled in Harvey's Lincoln home and very shortly afterwards Arlene became pregnant. She gave Harvey a daughter almost a year to the day of their marriage.

They christened her Rosalie. She was the apple of Harvey's eye, and he was very disappointed when a prolapse closely followed by a hysterectomy ensured that Arlene would not be able to bear him any more children. He sent Rosalie to Bennetts, the best girls' school in Washington, and from there she won a place at Vassar to major in English. This even pleased old man Hunter, who had grown to tolerate Harvey and adore his grand-daughter. After gaining her degree, Rosalie continued her education at the Sorbonne because of a fierce disagreement with her father concerning the type of friends she was keeping, particularly the ones with long hair who didn't want to go to Vietnam. The final crunch came when Rosalie suggested that morals were not decided only by the length of one's hair or one's political views.

Harvey, meanwhile, filled his home with beautiful antiques and paintings, becoming a connoisseur of the Impressionist period and finding a genuine love of the style, a love that had developed over many years and had been kindled in the strangest way. A client of Sharpley & Son was about to go bankrupt while still owing a fairly large sum of money to the company. Harvey got wind of it and went round to confront him, but the rot had set in and there was no hope of securing any cash. Harvey had no intention of leaving empty-handed and took with him the man's only tangible asset, a Renoir valued at $10,000.

It had been Harvey's intention to sell the picture before it could be proved that he was a preferred creditor, but he became entranced with the delicate pastel shades and from this newly acquired prize came a desire to own more. When he realized that pictures were not only a good investment, but that he actually liked them as well, his collection and his love grew hand in hand. By the early 1970s, Harvey had a Manet, two Monets, a Renoir, two Picassos, a Pissarro, a Utrillo, a Cézanne, and most of the recognized lesser names. His desire was to own a Van Gogh, and only recently he had failed to acquire *L'Hôpital de St Paul à St Rémy* at the Sotheby Parke Bernet Gallery in New York, when Dr Armand Hammer of Occidental Petroleum had outbid him—$1,200,000 had been just a little too much. Earlier, in 1966, he had failed to acquire Lot 49, *Mademoiselle Ravoux*, from Christie Manson & Woods, the London art dealers; the Rev. Theodore Pitcairn, representing the Lord's New Church in Bryn Athyn, Pennsylvania, had pushed him over the top and whetted his appetite further. The Lord giveth and on that occasion the Lord had taken away. Although it was not fully appreciated in Boston, it was recognized elsewhere that Harvey had one of the finest

Impressionist collections in the world, almost as good as that of Walter Annenberg, President Nixon's Ambassador to London, who like Harvey had been one of the few people to build up a major collection since the Second World War. Harvey's other love was his prize collection of orchids, and he had three times been a winner at the New England Spring Flower Show in Boston.

Harvey now travelled to Europe once a year. He had established a successful stud in Kentucky and liked to see his horses run at Longchamp and Ascot. He also enjoyed watching Wimbledon, which he felt was still the outstanding tennis tournament in the world. It amused him to do a little business in Europe, where he still had the opportunity to make money for his Swiss bank account in Zürich. He did not need a Swiss bank account, but somehow he got a kick out of doing Uncle Sam.

Although Harvey had mellowed over the years and cut down on his more dubious deals, he could never resist taking a risk if he thought the reward was likely to be high enough. Such a golden opportunity presented itself in 1964 when the British Government invited applications for exploration and production licences in the North Sea. At that time neither the British Government nor the civil servants involved had any idea of the future significance of North Sea oil, or the role it would eventually play in British politics. If the Government had known that in 1974 the Arabs would be holding a pistol to the heads of the rest of the world, and the British House of Commons would have eleven Scottish Nationalist Members of Parliament, it would surely have acted in a totally different way.

On May 13th, 1964, the Secretary of State for Power laid before Parliament 'Statutory Instrument—No. 708—Continental Shelf—Petroleum'. Harvey read this particular document with great interest as he thought it might well be a means of making an exceptional killing. He was particularly fascinated by Paragraph 4:

Persons who are citizens of the United Kingdom and Colonies and are resident in the United Kingdom or who are bodies corporate incorporated in the United Kingdom may apply in accordance with these Regulations for;
(a) a production licence; or
(b) an exploration licence.

When he had studied the Regulations in their entirety, he had sat back and thought hard. Only a small amount of money was required to secure a production and exploration licence. As Paragraph 6 had it:

> (1) With every application for a production licence there shall
> be paid a fee of two hundred pounds with an additional fee of
> five pounds for every block after the first ten in respect whereof
> that application is made.
> (2) With every application for an exploration licence there shall
> be paid a fee of twenty pounds.

How easily the possession of such a licence might, in Harvey's hands,
be used to create the impression of a vast enterprise. He could be
alongside such names as Shell, B.P., Total, Gulf, Occidental and all
the other major oil companies.

He went over the Regulations again and again, hardly believing that
the British Government would release such potential for so small an
investment. Only the application form, an elaborate and exacting
document, stood in his way. Harvey was not British, none of his
companies was British and he knew he would have presentation
problems. He decided that his application must be backed by a
British Bank and that he must set up a company whose directors
would give confidence to the British Government.

With this in mind, early in 1964 he registered a company in
England called Prospecta Oil, using Malcolm, Bottnick and Davis as
his solicitors and Barclays Bank as bankers, as they were already the
Lincoln Trust's representatives in Europe. Lord Hunnisett became
Chairman and several distinguished men joined the Board, including
two ex-Members of Parliament who had lost their seats when the
Labour Party won the 1964 Election. When Harvey discovered how
stringent the rules were for setting up a public company in England,
he decided to launch the main company on the Canadian Stock
Exchange and to use the English company only as a subsidiary.
Prospecta Oil issued 2,000,000 10 cent shares at 50 cents, which were
all acquired for Harvey by nominees. He also deposited $500,000 in
the Lombard Street branch of Barclays Bank.

Having thus created the front, Harvey then used Lord Hunnisett
to apply for the licence from the British Government. The new
Labour Government elected in October 1964 was no more aware of
the significance of North Sea oil than the earlier Conservative admini-
stration. The Government's requirements for a licence were a rent of
£12,000 a year for the first six years, and 12½ per cent revenue tax
with a further Capital Gains tax on profits, but as Harvey's plan did

22

not allow for any company profit, that was not going to be a problem.

On May 22nd, 1965, the Minister of Power published in the *London Gazette* the name of Prospecta Oil among the fifty-two companies granted production licences. On August 3rd, 1965, Statutory Instrument No. 1531 allocated the actual areas. Prospecta Oil's was 51° 50′ 00″ N: 2° 30′ 20″ E, a site adjacent to one of British Petroleum's holdings.

Hopefully, Harvey waited for one of the companies which had acquired North Sea sites to strike oil. It was a longish wait: not until June 1970 did British Petroleum make a big commercial strike in their Forties Field. British Petroleum had spent over $1 billion in the North Sea and Harvey was going to be one of the main beneficiaries. He was on to another winner, and set the second part of his plan in motion.

Early in 1972 he hired an oil rig which, with much flourish and publicity, he had towed out to the Prospecta Oil site. He hired the rig on the basis of being able to renew the contract if he made a successful strike, engaged the minimum number of people allowed by the Government Regulations, and proceeded to drill to 6,000 ft. After this drilling had been completed he released from employment all those involved, but told Reading & Bates, from whom he had rented the rig, that he would be requiring it again in the near future and therefore would continue to pay the rental.

Harvey then bought Prospecta Oil shares on the market at the rate of a few thousand a day for the next two months from his own nominees, and whenever the financial journalists of the British Press rang to ask why these shares were steadily rising, the young public relations officer at Prospecta Oil's office said, as briefed, that he had no comment to make at present but they would be making a press statement in the near future; some newspapers put two and two together and made about fifteen. The shares climbed steadily from 50 cents to nearly $3. Harvey's chief executive in Britain, Bernie Silverman, was only too aware of what the boss was up to—he had been involved in operations of this kind before. His main task was to ensure that nobody could prove a direct connection between Metcalfe and Prospecta Oil.

In January 1974 the shares stood at $6. It was then that Harvey was ready to move on to the third part of his plan, which was to use Prospecta Oil's new recruit, a young Harvard graduate called David Kesler, as the fall-guy.

23

TWO

David pushed his glasses back on to the bridge of his nose and read the advertisement in the Business Section of the *Boston Globe* again to be sure he was not dreaming. It could have been tailor-made for him:

> Oil Company based in Canada, carrying out extensive work in the North Sea off Scotland, requires a young executive with experience in the stock market and financial marketing. Salary $20,000 a year. Accommodation supplied. Based in London. Apply Box No. 217A.

Knowing it must lead to other openings in an expanding industry, David thought it sounded like a challenge. He recalled what his tutor in European affairs used to say: 'If you must work in Great Britain, better make it the North Sea. Nothing else great about the country. Lots of oil in lots of places equals lots of business opportunities for those who have the guts to invest with their balls.'

David Kesler was a lean, clean-cut young American, with a crew cut which would have been better suited to a lieutenant in the Marines, a fresh complexion and an unquenchable earnestness and he wanted to succeed in business with all the fervour of the new graduate from Harvard Business School. He had spent five years in all at Harvard, the first three studying Mathematics, and the last two across the Charles River, at the Business School. He had just graduated and, armed with an M.A. and an M.B.A.,* he was looking round for a job that would reward him for the exceptional capacity for hard work he knew he possessed. He had never been a brilliant scholar, and he envied the natural academics among his classmates who found post-Keynesian economic theories more like fun than hard work. David had worked ferociously, only lifting his

* In Harvard Business School or B School, 24 per cent of the 1971 intake came fresh from college, while 76 per cent had spent at least two years in business. David Kesler was in the 24 per cent.

nose far enough from the grindstone for a daily work-out at the gymnasium, and the occasional weekend watching Harvard Jocks defending the honour of the university on the football pitch or in the basketball court. He would have enjoyed playing himself, but that would have meant less time for study.

He read the advertisement again, and typed a neat letter to the box number. A few days passed before the reply came summoning him to an interview at a local hotel on the following Wednesday at 3.00. Talent scouts for big companies often used such a venue for interviews in a university city.

David arrived at 2.45 p.m. at the Copley Square Hotel in Huntingdon Avenue, the adrenalin pumping round his body. He repeated the Harvard Business School motto to himself as he was ushered into a small private room: look British, think Yiddish.

Three men, who introduced themselves as Silverman, Cooper and Elliott interviewed him. Bernie Silverman, a grey-haired, check-tied New Yorker with a solid aura of success, was in charge. Cooper and Elliott sat and watched David silently. It didn't throw him: he knew he looked keen and was coming over well.

Silverman spent considerable time giving David an enticing description of the company's background and its future aims. Harvey had trained Silverman well and he had at his well-manicured finger-tips all the glib expertise needed by the righthand man in a Metcalfe coup.

'So there you have it, Mr Kesler. We're involved in one of the biggest commercial opportunities in the world, looking for oil in the North Sea off Scotland. Our company, Prospecta Oil, has the backing of one of the largest banks in America. We have been granted licences from the British Government and we have the finance. But companies are made, Mr Kesler, by people, it's as simple as that. We're looking for a man who will work night and day to put Prospecta Oil on the map, and we'll pay the right man a top salary to do just that. If you were offered the position you would be working in our London office under the immediate direction of our no. 2, Mr Elliott.'

'Where are the company headquarters?'

'Montreal, Canada, but we have offices in New York, San Francisco, London, Aberdeen, Paris and Brussels.'

'Is the company looking for oil anywhere else?'

'Not at the moment,' answered Silverman. 'We're sinking millions into the North Sea after B.P.'s successful strike, and the fields around

25

us have so far had a one-in-five success rate, which is very high in our business.'

'When would you want the successful applicant to start?'

'Some time in January, when he has completed a Government training course on management in oil,' said Richard Elliott. The slim, sallow no. 2 sounded as if he was from Georgia. The Government course was a typical Harvey Metcalfe touch.

'And the company apartment,' said David, 'where's that?'

Cooper spoke:

'You will have the small company flat in the Barbican, a few hundred yards away from our London City office.'

David had no more questions—Silverman had covered everything and seemed to understand exactly what he wanted.

Ten days later he received a telegram from Silverman, inviting him to lunch at the 21 Club in New York. The plush air of the restaurant gave David confidence that these people knew what they were about. Their table was in one of the small alcoves selected by businessmen who prefer their conversations to remain confidential. He met Silverman in the bar at 12.55 p.m.

Silverman was genial and relaxed. He stretched the conversation out a little, discussing irrelevancies, but finally, over a brandy, offered David the position in London. David was delighted—$20,000 a year and the chance to be involved with a company which obviously had such exciting potential. He did not hesitate to agree to start his new appointment in London on January 1st.

David Kesler had never been to England: how green the grass was, how narrow the roads, how closed in by hedges and fences were the houses. He felt he was in Toy Town after the vast highways and large automobiles of New York. The small flat in the Barbican was clean and impersonal and, as Mr Cooper had said, convenient for the office a few hundred yards away in Threadneedle Street.

The small office building consisted of seven rooms, of which only Silverman's had a prestigious air about it. There was a tiny reception area, a telex room, two rooms for secretaries, a room for Mr Elliott and another for himself. It seemed very poky to David, but, as Silverman was quick to point out, office rent in the City of London was £15 a square foot compared with £5 in New York.

Bernie Silverman's secretary, Judith Lampson, ushered him through to the well-appointed office of the Chief Executive. Silverman sat in a large black swivel chair behind a massive desk, which made him look like a midget. By his side were positioned the telephones—three white and one red. David was later to learn that the important-looking red telephone was directly connected to a number in the States, but he was never quite sure to whom.

'Good morning, Mr Silverman. Where would you like me to start?'

'Bernie, please call me Bernie. Take a seat. Notice the change in the price of the company's shares in the last few days?'

'Oh yes,' enthused David, 'up 50 cents to nearly $6. I suppose it is because of our new bank backing and the other companies' successful strikes?'

'No,' said Silverman in a low tone designed to leave the impression that no one else must hear this part of the conversation, 'the truth is that we have made a big strike ourselves, but we have not yet decided when to announce it.'

David whistled under his breath. 'What are the company's plans at the moment?'

'We will announce it,' said Silverman quietly, picking at his india rubber as he talked, 'in about three weeks' time when we are certain of the full extent and capacity of the hole. We want to make some plans for coping with the publicity and the sudden inflow of money. The shares will go through the roof, of course.'

'Some people must already know as the shares have climbed so steadily. Is there any harm in getting in on the act?' asked David.

'No, as long as it doesn't harm the company in any way. Just let me know if anyone wants to invest. We don't have the problems of inside information in England—none of the restrictive laws we have in America.'

'How high do you think the shares will go?'

Silverman looked him straight in the eye. '$20.'

Back in his own office, David carefully read the geologist's report that Silverman had given him: it certainly seemed as if Prospecta Oil had made a successful strike, although the extent of the find was not as yet entirely certain. When he had completed the report, he glanced at his watch and cursed. The geologist's file had totally preoccupied him. He threw the report into his briefcase and took a taxi to Paddington Station, only just making the 6.15. He was due in Oxford for dinner with an old classmate from Harvard.

On the train down to the university city he thought about Stephen Bradley, who had been a friend in his Harvard days and had generously helped David and other students in the Mathematics class that year. Stephen, now a visiting Fellow at Magdalen College, was undoubtedly the most brilliant scholar of his generation. He had won the Kennedy Memorial Scholarship to Harvard and later in 1970 the Wister Prize for Mathematics, the most sought-after award in the mathematical faculty. Although in monetary terms this award was a derisory $80 and a medal, it was the reputation and offers that came after that made the competition so keen. Stephen had won it with consummate ease and nobody was surprised when he was successful in his application for a Fellowship at Oxford. He was now in his third year of research at Magdalen. Papers by Bradley on Boolean algebra appeared at short intervals in the *Proceedings of the London Mathematical Society*. He had just been elected to a Chair in Mathematics back at his Alma Mater, Harvard.

The 6.15 train from Paddington arrived in Oxford at 7.15 p.m. and the short taxi ride from the station, past Worcester College and down New College Lane, brought David to Magdalen at 7.30 p.m. One of the College porters escorted David to Stephen's rooms, which were spacious and ancient, and comfortably cluttered with books, cushions and prints. How unlike the antiseptic walls of Harvard, thought David. Stephen was there to greet him. He didn't seem to have changed an iota. His tall, thin, ungainly body made any suit look as if it was hanging on him; no tailor would ever have employed him to be a dummy. His heavy eyebrows protruded over his out-of-date round-rimmed spectacles, which he almost seemed to hide behind in his shyness. He ambled up to David to welcome him, one minute an old man, the next younger than his thirty years. Stephen poured David a Jack Daniels and they settled down to chat. Although Stephen had never looked upon David as a real friend at Harvard, he had enjoyed coaching a fellow-student so eager to learn, and anyway, he always welcomed any excuse to entertain Americans at Oxford.

'It has been a memorable three years, David. The only sad event has been the death of my father last year,' said Stephen. 'He took such an interest in my progress and gave my academic work so much support. I do miss him.

'He's left me rather well off, actually . . . You're the bright boy in business, David. Whatever can I do with a bequest of $250,000, which is just sitting on deposit with the bank? I never seem to have the time to do anything about it, and when it comes to investments I haven't a clue where to begin.'

28

That started David off about his exacting new job with Prospecta Oil.

'Why don't you invest your money in my company, Stephen? We've had a fantastic strike in the North Sea, and when we announce it the shares are going to go through the roof. The whole operation would only take a month or so. You will make the killing of a lifetime. I only wish I had money to put into it.'

'Have you the full details of the strike?' inquired Stephen.

'No, but I have the geologist's report, and that makes pretty good reading. The problem is that the shares are already going up fast and although I am convinced they will reach $20, there is little time to waste.'

Stephen glanced at the geologist's report, thinking he would study it carefully later.

'How does one go about an investment of this sort?' he inquired.

'Well, you find yourself a respectable stockbroker, buy as many shares as you can afford and then await the announcement of the strike. I'll keep you informed on how things are going and advise you when I feel it's the best time to sell.'

'That would be extremely thoughtful of you, David.'

'It's the least I can do after all the help you gave me with Math. at Harvard.'

'Oh, that was nothing. Let's go and have some dinner.'

Stephen led David to the college dining hall, an oblong, oak-panelled room covered in pictures of past Presidents of Magdalen, bishops and academics. The long wooden tables at which the under-graduates were eating filled the body of the hall, but Stephen shuffled up to the High Table and proffered David a comfortable seat. The undergraduates were a noisy, enthusiastic bunch—Stephen didn't notice them though David was enjoying the new experience.

The meal was formidable and David wondered how Stephen kept so thin with such daily temptations (he gathered that seven courses were not unusual at Magdalen High Table). When they reached the port, Stephen suggested they return to his rooms rather than join the crusty old dons in the Senior Common Room.

Late into the night, over the rubicund Magdalen port, they talked about North Sea oil and Boolean algebra, each admiring the other for his mastery of his subject. Stephen, like most academics, was fairly credulous outside the bounds of his own discipline. He began to think that an investment in Prospecta Oil would be a very astute move on his part.

29

In the morning, they strolled in the famous Addison's Walk near Magdalen where the grass grows green and lush by the Cherwell. Reluctantly, David caught the 11 a.m. train back to London. He had enjoyed his stay at Oxford and hoped he had been able to help his old Harvard friend, who had done so much for him.

'Good morning, David.'

'Good morning, Bernie.'

'I thought I ought to let you know I spent the evening with a friend at Oxford, and he may invest some money in the company. The sum could be as high as $250,000.'

'Well done, keep up the good work. You're doing a great job.'

Silverman showed no surprise at David's news, but once back in his office he picked up the red telephone.

'Harvey?'

'Yes.'

'Kesler seems to have been the right choice. He may have talked a friend of his into investing $250,000 in the company.'

'Good, now listen, brief my broker to put 40,000 shares on the market at just over $6 a share. If Kesler's friend does decide to invest in the company, mine will be the only shares available.'

After a further day's thought, Stephen noticed that the shares of Prospecta Oil moved from $5.75 to $6.05, and he decided the time had come to invest in what he was now convinced was a winner. He trusted David, and had been impressed by the geologist's report. He rang Kitcat & Aitken, a distinguished firm of stockbrokers in the City, and instructed them to buy $250,000-worth of shares in Prospecta Oil. Harvey Metcalfe's broker released 40,000 shares when Stephen's request came on to the floor of the market and the transaction was quickly completed. Stephen's purchase price of $6.10 cents included the dollar premium.

Stephen had invested everything he had and over the next few days he happily watched the shares climb to $7, even before the expected announcement. Though Stephen didn't realize it, it was his own investment that had caused the shares to rise. He began to wonder what he would spend his profit on even before he had made it. He decided he would not sell immediately, but hold on, as David thought the shares would reach $20.

At the same time, Harvey Metcalfe began to release a few more shares on to the market, because of the interest created by Stephen's investment. He was beginning to agree with Silverman that the choice of David Kesler, young, honest, with all the enthusiasm of a man in his first appointment, had been a good one. It was not the first time Harvey had used this ploy, keeping himself well away from the action and placing the responsibility on innocent shoulders.

Meanwhile Richard Elliott, acting as the company spokesman, leaked stories to the Press about large buyers coming into the market, which in itself occasioned a flood of small investors.

One lesson a man learns in the Harvard Business School is that an executive is only as good as his health. David didn't feel happy without a regular medical check-up: he rather enjoyed being told he was in good shape, but perhaps should take things a little easier. His secretary, Miss Rentoul, had therefore made an appointment for him with a Harley Street doctor.

Dr Adrian Tryner was a very successful man. At thirty-seven he was tall and handsome, with a head of dark hair that looked as if it would never go bald. He had a classic strong face and a self-assurance that came from proven success. He still played squash twice a week, which made him look enviably younger than his contemporaries. He had remained fit since his Cambridge days, which had equipped him with a Rugby Blue and an upper-second-class degree. He had completed his medical training at St Thomas's, where once again his Rugby football rather than his medical skill brought him into prominence. When he qualified, he went to work as an assistant to a highly successful Harley Street practitioner, Dr Eugene Moffat. Dr Moffat was successful not so much in curing the sick as in charming his patients, especially middle-aged women, who came to see him again and again however little was wrong with them. At 50 guineas a time that had to be regarded as success.

Moffat had chosen Adrian Tryner as his assistant for exactly those qualities which he had himself, and which made him so sought after. Adrian Tryner was good-looking, personable, well educated and just clever enough. He settled in very well to Harley Street and the Moffat system, and when the older man died suddenly in his early sixties, he took over his mantle much as a crown prince would take over a throne. He continued to build up the practice, losing none of Moffat's ladies, except by natural causes, and was doing remarkably well for himself. He had a comfortable country house just outside Newbury in Berkshire, a wife and two sons, and considerable savings

31

in blue chip securities. He wasn't complaining at his good fortune and he enjoyed his lifestyle, but he was a bored man. Occasionally he found the bland role of a sympathetic doctor almost intolerably cloying. How would it be if he admitted that he neither knew or cared just what was causing the minute patches of dermatitis on Lady Fiona Fisher's diamond-studded hands? Would the Heavens descend if he told the dreaded Mrs Page-Stanley that she was a malodorous old woman in need of nothing more medically taxing than a new set of dentures? And would he be struck off if he personally administered to the nubile Miss Lydia de Villiers a good dose of what she so clearly indicated that she wanted?

David Kesler arrived on time for his appointment. He had been warned by Miss Rentoul that doctors and dentists cancel if you are late and still charge you.

David stripped and lay on Adrian Tryner's couch. The doctor took his blood pressure, listened to his heart, and made him put out his tongue (an organ that seldom stands up well to public scrutiny). As he tapped and poked his way over David's body, they chatted.

'What brings you to work in London, Mr Kesler?'

'I'm with an oil company in the City. I expect you've heard of us— Prospecta Oil?'

'No,' said Adrian. 'Can't say I have. Bend your legs up please.' He hit David's knee-caps smartly, one after the other, with a patella hammer. The legs jumped wildly.

'Nothing wrong with those reflexes.'

'You will, Dr Tryner, you will. Things are going very well for us. Look out for our name in the papers.'

'Why,' said Adrian, smiling, 'struck oil have you?'

'Yes,' said David quietly, pleased with the impression he was creating, 'we have done just that, as a matter of fact.'

Adrian prodded David's abdomen for a few seconds. Good muscular wall, no fat, no sign of an enlarged liver. The young American was in good physical shape. Adrian left him in the examination room to get dressed and thoughtfully wrote out a brief report on Kesler for his records. An oil strike. Should he dig a little deeper?

Harley Street doctors, although they routinely keep private patients waiting for three-quarters of an hour in a gas-fired waiting-room equipped with one out-of-date copy of Punch, never let them feel rushed once they are in the consulting room. Adrian certainly didn't want to rush David.

32

'There is very little wrong with you, Mr Kesler. Some signs of anaemia, which I suspect are caused by overwork and your recent rushing about. I am going to give you some iron tablets which should take care of that. Take two a day, morning and night.' He scribbled an illegible prescription for tablets and handed it to David.

'Many thanks. It is kind of you to give me so much of your time.'

'Not at all. How do you like London?' said Adrian. 'Very different from America, I expect.'

'Sure—the pace is much slower. Once I have mastered how long it takes to get something done here I will be halfway to victory.'

'Do you have any friends in London?'

'No,' replied David, 'I have one or two buddies at Oxford from my Harvard days, but I have not yet made contact with many people in London.'

Good, thought Adrian, here was a chance for him to find out a bit more about this oil, and to spend some time with someone who made most of his patients look as if they had both feet in the grave. It might even shake him out of his present lethargy. He continued, 'Would you care to join me for lunch later in the week? You might like to see one of our antique London clubs.'

'How very kind of you.'

'Excellent. Will Friday suit you?'

'It certainly will.'

'Then make it 1 o'clock at the Athenaeum Club in Pall Mall.'

David returned to his City desk, picking up his tablets on the way. He took one immediately for luck. He was beginning to enjoy his stay in London. Silverman seemed pleased with him, Prospecta Oil was doing well and he was already meeting some interesting people. Yes, he felt this was going to be a very happy period in his life.

On Friday at 12.45 p.m., he arrived at the Athenaeum, a massive white building on the corner of Pall Mall, overlooked by a statue of the Duke of Wellington. David was amazed by the vast rooms and his commercial mind could not help wondering what price they would fetch as office space. The place seemed to be full of moving waxworks who, Adrian later assured him, were distinguished generals and diplomats.

They lunched in the Coffee Room, dominated by a Rubens of Charles II. Over coffee, David readily told Adrian the details of the geologist's findings on the Prospecta Oil site. The shares were now at $7.15 on the Montreal Stock Exchange, and were still going up.

'Sounds like a good investment,' said Adrian, 'and as it's your own company, it might be worth a risk.'

'I don't think there is much risk,' said David, 'as long as the oil is actually there.'

'Well, I will certainly consider it most seriously over the weekend.'

They parted after lunch, David to a conference on the Energy Crisis organized by the *Financial Times*, Adrian to his home in Berkshire. His two young sons were back from prep school for the weekend and he was looking forward to seeing them again. How quickly they had passed from babies to toddlers to boys, he thought, and how reassuring to know their future was secure.

Bernie Silverman was pleased to hear of the possibility of a further investment.

'Congratulations, my boy. We are going to need a lot of capital to finance our pipe-laying operations, you know. Pipe-laying can cost $2 million per mile. Still, you are playing your part. I have just had word from head office that we are to give you a $5,000 bonus for your efforts. Keep up the good work.'

David smiled. This was business in the proper Harvard way. If you do the work, you get the rewards. No messing about.

'When is the announcement on the strike being made?' he asked.

'Some time in the next few days.'

David left Silverman's office with a glow of pride.

Silverman immediately contacted Harvey Metcalfe, who set the routine in motion again. Metcalfe's brokers released on to the market 35,000 shares at $7.23 and approximately 5,000 each day on to the open market, always being able to feel when the market had taken enough so that the price remained steady. Once again, the shares climbed because of Dr Tryner's substantial investment, this time to $7.40, keeping David, Adrian and Stephen all happy. They did not know that Harvey was releasing more shares each day because of the interest they had caused, which had created a market of its own.

David decided to spend some of his bonus on a painting for his little flat in the Barbican, which he felt was rather grey. About $2,000, he thought, something that was going to appreciate. David quite enjoyed art for art's sake, but he liked it even better for business's sake. He spent the Friday afternoon tramping round Bond Street, Cork Street and Bruton Street, the home of the London art galleries. The Wildenstein was too expensive for his pocket and the

Marlborough too modern for his taste. The painting he finally picked out was at the Lamanns Gallery in Bond Street.

The gallery, just three doors away from Sotheby's, consisted of one vast room with a worn grey carpet and red faded wallpaper. The more worn the carpet, the more faded the walls, the greater the success and reputation of the gallery (or at least that is the theory). There was a staircase at the far end of the room, against which some unregarded paintings were stacked, backs to the world. David sorted through them on a whim and found, to his surprise, the sort of painting he was after.

It was an oil by Leon Underwood called *Venus in the Park*. The large, rather sombre canvas contained about six men and women sitting on metal chairs at circular tea-tables. Among them, in the foreground, was a comely naked woman with generous breasts and long hair. Nobody was paying her the slightest attention and she sat gazing out of the picture, face inscrutable, a symbol of warmth and love in indifferent surroundings. David found her utterly compelling.

The gallery proprietor, Jean-Pierre Lamanns wore an elegantly tailored suit, as befitted a man who rarely received cheques for less than a thousand pounds. At thirty-five, he could afford the little extravagances of life and his Gucci shoes, Yves St Laurent tie, Turnbull & Asser shirt and Piaget watch left no one, especially women, in any doubt that he knew what he was about. He was an Englishman's vision of a Frenchman, slim and neat with longish, dark wavy hair and deep brown eyes that hinted at being a little sharp. He could be pernickety and demanding, with a wit that was often as cruel as it was amusing, which may have been one of the reasons he was still a bachelor. There certainly had not been any shortage of applicants. When it came to customers only his charm was on display. As David wrote out his cheque, Jean-Pierre rubbed his forefinger backwards and forwards over his fashionable moustache, only too happy to discuss the picture.

'Underwood is one of the greatest sculptors and artists in England today. He even tutored Henry Moore, you know. I believe he is under-estimated because of his treatment of journalists and the Press, whom he will describe as drunken scribblers.'

'Hardly the way to endear himself to the media,' murmured David, as he handed over the cheque for £850, feeling agreeably prosperous. Although it was the most expensive purchase he had ever made, he felt it had been a good investment and, more important, he liked the painting.

Jean-Pierre took David downstairs to show him the Impressionist and Modern collection he had built up over many years, and continued to enthuse about Underwood. They celebrated David's acquisition over a whisky in Jean-Pierre's office.

'What line of business are you in, Mr Kesler?'

'I work with a small oil company called Prospecta Oil, who are exploring prospects in the North Sea.'

'Had any success?' inquired Jean-Pierre.

'Well, confidentially, we are rather excited about the future. It is no secret that the company shares have gone from $3 to $7 in the last few weeks, but no one knows the real reason.'

'Would it be a good investment for a little art dealer like myself?' asked Jean-Pierre.

'I'll tell you how good an investment I think it is,' said David. 'I am investing $3,000 in the company on Monday, which is all I have in the world—now that I have captured Venus, that is. We are shortly to make a rather special announcement.'

A twinkle came into Jean-Pierre's eye. A nod was as good as a wink to one of his Gallic subtlety. He did not pursue the line any longer.

'When is the strike going to be announced, Bernie?'

'We expect it to be early next week. We've had a few problems. Nothing we can't lick, though.'

That gave David some relief, as he had taken up 500 shares himself that morning, investing the remaining $3,000 from his bonus. Like the others, he was hoping for a quick profit.

'Rowe Rudd.'

'Frank Watts, please. Jean-Pierre Lamanns.'

'Good morning, Jean-Pierre. What can we do for you?'

'I want to buy 25,000 Prospecta Oil.'

'Never heard of them. Hold on a minute . . . Canadian company, very low capital. A bit risky, J.-P. I wouldn't recommend it.'

'It's all right, Frank, I only want them for two or three weeks then you can sell them. I'm not going to hold on to them. When did the account start?'

'Yesterday.'

'Right. Buy them today and sell them by the end of the account, or earlier. I'm expecting an announcement next week, so when they go over $10 you can get rid of them. I'm not trying to be clever, but buy

36

them in my share company name, as I don't want the deal traced back to me—it might embarrass the informant.'

'Right, sir. Buy 25,000 Prospecta Oil and sell during the last few days of the account, or sooner if instructed.'

'I will be in Paris all next week, so don't forget to sell if they go over $10.'

'Right, J.-P., have a good trip.'

The red telephone rang.

'Rowe Rudd are looking for shares. Do you know anything about it?'

'No, Harvey. It must be David Kesler again. Do you want me to speak to him?'

'No, say nothing. I have released 25,000 shares at $7.80. Kesler's only got to do one more big one and I'll be out. Prepare our plan for a week before the end of this account.'

'Right, boss. Quite a few people are also buying small amounts.'

'Yes, just as before, they all have to tell their friends they're on to a good thing. Say nothing to Kesler.'

'You know, David,' said Richard Elliott, 'you work too hard. Relax. We're going to be busy once the announcement's made.'

'I guess so,' said David. 'Work's just a habit with me now.'

'Well, take tonight off. How about a spot of something at Annabel's?'

David was flattered by the invitation to London's most exclusive nightclub and accepted enthusiastically.

David's hired Ford Cortina looked out of place that evening in Berkeley Square with so many Rolls Royces and Mercedes double-parked. He made his way down the little iron staircase into the basement, which must have been at one time no more than the servant's quarters of the elegant town house above. Now it was a splendid club, with a restaurant, discotheque and a small plush bar, the walls covered in prints and pictures. The main dining-room was dimly lit and crowded with small tables, most of them already occupied. The decor was Regency and extravagant. Mark Birley, the owner, had in the short period of ten years made Annabel's the most sought-after club in London with a waiting list for membership of over a thousand. The discotheque was playing in the far corner, and the dance floor, on which you couldn't have parked two Cadillacs, was crowded. Most of the couples were dancing very close to each other—they didn't have much choice. David was somewhat surprised to notice that most of the men on the floor were about twenty years older than the girls. The head waiter, Louis, showed David to Richard Elliott's table, realizing it was David's first visit to the club by the way he was staring at all the personalities of the day. Oh well, thought David, perhaps one day they will stare at me.

After an exceptional dinner Richard Elliott and his wife joined the masses on the dance floor while David returned to the little bar surrounded by comfortable red settees. He struck up a conversation with someone who introduced himself as James Brigsley. Even if he did not treat the whole world as such, certainly he treated Annabel's as a stage. Tall, blond and cool, his eyes were alight with good humour and he seemed at ease with everyone round him. David admired his assured manner, something he had never acquired and feared he never would. His accent, even to David's unskilled ears, was resonantly upper class.

David's new acquaintance talked of his visits to the States, flattering him by remarking how much he had always liked the Americans. After some time, David was able quietly to ask the head waiter who the Englishman was.

'He's Lord Brigsley, the eldest son of the Earl of Louth, sir.'

What do you know, thought David, lords look like anyone else, especially when they have had a few drinks. Lord Brigsley was tapping David's glass.

'Would you care for another?'

'Thank you very much, my lord,' said David.

'Don't bother with all that stupidity. The name's James. What are you doing in London?'

'I work for an oil company. You probably know my Chairman, Lord Hunnisett. I have never met him myself, to tell you the truth.'

'Sweet old buffer,' said James. 'His son and I were at Harrow together. If you are in oil, you can tell me what to do with my Shell and B.P. shares.'

'Hold on to them,' said David. 'It's going to be very safe to be in any commodities, especially oil, as long as the British Government don't get greedy and try and take control of it themselves.'

Another double whisky arrived. David was beginning to feel just slightly tipsy.

'What about your own company?' inquired James.

'We're only small,' said David, 'but our shares have gone up more than any other oil company in the last three months, though I suspect they have nowhere near reached their zenith.'

'Why?' demanded James.

David glanced round and lowered his voice to a confidential whisper.

'Well, I expect you realize that if you make an oil strike in a big company it can only put the percentage of your profits up by a tiny amount, but if you make a strike in a small company, naturally that profit will be reflected as a considerably larger percentage of the whole.'

'Are you telling me you have made a strike?'

'Perhaps I shouldn't have said that,' said David. 'I would be obliged if you will treat that remark in confidence.'

David could not remember how he arrived home or who put him to bed, and he appeared late in the office the next morning.

'I am sorry, Bernie, I overslept after a little celebration with Richard at Annabel's.'

'Doesn't matter a bit. Glad you enjoyed yourself.'

'I hope I wasn't indiscreet, but I told some lord, whose name I can't remember, that he ought to invest in the company. I may have been a little too enthusiastic.'

'Don't worry, David, we're not going to let anyone down and you needed the rest. You've been working your ass off.'

James Brigsley left his London flat in Chelsea and took a taxi to his bank, Williams & Glyn's. James was an extrovert by nature and at Harrow his only real interest had been acting, but when he had left school, his father would not allow him to go on the stage and insisted that he complete his education at Christ Church, Oxford, where again he took a greater interest in the Dramatic Society than in gaining his degree in Politics, Philosophy and Economics. In fact he had never mentioned to anyone since leaving Oxford the class of degree he managed to secure. (The fourth-class Honours degree, for which James was such a natural, has since been abolished.) From Oxford he joined the Grenadier Guards, which gave him considerable scope for his histrionic talents. This was James's introduction to society life in London, and he succeeded as well as a personable young viscount might be expected to do in the circumstances.

When he had completed his two years in the Guards, the earl gave him a 500-acre farm in Hampshire to occupy his time, but James did not care for the coarser country life. He left the running of the farm to a manager and concentrated on his social life in London. He would dearly have liked to go on the stage, but he knew the old man thought Mrs Worthington's daughter's ambition an improper one for a peer of the realm. The fifth earl didn't think much of his eldest son, one way and another, and James did not find it easy to persuade his father that he was shrewder than he was given credit for. Perhaps the inside information David Kesler had let slip would provide him with the opportunity.

In Williams & Glyn's fine old buildings in Birchin Lane, James was shown into the manager's office.

'I should like to borrow some money against my farm in Hampshire,' said Lord Brigsley.

Philip Izard, the manager, knew Lord Brigsley well and also his father. Although he had respect for the earl's judgment, he did not have a great deal of time for the young lord. Nevertheless, it was not for him to query a customer's request, especially when the customer's father was one of the longest-standing the bank had.

'Yes, my lord, how much do you have in mind?'

'Well, it seems that farmland in Hampshire is worth about £1,000 an acre and is still climbing. Why don't we say £150,000? I should like to invest it in shares.'

'Will you agree to leave the deeds in the bank as security?' inquired Izard.

'Yes, of course. What difference does it make to me where they are?'

'Then I am sure we will find it acceptable to advance you a loan at 2 per cent above base rate.'

James was not at all sure of the going rate, but he knew that Williams & Glyn's were competitive with everyone else, and that their reputation was beyond discussion.

'And will you acquire for me 35,000 shares in a company called Prospecta Oil.'

'Have you checked carefully into this company?' inquired Izard.

'Yes, of course I have,' said Lord Brigsley, very sharply. He was not in awe of the bank-managerial class.

In Boston, Harvey Metcalfe was briefed over the telephone by

Silverman of the meeting in Annabel's between David Kesler and a nameless contact who appeared to have more money than sense. Harvey released 40,000 shares on to the market at $8.80. Williams & Glyn's took up 35,000 of them and, once again, the remainder was taken up by small investors. The shares rose a little. Harvey Metcalfe was now left with only 30,000 shares, and over the next four days he was able to dispose of them all. It had taken fourteen weeks to off-load his entire stock in Prospecta Oil at a profit of just over $6 million.

On the Friday morning, the shares stood at $9.10 and Kesler had, in all innocence, occasioned four large investments:

Stephen Bradley had bought 40,000 shares at $6.10
Dr Adrian Tryner had bought 35,000 shares at $7.23
Jean-Pierre Lamanns had bought 25,000 shares at $7.80
James Brigsley had bought 35,000 shares at $8.80
David Kesler himself had bought 500 shares at $7.25.

Between them they had purchased 135,000 shares at an investment of just over $1 million. They had also kept the interest alive, giving Harvey the chance to off-load all his shares in a natural market.

Harvey Metcalfe had done it again. His name was not on the letter paper and now he owned no shares. Nobody was going to be able to fix any blame on him. He had done nothing illegal; even the geologist's report had enough ifs and buts to get by in a court of law. As for David Kesler, Harvey could not be blamed for his youthful enthusiasm. He had never even met the man. Harvey Metcalfe opened a bottle of Krug Privée Cuvée 1964, imported by Hedges and Butler of London. He sipped it slowly, then lit a Romeo y Julieta Churchill, and settled back for a mild celebration.

David, Stephen, Adrian, Jean-Pierre and James celebrated the weekend as well. Why not, the shares were at $9.10 and David had assured them they would reach $20. On Saturday morning David ordered himself a bespoke suit from Aquascutum, Stephen tut-tutted his way through the end-of-vacation examination papers he had set his freshmen students, Adrian went to his son's prep school to watch them taking part in their school Sports Day, Jean-Pierre re-framed a Renoir and James Brigsley went shooting, convinced that at last he had one in the eye for his father.

THREE

David arrived at the office at 9 a.m. on the Monday to find the front door locked, which he could not understand. The secretaries were supposed to be in by 8.45.

After waiting for over an hour, he went to the nearest telephone box and dialled Bernie Silverman's home number. There was no reply. He then rang Richard Elliott at home—again, no reply. He rang the Aberdeen office. As before, no reply. He decided to return to the office. There must be some simple explanation, he thought. Was he day-dreaming? Or was it Sunday? No—the streets were jammed with people and cars.

When he arrived at the office for a second time a young man was putting up a board. '2,500 sq. ft to let. Apply Conrad Ritblat.'

'What in hell's name are you up to?'

'The old tenants have given notice and left. We shall be looking for new ones. Are you interested in seeing over the property?'

'No,' said David, 'no, thank you,' backing away in panic. He raced down the street, sweat beginning to show on his forehead, praying that the telephone box would be empty.

He looked up Bernie Silverman's secretary, Judith Lampson, in the directory. This time there was a reply.

'Judith, in God's name what's going on here?' His voice could have left no doubt about how anxious he was.

'No idea,' replied Judith, 'I was given my notice on Friday night with a month's pay in advance and no explanation.'

David dropped the telephone. The truth was beginning to dawn on him. Whom could he turn to? What should he do?

He returned in a daze to his flat in the Barbican. The morning post had arrived in his absence. It included a letter from the landlords of his flat:

Corporation of London,
Barbican Estate Office,
London EC2.
Telephone 01-628 4341
Dear Sir,

We are sorry to learn you will be leaving at the end of the month, and would like to take this opportunity of thanking you for the month's payment of rent in advance.

We should be pleased if you would kindly deposit the keys at this office at your earliest convenience.

Yours faithfully,
C. J. Caselton
Estate Manager

David stood frozen in the middle of the room, gazing at his new Underwood with sudden loathing.

Finally, fearfully, he rang his stockbrokers.

'What price are Prospecta Oil this morning?'

'They have fallen to $7.40,' replied the broker.

'Why have they fallen?'

'I have no idea, but I will make inquiries and ring you back.'

'Please put 500 shares on the market for me immediately.'

'500 Prospecta Oil at market price, yes sir.'

David put the phone down. It rang a few minutes later. It was his broker.

'They have only made $7.25—exactly what you paid for them.'

'Would you credit the sum to my account at Lloyds Bank, Moorgate?'

'Of course, sir.'

David did not leave the flat for the rest of the day and night. He lay chain-smoking on his bed, wondering what he was going to do next, sometimes looking out of his little window over a rain-drenched City of banks, insurance companies, stockbrokers and public companies— his own world, but for how much longer? In the morning, as soon as the market opened, he rang his broker again, in the hope that they would have some new information.

'Can you give me any news on Prospecta Oil?' His voice was now tense and weary.

'The news is bad, sir. There has been a spate of heavy selling and the shares have dropped to $5.90 on the opening of business this morning.'

'Thank you.'

He replaced the receiver. All those years at Harvard were going to be blown away in a puff of smoke. An hour passed, but he did not notice it. Disaster had stepped in and made everything timeless.

He ate lunch in an insignificant restaurant and read a disturbing report in the London *Evening Standard* by its City editor, David Malbert, headlined 'The Mystery of Prospecta Oil'. By the close of the Stock Exchange at 4 p.m. the shares had fallen to $3.15.

David spent a restless night. He thought with pain and humiliation of how easily some smooth talk, two months of a good salary and a quick bonus had bought his unquestioning belief in an enterprise that should have excited all his business suspicion. He felt sick as he recalled his man-to-man tips on Prospecta Oil, whispered confidentially into willing ears.

On Wednesday morning David, dreading what he knew he must hear, once again rang the broker. The shares had fallen to $2 and there was no market. He left the flat and went to Lloyds Bank, where he closed his account and drew out the remaining £1,345. He was not sure why. He just felt he would rather have it with him than tied up in a bank. He had lost his faith in everything.

He picked up the final edition of the *Evening Standard* (the one marked '7RR' in the right-hand corner). Prospecta Oil had fallen to 50 cents. Numbly, he returned to his flat. The housekeeper was on the stairs.

'The police have been round inquiring after you, young man.'

David climbed the stairs, trying to look unperturbed.

'Thank you, Mrs Pearson, I guess it's another parking fine.'

Panic had now taken over completely: he had never felt so small, so lonely and so ill in his life. He packed everything in a suitcase, except the painting, which he left, and booked the first flight back to New York.

FOUR

Stephen Bradley was delivering a lecture on group theory at the Mathematics Institute in Oxford to third-year undergraduates. He had read with horror that morning in the *Daily Telegraph* of the collapse of Prospecta Oil. He had immediately rung his broker, who was still trying to find out the full facts. David Kesler seemed to have vanished without trace.

The lecture Stephen was giving was not going well. He was pre-occupied to say the least. He only hoped that the undergraduates would misconstrue his absent-mindedness for genius rather than recognize it for what it was—total despair. He was at least thankful that it was his final lecture of the Hilary Term.

At last it ended and he was able to return to his rooms in Magdalen College, wondering where to start. Why the hell did he put everything into one basket? How could he, the logical, calculating don, have been so reckless and so greedy? Mainly because he trusted David, and he still found it hard to believe that his friend was in any way involved. Perhaps he shouldn't have taken for granted that someone he had helped at Harvard would automatically be right. Damn it all, he hadn't been a brilliant mathematician. There must be a simple explanation. He must be able to get his money back. The telephone rang. Perhaps it was his broker at last?

As he picked up the phone, he realized for the first time that the palms of his hands were slippery with sweat.

'Stephen Bradley.'

'Good morning, sir. My name is Detective Inspector Clifford Smith of the Fraud Squad, Scotland Yard. I was wondering if you would be kind enough to see me this afternoon?'

Stephen hesitated, thinking wildly for a minute that he had done something criminal by his investment in Prospecta Oil.

'Certainly, Inspector,' he said uncertainly, 'would you like me to travel to London?'

'No, sir,' replied the Inspector, 'we will come down to you. We can be with you by 4 p.m. if that is convenient.'

45

'I'll expect you then. Goodbye, Inspector.'

Stephen replaced the receiver. What did they want? He knew little of English law and hoped he was not going to be involved with the police as well. All this just six months before he was due to return to Harvard. Stephen was now beginning to wonder if that would ever materialize.

The Detective Inspector was about 5 ft 11 in. tall, somewhere between forty-five and fifty. His hair was turning grey at the sides, but brilliantine toned it in with the original black. He was dressed in a shabby suit more indicative, Stephen thought, of a policeman's pay than of the Inspector's personal taste. His heavy frame would have fooled most people into thinking he was rather slow. In fact, Stephen was in the presence of one of the few men in England who fully understood the criminal mind. Time and time again he had been behind the arrest of international defrauders. He had a tired look that had come from years of putting men behind bars for major crimes, and seeing them freed again after only two or three years, to live off the spoils of their various shady transactions. The Force was so under-staffed that some of the smaller fry even got away scot-free because the office of the Director of Public Prosecutions had decided it would be too expensive to follow the case through to a proper conclusion. On other occasions, the Fraud Squad just did not get the back-up staff to finish the job properly.

The Detective Inspector was accompanied by Detective Sergeant Ryder, a considerably younger man—6 ft 1 in., thin in body and face. His large brown eyes had a haunted look against his sallow skin. He was at least dressed a little better than the Inspector, but then, Stephen thought, he probably wasn't married.

'I am sorry about this intrusion, sir,' began the Inspector, after he had settled himself comfortably in the large armchair usually occupied by Stephen, 'but I'm making inquiries into a company called Prospecta Oil. Now before you say anything, sir, we realize that you had no personal involvement in the running of this company. But we do need your help, and I would prefer to ask you a series of questions which will bring out the points I need answered, rather than have you just give me a general assessment.'

Stephen nodded his agreement.

'First, sir, why did you invest such a large amount in Prospecta Oil?'

The Inspector had in front of him a sheet of paper with a list of all the investments made in the company over the past four months.

'On the advice of a friend,' replied Stephen.

'Would the friend be a Mr David Kesler?'

'Yes.'

'How do you know Mr Kesler?'

'We were students at Harvard together in the Maths faculty, and when he took up his appointment in England to work for an oil company, I invited him down to Oxford for old times' sake.'

Stephen went on to explain the full background of his association with David, and the reason he had been willing to invest such a large amount. He ended his explanation by asking if the Inspector considered David was criminally involved in the rise and fall of Prospecta Oil.

'No, sir. My own view is that Kesler, who incidentally has made a run for it and left the country, is no more than a dupe of bigger men, but we would like to question him, so if he contacts you please let me know immediately.

'Now, sir,' he continued, 'I'm going to read you a list of names and I would be obliged if you could tell me whether you have evei met, spoken to or heard of any of them . . . Harvey Metcalfe?'

'No,' said Stephen.

'Bernie Silverman?'

'I have never met or spoken to him, but David did mention his name in conversation when he dined with me here in college.'

The Detective Sergeant was writing down everything Stephen said, slowly and methodically.

'Richard Elliott?'

'The same applies to him as Silverman,' murmured Stephen.

'Alvin Cooper?'

'No,' said Stephen.

'Have you had any contact with anyone else who invested in this company?'

'No,' said Stephen.

For well over an hour the Inspector quizzed Stephen on minor points, but he was unable to give very much help, although he had kept a copy of the geologist's report.

'Yes, we have one of those, sir,' said the Inspector, 'but it's carefully worded and we won't be able to rely much on that for evidence.'

'Evidence against whom or for what, Inspector?' Stephen leaned forward. 'It's clear to me that I have been taken for a great big ride. I probably don't need to tell you what a fool I have been. I put my shirt on Prospecta Oil because it sounded like a sure-fire winner. Now I have lost everything I had and I don't know where to turn. What in Heaven's name has been going on in Prospecta Oil?'

He offered the two men some whisky and poured himself a donnish dry sherry.

'Well, sir,' said the Inspector, 'you'll appreciate there are aspects of the case I can't discuss with you. Indeed, there are aspects that aren't very clear to us yet. However, the game is an old one, and this time it has been played by an old pro, a very cunning old pro. It works like this: a company is set up or taken over by a bunch of villains who acquire most of the shares. They make up a good story about a new find or product that will send the shares up, whisper it in a few ears, release their own shares on to the market where they are snapped up by the likes of you, sir, at a good price. Then they clear off with the profit they have made and the shares collapse. As often as not, it ends in dealings in the company's shares being suspended on the stock market, and finally in the compulsory liquidation of the company. That has not yet happened in this case, and may not. The Montreal Stock Exchange is only just recovering from the Aquablast fiasco and they don't want another scandal. I'm sorry to say, we can hardly ever recover the money, even if we get the evidence to nail the villains. They have it all stashed away halfway round the world before you can say Dow Jones Index.'

Stephen groaned. 'My God, you make it all sound so appallingly simple, Inspector. The geologist's report was a fake, then?'

'No, very impressively set up, with plenty of ifs and buts; and one thing is for certain, the D.P.P.'s office is not going to spend millions finding out if there *is* oil in their part of the North Sea.'

Stephen buried his head in his hands and mentally cursed the day he met David Kesler.

'Tell me, Inspector, who put Kesler up to this? Who was the brains behind that nest of sharks?

The Inspector realized only too well the terrible predicament Stephen was in. During his career he had faced many men in the same position, and he was grateful for Stephen's co-operation.

'I can answer any questions I feel cannot harm my own inquiry,' said the Inspector. 'The man we would like to nail is Harvey Metcalfe.'

'Who's Harvey Metcalfe, for God's sake?'

'He's a first-generation American who's had his hands in more dubious deals in Boston than you've had hot dinners. Made himself a multi-millionaire and a lot of other people bankrupt on the way. His style is now so professional and predictable we can smell the man a mile off. It won't amuse you to learn he is a great benefactor of Harvard—does it to ease his conscience, I suppose. We have never been able to pin anything on him in the past, and I doubt if we will be able to this time either. He was never a director of Prospecta Oil. He only bought and sold shares on the open market, and he never, as far as we know, even met David Kesler. He hired Silverman, Cooper and Elliott to do the dirty work, and they found a bright young man all freshly washed behind the ears to sell their story for them. Just a bit unlucky for you sir, wasn't it, that the young man in question was your friend, David Kesler?'

'Never mind him, poor sod,' said Stephen. 'What about Harvey Metcalfe? Is he going to get away with it again?'

'I fear so,' said the Inspector. 'We have warrants out for Silverman, Elliott and Cooper. They all beat it for South America. After the Ronald Biggs fiasco* I doubt if we will ever get an extradition order to bring them back, despite the fact that the American and Canadian police also have warrants out for them. They were fairly cunning too. They closed the London office of Prospecta Oil, surrendered the lease and returned it to Conrad Ritblat, the estate agents, and gave notice to both secretaries with one month's pay in advance. They cleared the bill on the oil rig with Reading & Bates. They paid off their hired hand, Mark Stewart in Aberdeen, and took the Sunday morning flight to Rio de Janeiro, where there was $1 million in a private account waiting for them. Harvey Metcalfe rewarded them well and left David Kesler holding the baby.'

'Clever boys,' said Stephen.

'Oh yes,' said the Inspector, 'it was a neat little operation. Worthy of the talents of Harvey Metcalfe.'

'Are you trying to arrest David Kesler?'

'No, but as I said we would like to question him. He bought and

---

* Ronald Biggs was involved in the Great Train Robbery of £2,595,998 in 1963 and had settled in Brazil. Scotland Yard were unable to obtain extradition papers for him, and when Chief Superintendent Jack Slipper and Detective Inspector Peter Jones went out to Brazil in 1974 to arrest him, they returned empty-handed.

sold 500 shares, but we think that was only because he believed in the oil strike story himself. In fact, if he was wise he would return to England and help the police with their inquiries, but I fear the poor man has panicked under pressure and made a bolt for it. The American police are keeping an eye out for him.'

'One last question,' said Stephen. 'Are there any other people who have made such fools of themselves as I have?'

The Inspector gave this question long consideration. He had not had as much success with the other big investors as he had had with Stephen. They had all been evasive about their involvement with Kesler and Prospecta Oil. Perhaps if he released their names it might bring them out in some way. The police have many ways of gaining information.

'Yes, sir, but . . . please understand that you never heard about them from me.'

Stephen nodded.

'For your own interest you could find out what you want to know if you made some thorough inquiries at the Stock Exchange. There were four main punters, of whom you were one. Between you you lost approximately $1 million. The others were a Harley Street doctor, Adrian Tryner, a London art dealer called Jean-Pierre Lamanns, and a farmer, whom I feel the sorriest of all for, really. He mortgaged his farm to put up the money, as far as I can gather. Titled young man: Viscount Brigsley. Metcalfe's snatched the silver spoon out of his mouth all right.'

'No other big investors?'

'Yes, two or three banks burnt their fingers badly, but there were no other private investors above $25,000. What you, the banks and the other big investors did was to keep the market going long enough for Metcalfe to off-load his entire holding.'

'I know, and I was foolish enough to advise friends to invest in the company as well.'

'Uhm, there are two or three small investors from Oxford,' said the Inspector, looking down at the sheet of paper in front of him, 'but don't worry, sir, we won't be approaching them. Well, that seems to be all. It only leaves me to thank you for your co-operation and say we may be in touch again some time in the future, but in any case, we will keep you informed of developments, and hope you will do the same for us.'

'Of course, Inspector. I do hope you have a safe journey back to town.' The two policemen downed their drinks and left to catch their train.

Stephen was not sure if it was sitting in his armchair looking out at the Cloisters, or later in bed that night, that he decided to employ his academic mind to carry out a little research on Harvey Metcalfe and his fellow dupes. His grandfather's advice to him, when as a small child he could seldom win their nightly game of chess, floated through his mind: Stevie, don't get cross, get even. When he finally fell asleep at 3 a.m. that was his plan. He was pleased he had given his final lecture and finished work for the term, and he slept soundly, almost relieved by knowing the truth.

FIVE

Stephen awoke at about 5.30 a.m. He seemed to have been heavily, dreamlessly asleep, but as soon as he came to, his nightmare started again. He forced himself to use his mind constructively, to put the past firmly behind him and see what he could do about the future. He washed, shaved, dressed and missed college breakfast, pedalling to Oxford on his ancient bicycle, the preferred mode of transportation in a city blocked solid with juggernaut lorries in one-way systems. He left Ethelred the Unsteady padlocked to the station railings. There were as many bicycles standing in the ranks as there are cars in other railway stations.

He caught the 8.17 so favoured by those who commute from Oxford to London every day. All the people having breakfast seemed to know each other and Stephen felt like an uninvited guest at a party. The ticket collector bustled through the buffet car and clipped Stephen's first-class ticket. The man opposite Stephen produced a second-class ticket from behind his copy of the *Financial Times*. The collector clipped it grudgingly.

'Have to go back to a second-class compartment when you've finished your breakfast, sir. The restaurant car is first class, you know.'

Stephen considered the implication of these remarks, watching the flat Berkshire countryside jolt past as his coffee-cup lurched unsampled in its saucer before he turned to the morning papers. *The Times* carried no news of Prospecta Oil that morning. It was, he supposed, only a little story, even a dull one. Just another shady business enterprise collapsed in double-quick order, not kidnap or arson or even rape: nothing there to hold the attention of the front page for long. Not a story he would have given a second thought to but for his own involvement, which gave it all the makings of a personal tragedy.

At Paddington he pushed through the ants rushing round the forecourt. He was glad he had chosen the closeted life of Oxford or, more accurately, that it had chosen him. He had never come to terms with London—he found it large and impersonal, and he always took a taxi everywhere for fear of getting lost on the buses or the underground. Why ever didn't they number their streets so Americans would know where they were?

'*The Times* office, Printing House Square.'

The cabby nodded and moved his black Austin deftly down the Bayswater Road, alongside a rain-sodden Hyde Park. The crocuses at Marble Arch looked sullen and battered, splayed wetly on the close grass. Stephen was impressed by London cabs: they never had a scrape or mark on them (cab-drivers are not allowed to pick up fares unless their vehicles are in perfect condition). How different from New York's battered yellow monsters, he thought. The cabby swung down Park Lane to Hyde Park Corner, past the House of Commons and along the Embankment. The flags were out in Parliament Square. Stephen frowned to himself. What was the lead story he had read so inattentively in the train? Ah yes, a meeting of Commonwealth leaders. He supposed he must allow the world to go about its day's business as usual.

Stephen was unsure how to tackle the problem of checking Harvey Metcalfe out. Back in Harvard he would have had no trouble: he would have made a bee-line for the offices of the *Herald American* and his father's old friend the business correspondent, Hank Swaltz, would have given him the dope. The diary correspondent of *The Times*, Richard Compton-Miller, was by no means so appropriate a contact, but he was the only British Press man Stephen had ever met. Compton-Miller had visited Magdalen the previous spring to write a feature on the time-honoured observance of May Day in Oxford. The choristers on the top of the College tower sang the Miltonian salute as the sun peeped over the horizon on May 1st:

> Hail, bounteous May, that doth inspire
> Mirth and youth and warm desire.

On the banks of the river beneath Magdalen bridge where Compton-Miller and Stephen had stood, several couples were clearly inspired.

Later, Stephen was more embarrassed than flattered by his appearance in the resulting piece on May Day at Magdalen that Compton-Miller had written for *The Times* Diary: academics are sparing with the word brilliant, but journalists are not. The more self-important of Stephen's Senior Common Room colleagues were not amused to see him described as the brightest star in a firmament of moderate luminescence.

The taxi pulled into the forecourt and came to a stop by the side of a massive hunk of modern sculpture by Henry Moore. *The Times* and the *Observer* shared a building with separate entrances, *The Times*'s by far the more impressive. Stephen inquired of the sergeant behind the desk for Richard Compton-Miller, and was shown up to the fifth floor and along to his little private cubicle at the end of the corridor.

It was still only just after 10 a.m. when Stephen arrived and the building was practically deserted. A national newspaper does not begin to wake up until 11 a.m. and generally indulges itself in a long lunch hour until about 3 p.m. Between then and putting the paper to bed, about 8.30 p.m. for all but the front page, the real work is done. There is usually a change of staff, staggered from 5 p.m. onwards, whose job it is to watch for major news stories breaking during the night. They always have to keep an eye on what is happening in America because if the President makes some important statement in the afternoon in Washington it is already late in the evening in London. Sometimes the front page can change as often as five times during the night and in a case like the assassination of President Kennedy, news of which first reached England about 7 p.m. on the evening of November 22nd, 1963, the whole existing front page is scrapped to make way for the sensation.

'Richard, it was kind of you to come in early for me. I didn't realize that you start work so late. I rather take my daily paper for granted.'

Richard laughed, 'That's O.K. You must think we're a lazy bunch, but this place will be buzzing at midnight when you are in bed sound asleep. How can I help you?'

'I'm trying to do some research on a fellow countryman of mine called Harvey Metcalfe. He's a substantial benefactor of Harvard, and I want to flatter the old boy by knowing all about him when I return.' Stephen didn't care very much for the lie, but these were strange circumstances he found himself in.

'Hang on here and I'll go and see if we have any cuttings on him.'

Stephen amused himself by reading the headlines pinned up on Compton-Miller's board—obviously stories he had taken some pride in: 'Prime Minister to Conduct Orchestra at Royal Festival Hall', 'Miss World loves Tom Jones', 'Muhammad Ali says "I will be Champion Again"'.

Richard returned with a largish file for Stephen fifteen minutes later.

'Have a go at that, Descartes, I'll be back in an hour and we'll have some coffee.'

Stephen nodded and smiled thankfully. Descartes never had the problem he was facing.

Everything Harvey Metcalfe wanted the world to know was in that file, and a little bit he didn't want the world to know. Stephen learned of his yearly trips to Europe to see Wimbledon, of the success of his horses at Ascot and of his pursuit of pictures for his private art collection. William Hickey of the *Daily Express* had titillated his readers with a plump Harvey clad in Bermuda shorts over the information that he spent two or three weeks a year on his private yacht at Monte Carlo, gambling at the Casino. Hickey's tone was something less than fulsome. The Metcalfe fortune was too new to be respectable. Stephen wrote down all the facts he thought relevant and was studying the photographs when Richard returned.

They went to have some coffee in the canteen on the same floor. The cigarette smoke swirled mistily round the girl at the cashier's desk at the end of the self-service counter.

'Richard, I don't quite have all the information I need. Harvard want to touch this man for quite a bit: I believe they are thinking in terms of about $1 million. Where can I find out some more about him?'

'*New York Times*, I should think,' said Compton-Miller, 'come on, we'll give Terry Robards a visit.'

The *New York Times*'s office in London was also on the fifth floor of *The Times*'s building in Printing House Square. Stephen thought of the vast *New York Times* building in 43rd Street and wondered if the London *Times*, on a reciprocal arrangement, was secreted in the basement there. Terry Robards was a wiry creature with a perpetual smile on his face. Stephen felt at ease with him immediately, a knack Terry had developed almost subconsciously over the years and which was a great asset to him when digging for stories.

Stephen repeated his piece about Metcalfe. Terry laughed.

'Harvard aren't too fussy where they get their money from, are they? That guy knows more legal ways of stealing money than the Internal Revenue Service.'

'You don't say,' said Stephen innocently.

The *New York Times*'s file on Harvey was voluminous. 'Metcalfe's rise from Messenger Boy to Millionaire', as one headline had it, was documented admirably. Stephen took careful notes. The details of Sharpley & Son fascinated him, as did the arms dealing and the few facts on his wife Arlene and their daughter Rosalie. There was a picture of both of them, but the daughter was only fifteen at the time. There were also long reports of two court cases some twenty-five years before in which Harvey had been charged but never convicted, and a more recent one in 1956 concerning a share transaction in Boston. Again Harvey had escaped the law, but the District Attorney had left the jury in little doubt of his views on Mr Metcalfe. The most recent Press stories were in the gossip columns: Metcalfe's paintings, his horses, his orchids, his daughter doing well at Vassar and his trips to Europe. Of Prospecta Oil there was not a word. Stephen admired Harvey's ability in later years to conceal from the Press the more dubious of his activities.

Terry invited his fellow expatriate to lunch. Newsmen always like new contacts and Terry thought Stephen looked a promising one. He told the cabby to go to Whitfield Street. As they inched their way out of the City into the West End, Stephen hoped that the meal would be worthy of the journey. He was not disappointed.

Lacy's restaurant was airy and bedecked with clean linen and young daffodils. Terry said it was greatly favoured by Press men. Margaret Costa, the well-known cookery writer and her chef husband, Bill Lacy, certainly knew their onions. Over delicious watercress soup followed by *Médaillons de veau à la crème au calvados* and a bottle of *Château de Péronne 1972*, Terry became quite expansive on Harvey Metcalfe. He had interviewed him at Harvard on the occasion of the opening of Metcalfe Hall, which included a gymnasium and four indoor tennis courts.

'Hoping to get an honorary degree one day,' said Terry cynically, 'but not much hope, even if he gives a billion.'

Stephen noted the words thoughtfully.

'I guess you could get some more facts on the guy at the American Embassy,' said Terry. He glanced at his watch. 'No, hell, the library closes at 4 p.m. Too late today. Time I got back to the office for an afternoon's work.'

Stephen wondered if Press men ate and drank like that every day. If they did, however did they ever manage to get a paper out?

He fought his way on to the 5.15 train back with the Oxford-bound commuters and only when he was alone in his room did he begin to

56

study the results of his day's work. He was exhausted, but he forced himself to sit at his desk until the first neat draft of a dossier on Harvey Metcalfe was prepared.

Next day Stephen again caught the 8.17 to London, this time buying a second-class ticket. The ticket collector repeated his piece about leaving the restaurant car after he had finished his meal.

'Sure,' said Stephen, but he toyed with the remains of his coffee-cup for the rest of the hour-long journey and never shifted from first class. He was pleased with himself: he had saved £2 and that was exactly how Harvey Metcalfe would have behaved.

At Paddington he followed Terry Robard's advice and took a taxi to the American Embassy, a vast and monolithic building which sprawls over 250,000 sq. ft and is nine storeys high, stretching the entire length of one side of Grosvenor Square. Not as elegant as the American Ambassador's magnificent official residence in Regent's Park, where he had been summoned to drinks last year, which was once the private home of Barbara Hutton before it was sold to the American government in 1946. Certainly either of them was large enough for seven husbands, thought Stephen.

The entrance to the Embassy Reference Library on the ground floor was firmly shut. Stephen was reduced to a close study of the plaques on the wall in the corridor outside, honouring recent Ambassadors to the Court of St James. Reading backwards from Walter Annenberg, he had got as far as Joseph Kennedy when the doors of the Library swung open, rather like a bank. The prim girl behind a sign marked 'Inquiries' was not immediately forthcoming on the subject of Harvey Metcalfe.

'Why do you want this information?' she asked sharply.

This threw Stephen for a moment, but he quickly recovered. 'I am returning to Harvard as a Professor and I feel I should know more about his involvement with the university. I am at present a Visiting Fellow at Oxford.'

Stephen's answer motivated the girl to action and she produced a file within a few minutes. It was by no means as racy as the *New York Times*'s, but it did put figures on the amount Harvey Metcalfe had donated to charity and gave exact details of his gifts to the Democratic Party. Most people do not divulge the exact amount they give to political parties, but Harvey only knew about lights—no one seemed to have told him about bushels.

Having finished his research at the Embassy, Stephen took a taxi to the Cunard offices in St James's Square and from there went on to Claridge's in Brook Street and spent a few minutes with the manager. A telephone call to Monte Carlo completed his research. He returned to Oxford on the 5.15.

Stephen went immediately to his college rooms. He felt he knew as much about Harvey Metcalfe as anyone other than perhaps Arlene and Detective Inspector Smith of the Fraud Squad. Once again he stayed up into the night completing his dossier which now numbered over forty typewritten pages.

When the dossier was finally completed he went to bed and fell into a deep sleep. He rose again early in the morning, walked across the Cloisters to a Common Room breakfast and helped himself to eggs and bacon, coffee and toast. Then he took his dossier to the Bursar's office where he made four copies of every document, ending up with five dossiers in all. He strolled across Magdalen Bridge, admiring, as he always did, the trim flower beds of the University Botanic Gardens beneath him on his right, and called in at Maxwells Bookshop on the other side of the bridge.

He returned to his rooms with five smart files of different colours. He then made up the five dossiers in the separate files and placed them in a drawer of his desk which he kept locked. He had a tidy and methodical mind, as a mathematician must: a mind the like of which Harvey Metcalfe had never yet come up against.

Stephen then referred to the notes he had written after his meeting with Detective Inspector Smith and rang Directory Enquiries, asking for the London addresses and telephone numbers of Dr Adrian Tryner, Jean-Pierre Lamanns and Lord Brigsley. Directory Enquiries would not give him more than two numbers at any one time. Stephen wondered how, or indeed if, the G.P.O. made any money at all. In the States the Bell Telephone Company would happily have given him a dozen telephone numbers and still ended with the invariable 'You're welcome.'

The two he managed to wheedle out of his reluctant informant were Dr Adrian Tryner at 122 Harley Street, London W1., and Jean-Pierre Lamanns at the Lamanns Gallery, 40 New Bond Street, W1. Stephen then dialled Directory Enquiries a second time and requested the number and address of Lord Brigsley.

'No one under Brigsley in Central London,' said the operator. 'Maybe he's ex-Directory. That is, if he really is a lord,' she sniffed.

Stephen left his study for the Senior Common Room where he

thumbed through the latest copy of *Who's Who* and found the noble lord:

BRIGSLEY, **Viscount; James Clarence Spencer;** *b* 11 Oct. 1942; Farmer, *s* and *heir* of 5th Earl of Louth, *cr* 1764, *qv*. *Educ:* Harrow; Christ Church, Oxford (BA). Pres. Oxford University Dramatic Society. Lt Grenadier Guards 1966–8. *Recreations:* polo (not water), shooting. *Address:* Tathwell Hall, Louth, Lincs. *Clubs:* Garrick, Guards.

Stephen then strolled over to Christ Church and asked the secretary in the Treasurer's office if she had a London address for James Brigsley, matriculated 1963, in the records. It was duly supplied as 119 King's Road, London SW3.

Stephen was beginning to warm to the challenge of Harvey Metcalfe. He left Christ Church by Peckwater and the Canterbury Gate, out into the High and back to Magdalen, hands in pockets, composing a brief letter in his mind. Oxford's nocturnal slogan-writers had been at work on a college wall again, he saw. 'Deanz means feinz' said one neatly painted graffito. Stephen, the reluctant Junior Dean of Magdalen, responsible for undergraduate discipline, smiled. When back at his desk he wrote down what had been in his mind.

Magdalen College,
Oxford.
April 15th
Dear Dr Tryner,
    I am holding a small dinner party in my rooms next Thursday evening for a few carefully selected people.
    I would be very pleased if you could spare the time to join me, and I think you would find it worth your while to come.
Yours sincerely,
Stephen Bradley.
Black Tie. 7.30 for 8 p.m.

Stephen changed the sheet of letter paper in his typewriter and addressed similar letters to Jean-Pierre Lamanns and Lord Brigsley. Then he thought for a little and picked up the internal telephone.

'Harry?' he said to the head porter. 'If anyone rings the lodge to ask if the college has a member called Stephen Bradley, I want you to say, "Yes, sir, a new Mathematics Fellow already famous for his dinner parties." Got that?'

'Yes, sir,' said the head porter, Harry Woodley. He had never understood Americans and Dr Bradley was no exception.

All three men did ring and inquire as Stephen had anticipated they would. He himself would have done the same. Harry remembered his message and repeated it, although the callers seemed a little baffled.

'No more than me, or is it I?' muttered the head porter.

Stephen received acceptances from all three. James Brigsley's arrived last, on the Monday. The crest on his letter paper announced a promising motto: *ex nihilo omnia*.

The butler to the Senior Common Room and the college chef were consulted, and a meal to loosen the tongues of the most taciturn was planned:

Coquilles St Jacques	Pouilly Fuissé 1969
Carrée d'agneau en croûte	Feux St Jean 1970
Casserole d'artichauds et champignons	
Pommes de terre boulangère	
Griestorte with raspberries	Barsac Ch. d'Yquem 1927
Camembert frappé	Port Taylor 1947
Café	

Everything was now planned; all Stephen could do was wait for the appointed hour.

On the stroke of 7.30 p.m. on Thursday Jean-Pierre arrived. Stephen admired the elegant dinner-jacket and floppy bow-tie that his guest wore, and fingered his own little clip-on, surprised that Jean-Pierre Lamanns, with such apparent savoir-faire, could also have fallen victim to Prospecta Oil. Stephen plunged into a monologue on the significance of the isosceles triangle in modern art. Not a subject he would normally have chosen to speak on without a break for five minutes, but he was saved from the inevitability of questions from Jean-Pierre by the arrival of Dr Adrian Tryner. He had lost a few pounds in the past days, but Stephen could see why his practice in Harley Street would be a success. He was, in the words of H. H. Munro, a man whose looks made it possible for women to forgive any other little inadequacies. Adrian studied his shambling host and asked himself if he dared to inquire immediately if they had ever met before. No, he would leave it a little and perhaps some clue would materialize during dinner.

Stephen introduced him to Jean-Pierre and they chatted while the host checked the dinner table. Once again the door opened and with a little more respect than previously displayed the porter announced, 'Lord Brigsley'. Stephen greeted him, suddenly unsure whether he should bow or shake hands. Although James did not know anyone present (a very strange gathering, he thought), he showed no signs of discomfort and entered easily into the conversation. Even Stephen was struck by James's relaxed line of small talk, but he couldn't help recalling his academic results at Christ Church and he wondered whether the noble lord would be an asset to his plans.

The meal worked the magic that had been intended. No guest could possibly have asked his host why the dinner party was taking place at all while such delicately garlic-flavoured lamb, such tender almond pastry, were to hand.

Finally, when the servants had cleared the table and the port was on its way round for the second time, Adrian could stand it no longer:

'If it's not a rude question, Dr Bradley.'

'Do call me Stephen.'

'Stephen, what in hell's name is the purpose of this select gathering?'

Six eyes bored into him asking the same question.

Stephen rose and surveyed his guests. He started by recalling the entire happenings of the past few weeks. He told them of his meeting with David Kesler, his investment in Prospecta Oil and the visit of the Fraud Squad. He ended his carefully prepared speech with the words, 'Gentlemen, the truth is that the four of us are all in the same bloody mess.'

Jean-Pierre reacted before Stephen could finish what he was saying:

'Count me out. I would not be involved in anything quite so stupid as that. I am a humble art dealer, not a speculator.'

Adrian Tryner joined in even before Stephen was given the chance to reply:

'Never heard anything so preposterous. You must have got the wrong man. I am a Harley Street doctor—I know nothing about oil.'

Stephen could see why the Fraud Squad had had trouble with those two and why they had been so thankful for his co-operation. They all looked at Lord Brigsley, who raised his eyes and said very quietly:

'Absolutely right to the detail, Mr Bradley, and I am in more of a pickle than you. I borrowed £150,000 to buy the shares against the security of my small farm in Hampshire and I don't think it will be long before the bank insist that I sell it, and when they do and my dear

61

old pa, the fifth earl, finds out, it's curtains for me or I become the sixth earl overnight.'

'Thank you,' said Stephen. As he sat down, he turned to Adrian and raised his eyebrows interrogatively.

'What the hell,' said Adrian, 'you are quite right about my involvement. I met David Kesler as a patient and in a rash moment invested £100,000 in Prospecta Oil as a loan against my securities. God only knows what made me do it. As the shares are only worth 50 cents now no one will buy them, and I have a shortfall at my bank which they are beginning to fuss about. I also have a large mortgage on my country home in Berkshire and a heavy rent on my Harley Street consulting-room, a wife with expensive tastes and two boys at the best private prep school in England. I have hardly slept a wink since Detective Inspector Smith visited me two weeks ago.' He looked up. His face had drained of colour and the assured suavity of Harley Street had gone. Slowly, they turned and looked at Jean-Pierre.

'All right, all right,' he admitted, 'me too. I was in Paris when the damned thing folded under me and I got stuck with the useless shares. £80,000 borrowed against my stock at the gallery—stock I cannot move at the moment because of the drop in values in the art market. The bank are asking me to consider selling my gallery. And what is worse, I told some of my friends to invest in the bloody company.'

Silence enveloped the room. It was Jean-Pierre who broke it again:

'So what do you suggest, Professor,' he said sarcastically, 'hold an annual dinner to celebrate what fools we have been?'

'That was not my plan,' Stephen realized that what he was about to suggest would shock, so he rose again to his feet, and quietly and deliberately said:

'We have had our money stolen by a very clever man who is an expert in share fraud. We are not knowledgeable about stocks and shares, but we are all experts in our own fields. Gentlemen I therefore suggest we steal it back.

NOT A PENNY MORE AND NOT A PENNY LESS.'

A few seconds' silence was followed by uproar.

'Just walk up and take it, I suppose?' said Adrian.

'Kidnap him,' mused James.

'Why don't we just kill him?' said Jean-Pierre.

62

Several minutes passed. Stephen waited until he had complete silence again and then he handed round the four dossiers marked 'Harvey Metcalfe' with each individual name below. The green dossier for Adrian, the blue one for James and the yellow for Jean-Pierre. The red master copy Stephen kept for himself. They were all impressed. While they had been wringing their hands in unproductive dismay, it was obvious that Stephen Bradley had been hard at work.

Stephen continued:

'Please read your dossier carefully. It gives you full details of everything that is known about Harvey Metcalfe. Each of you must take it away and study the information, and return with a plan of how we are, between us, to extract $1,000,000 from him without his ever becoming aware of it. All four of us must come up with a separate plan. Each may involve the other three in his operation. We will return here in fourteen days' time and present our ideas. Each member of the team will put $10,000 into the kitty as a float and I, as the mathematician, will keep a running account. All expenses incurred in retrieving our money will be added to Mr Metcalfe's bill, starting with your journey down here this evening and the cost of the dinner tonight.'

Jean-Pierre and Adrian protested. Again it was James who stopped the proceedings by saying simply:

'I agree. What else have we got to lose if we fail? On our own we have no chance: together we might just beat the bastard.'

Adrian and Jean-Pierre looked at each other, shrugged and nodded.

The four of them settled down to a long discussion about the material Stephen had acquired over the past few days. They left the college just before midnight, agreeing that they would each have a plan ready in fourteen days' time. None of them was quite sure where it was all going to end, but each was relieved to find he was no longer on his own.

Stephen thought that the first part of the Team versus Harvey Metcalfe had gone as well as he could have wished. He only hoped his conspirators would get down to work. He sat in his armchair, lit a Winston and started thinking.

SIX

Adrian retrieved his car from the High Street, not for the first time in his life thanking its 'Doctor on Call' sticker for the extra degree of freedom it gave him in parking. He drove back to his home in Berkshire. There was no doubt about it, he had been impressed by Stephen Bradley, and he was determined to come up with something that would ensure he played his full part.

He let his mind linger a little on the delightful prospect of recovering the money he had so ill-advisedly entrusted to Prospecta Oil and Harvey Metcalfe. It seemed worth a try: after all, he might as well be struck off the register of the General Medical Council for attempted robbery as for bankruptcy. He wound the window of the car down a little way to dispel the last delicious effects of the claret and thought.

The journey between Oxford and his country house passed very quickly. His mind was so preoccupied that when he arrived home to his wife there were large sections of the route he could not even remember. He had only one card to play, other than his natural charm, and he hoped that he was right in thinking that card was the strength in his armour and the weakness in Harvey Metcalfe's. He began to repeat out loud something that was written on page 16 of Stephen's dossier, 'One of Harvey Metcalfe's recurrent worries is . . .'

'What was it all about, darling?'

His wife's voice brought Adrian quickly to his senses and he locked the briefcase which contained the green Metcalfe dossier.

'You still awake, Mary?'

'Well, I'm not talking in my sleep, love.'

Adrian had to think quickly. He had not yet steeled himself to tell Mary of his foolish investment, but he had let her know about the dinner in Oxford, not realizing it was in any way connected with Prospecta Oil.

'It was a tease, sweetheart. An old friend of mine from Cambridge has become a lecturer at Oxford, so he dragged a few of his contemporaries down for dinner and we had a damn good evening. Jim and Fred from my old college were there, but I don't expect you remember them.'

A bit weak, thought Adrian, but the best he could do at 1.15 a.m.

'Sure it wasn't some beautiful girl?' said Mary.

'I'm afraid Jim and Fred could hardly be described as beautiful, even by their loving wives.'

'Do lower your voice, Adrian, or you'll wake the children.'

'I'm going down again in two weeks' time to . . .'

'Oh, do come to bed and tell me about it at breakfast.'

Adrian was relieved to be let off the hook until the morning. He clambered in beside his fragrant silk-clad wife and ran his finger hopefully down her vertebral column to her coccyx.

'You'll be lucky, at this time of night,' she said.

They both slept.

Jean-Pierre had booked in at the Eastgate Hotel in the High. There was an undergraduate exhibition the next day at the Christ Church Art Gallery. Jean-Pierre hoped to find some new young talent which he could contract to the Lamanns Gallery. It was the Marlborough Gallery, a few doors away from him in Bond Street, that had taught the London art world the astuteness of buying up young artists and being closely identified with their careers. But for the moment, the artistic future of his gallery was not uppermost in Jean-Pierre's mind: its very survival was threatened and the quiet American don at Magdalen had offered a chance of redress. He settled down in his comfortable hotel bedroom, oblivious to the late hour, to go over his dossier and work out where he could fit into the jig-saw. He was not going to allow two Englishmen and a Yank to beat him. His French father had been relieved at Rochefort by the British in 1918 and released from a prisoner-of-war camp near Frankfurt by the Americans in 1945. There was no way he was not going to play his part in this operation. He read the yellow dossier late into the night: the germ of an idea was beginning to form in his mind.

James made the last train from Oxford and looked for an empty carriage where he could settle down to study the blue dossier. He was a worried man: he was sure the other three would come up with some brilliant plan and, as had always seemed to happen to him in his life, he would be found lacking. He had never been under pressure before —everything had come to him so easily. A foolproof scheme for relieving Harvey Metcalfe of some of his excess profits was not going to come anything like so readily. Still, the awful vision of his father finding out that the Hampshire farm was mortgaged up to the hilt was there to keep his mind on the job. Fourteen days was not very long: where on earth would he begin? He was not a professional man like the other three and had no particular skills to offer. He could only hope that his stage experience might be of use in some way.

He bumped into the ticket collector, who was not surprised to find James the holder of a first-class ticket. The quest for an unoccupied compartment ended in failure. James concluded that Richard Marsh was trying to run the railways at a profit. Whatever would happen next? What was more aggravating, they would probably give him a knighthood for his trouble.

The next best thing to an empty compartment, James always considered, was one containing a beautiful girl—and this time his luck was in. One of the compartments was occupied by a truly stunning creature who looked as if she was on her own. The only other person in the carriage was a middle-aged lady reading *Vogue*, who showed no signs of knowing her travelling companion. James settled down in the corner with his back to the engine, realizing he could not study the Metcalfe dossier on the train. They had all been sworn to total secrecy, and Stephen had cautioned them against reading the dossiers in anyone else's company. James feared that of the four of them he was going to find it most difficult to keep silent: a companionable man, he found secrets rather tedious. He patted his overcoat pocket holding the dossier in the envelope supplied by Stephen Bradley. What an efficient man he was, thought James. Alarmingly brainy, too. He would no doubt have a dozen clever plans ready for the next meeting. James frowned and stared out of the window in the hope of some serendipitous ideas. Instead he found himself studying the reflection of the beautiful profile of the girl sitting opposite him.

She had a shiny nob of dark brown hair, a slim straight nose and her long lashes lay demurely on her cheeks as she read the book she held in her lap. James wondered if she was as entirely oblivious of his presence as she appeared to be, and reluctantly (and wrongly) decided that she was. His eyes slipped down to the gentle curve of her breast, softly encased in angora. He craned his neck slightly to see

66

what sort of legs the reflection had. Damn it, she was wearing boots. He looked back at the face again. It was looking at him, faintly amused. Embarrassed, he switched his attention to the third occupant of the carriage, the unofficial chaperon in front of whom James had not the courage to strike up a conversation with the girl.

Suddenly he realized that the model on the front cover of the middle-aged lady's *Vogue* was the exact image of the girl he was sitting opposite. To begin with, he could hardly believe his eyes, but a quick check against the real McCoy left him in no doubt. As soon as *Vogue* was relinquished in favour of *Queen*, James leant across and asked the chaperon if he might have a look.

'Left my briefcase on the station by mistake,' he said idiotically. 'I haven't got anything to read.'

He turned to the second page. 'Cover: Picture yourself like this ... black silk georgette dress with chiffon handkerchief points. Ostrich-feather boa. Turban with flower matching dress. Made to measure by Zandra Rhodes. Anne's hair by Jason at Vidal Sassoon. Photograph by Lichfield. Camera: Hasselblad.'

James could not picture himself like that with any degree of success. At least he knew the beautiful cover-girl's name, Anne. The next time the real-life version looked up, he showed her by sign language that he had seen the photograph. She smiled briefly at James and then went back to *The Odessa File*.

At Reading station the middle-aged lady left, bearing off *Vogue* with her. Couldn't be better, mused James. Anne looked up, faintly embarrassed, and smiled hopefully at the few passers-by in the corridor looking for a seat. James glared at them as they passed. No one entered the carriage. James had won the first round. As the train gathered speed he tried his opening gambit, which was quite good by his normal standards:

'What a super picture on the front of *Vogue* taken by my old mate Patrick Lichfield.'

Anne Summerton looked up. She was even more beautiful than the picture James had referred to. Her dark hair, cut softly in the latest Vidal Sassoon style, her big hazel eyes and faultless skin gave her a gentle look that James found irresistible. She had that slim, graceful body that all leading models need in order to earn their living, but Anne had a presence that most of them would never have. James was quite stunned and wished she would say something.

Anne was used to men trying to pick her up, but she was rather taken aback by the remark about Lord Lichfield. If he was a friend it would be offhand not to be at least polite. On a second glance she found James's diffidence rather charming. He had used the self-deprecating approach many times with great success, but this time it was perfectly genuine. He tried again.

'It must be a hell of a job being a model.'

What a bloody silly line, he thought. Why couldn't he just say to her, I think you are absolutely fantastic. Can we talk a little and if I still think you are fantastic perhaps we'll take it from there. But it never was possible that way and he would have to go through the usual routine.

'It's rather fun if the contracts are good,' she replied, 'but today's been particularly tiring.' Her voice was gentle, and her faint transatlantic accent appealed to James. 'I've been smiling my head off all day, modelling a toothpaste advertisement for Close-Up: the photographer never seemed to be satisfied. The only good thing was that it ended earlier than expected. How do you know Patrick?'

'We were fags together at Harrow in our first year. He was rather better than me at getting out of work.'

Anne laughed—a gentle, warm laugh. It was obvious he did know Lord Lichfield.

'Do you see much of him now?'

'Occasionally at dinner parties, but not regularly. Does he photograph you a lot?'

'No,' said Anne, 'the cover picture for *Vogue* is the only occasion I have been shot by him.'

They chatted on and the thirty-five minute journey between Reading and London seemed to pass in a flash for James. As they walked down the platform of Paddington Station together he ventured:

'Can I give you a lift home? My car is parked in Craven Street.'

Anne accepted. She was relieved not to have to search for a taxi at that late hour.

James drove her home in his Alfa Romeo. He had already decided that he could not hold on to that for much longer with petrol going up and the cash flow going down. He chattered merrily all the way to her destination in a block of flats overlooking the Thames in Cheyne Row, and much to Anne's surprise just dropped her off at the front door and said goodnight. He did not even ask for her telephone number and he only knew her Christian name. In fact, she did not have any idea what his name was. Pity, she thought, he had been a rather pleasant change from the men who worked on the fringe of the advertising media, who imagined they had an automatic right to a girl's compliance just because she posed in a bra.

James knew exactly what he was doing. He always found a girl was more flattered if he called her when she least expected it. His tactics were to leave the impression that she had seen the last of him, especially when the first meeting had gone well. He returned to his home in the King's Road and thought for a while. But unlike Stephen, Adrian and Jean-Pierre, with thirteen days to go, he had no ideas for defeating Harvey Metcalfe: he was developing plans for Anne.

On waking in the morning, Stephen began to do a little more research. He started with a close study of the way the university was administered. He visited the Vice-Chancellor's office in the Clarendon Building, where he spent some time asking strange questions of the personal secretary, Miss Smallwood. She was most intrigued. He then left for the office of the University Registrar, where he was equally inquisitive. He ended the day by visiting the Bodleian Library, and copying out some of the University Statutes. Among other outings during the next fourteen days was a trip to the Oxford tailors Shepherd and Woodward, and a full day at the Sheldonian Theatre to watch a batch of students take their B.A. degrees in a brief ceremony. Stephen also studied the layout of the Randolph, the largest hotel in Oxford. This he took considerable time over, so much so that the manager became inquisitive, but Stephen left before this turned to suspicion. His final trip was a return journey to the Clarendon to meet the Secretary of the University Chest, and to be taken on a guided tour of the building by the porter. Stephen warned him that he anticipated showing an American the building on the day of Encaenia, but remained vague.

'Well, that won't be easy . . .' began the porter. Stephen carefully and deliberately folded a pound note and passed it to the porter '. . . though I'm sure we will be able to work something out, sir.'

In between the trips all over the university city, Stephen did a lot of thinking in his big leather chair and a lot more writing at his desk. By the fourteenth day his plan was perfected and ready for presentation to the other three. He had put the show on the road, as Harvey Metcalfe might have said, and he intended to see it had a long run.

*

Adrian rose early on the morning after the Oxford dinner, and avoided awkward questions from his wife at breakfast about his experience the night before. He travelled to London as quickly as he could get away and on arrival in Harley Street was greeted by his efficient secretary-cum-receptionist, Miss Meikle.

Elspeth Meikle was a dedicated, dour Scot who looked upon her work as a vocation. Her devotion to Adrian, not that she ever called him that even in her own mind, was obvious for all to see.

'I want as few appointments as possible over the next fourteen days, Miss Meikle.'

'I understand, Dr Tryner,' she said.

'I have some research to do and do not want to be interrupted when I am alone in my study.'

Miss Meikle was a little surprised. She had always thought that Dr Tryner was a good doctor, but had never known him in the past to indulge in research work. She padded off noiselessly in her white-shod feet to let in the first of a bunch of admirably healthy ladies for Dr Tryner's clinic.

Adrian entered his consulting-room. He started the morning by making several telephone calls, among them two overseas calls to the Boston Infirmary and several to a leading gastroenterologist for whom he had been a houseman at Cambridge. Then he pressed the buzzer to summon Miss Meikle.

'Pop round to H. K. Lewis, would you, Miss Meikle, and get two books on my account. I want the latest edition of Polson and Tatter-sall's *Clinical Toxicology* and Harding Rain's book on the bladder and abdomen.'

'Yes, sir,' she said imperturbably, and thought nothing of delaying her lunchtime sandwich to fetch them in time for Adrian's return from his habitual Club lunch.

They were on his desk when he returned, and he started a careful reading of them. The following day he spent at St Thomas's Hospital, not taking his morning clinic as usual, but closely watching two of his colleagues at work. His confidence in the plan he was formulating was growing. He returned to Harley Street and wrote some notes on the techniques he had observed as he had done in his student days. He remembered the words Stephen had used:

'Think as Harvey Metcalfe would. Think not as a cautious professional man, but as a risk-taker, as an entrepreneur.'

Adrian was getting on to Harvey Metcalfe's wavelength, and he would be ready for the American, the Frenchman and the lord when his plan was called for: he looked forward to their next meeting.

Jean-Pierre returned from Oxford the next day. None of the youthful artists had greatly impressed him, though he felt Anthony Bamber's watercolours showed considerable promise and he made a mental note to keep an eye on his future work. When he arrived in London he started, like Adrian and Stephen, on his research. The tentative idea that had come to him in the Eastgate Hotel was beginning to develop. Through his numerous contacts in the art world he checked all the buying and selling of major Impressionist paintings over the previous twenty years. He made a list of the pictures which were currently thought to be on the market. He then contacted the one person who had it in his power to set Jean-Pierre's plan in motion. The man whose help he most needed, David Stein, was luckily in England and free to visit him: but would he fall in with the plan?

Stein arrived late the next afternoon and spent two hours with Jean-Pierre privately in his little room in the basement of the Lamanns Gallery. When he departed Jean-Pierre was smiling to himself. A final afternoon spent at the German Embassy in Belgrave Square, followed by a call to Dr Wormit of the Preussischer Kulturbesitz in Berlin and a further one to Mme Tellegen at the Rijksbureau in The Hague, gave him all the information he needed. Even Metcalfe would have praised him for that touch. There would be no relieving the French this time. The American and the Englishmen had better be up to scratch when he presented his plan.

On waking in the morning the last thing James had on his mind was a plan for outwitting Harvey Metcalfe. His thoughts were fully occupied with Anne. He telephoned Patrick Lichfield at home.

'Patrick?'

'Yes.'

'James Brigsley.'

'Oh, hello James. Haven't seen you for some time. What are you doing waking me up at this filthy hour?'

'It's 10 a.m. Patrick.'

'Is it? I had a hell of a night last night. What can I do for you?'

'You took a picture for *Vogue* of a girl whose first name was Anne.'

'Summerton,' said Patrick without hesitation. 'Got her from the Stacpoole Agency.'

'What's she like?'

'No idea,' said Patrick. 'I thought she was awfully nice. She just didn't think I was her type.'

'I can't say I blame her. Go back to bed, Patrick. See you soon.'

Anne Summerton was not in the telephone directory so that ploy had failed. James stayed in bed, scratching the stubble on his chin, when a triumphant look came into his eye. A quick flip through the S–Z directory revealed the number he required.

'The Stacpoole Agency.'

'Can I speak to the manager?'

'Who's calling?'

'Lord Brigsley.'

'I'll put you through, my lord.'

James heard the phone click and the voice of the manager, Michael Stacpoole.

'Good morning, my lord, can I help you?'

'I hope so. I'm looking for a model for the opening of an antique shop and I want a classy sort of a bird. You do understand?'

James then described Anne as if he had never met her.

'We have two models who I think would suit you, my lord,' said Stacpoole. 'Paulene Stone and Anne Summerton. Unfortunately, Paulene is in Birmingham today for the launching of the new Allegro car and Anne is completing a toothpaste ad. in Oxford.'

'I need a girl today,' James said. How he would have liked to have told Stacpoole that Anne was back in town. 'If you find either of them is free, perhaps you would ring me at 352 2109, Mr Stacpoole.'

James rang off, a little disappointed. At least, he thought, if nothing comes of it today I can start planning my part in the Team versus Harvey Metcalfe. He was just resigning himself to it when the phone rang. A shrill, high-pitched voice announced:

'This is the Stacpoole Agency. Mr Stacpoole would like to speak to Lord Brigsley.'

'Speaking,' said James.

'I'll put you through, my lord.'

'Lord Brigsley?'

'Yes.'

'Stacpoole here, my lord. It seems Anne Summerton is free today. When would you like her to come to your shop?'

'Oh,' said James, taken aback for a second. 'My shop is in Berkeley Street, next to the Empress Restaurant. It's called Albemarle

Antiques. Perhaps we could meet outside at 12.45?'

'I'm sure that will be acceptable, my lord. If I don't ring you back in the next ten minutes you can assume the meeting is on. Perhaps you would be kind enough to let us know if she is suitable. We normally prefer you to come to the office, but I am sure we can make an exception in your case.'

'Thank you,' said James and put the phone down, pleased with himself.

James stood on the west side of Berkeley Street in the doorway of the May Fair Hotel so that he could watch Anne arriving. When it came to work, Anne was always on time, and at 12.40 p.m. she appeared from the Piccadilly end of the street. Her skirt was of the latest elegant length but this time James could see that her legs were as slim and shapely as the rest of her. She stopped outside the Empress Restaurant and looked in puzzlement at the Brazilian Trade Centre on her right and the Rolls Royce showrooms of H. R. Owen on her left.

James strode across the road, a large grin on his face.

'Good morning,' he said casually.

'Oh hello,' said Anne, 'what a coincidence.'

'What are you doing all alone?' said James.

'I'm trying to find a shop called Albemarle Antiques. You don't know it by any chance? I am supposed to be doing an assignment for them. I'm waiting for the owner, Lord Brigsley.'

James smiled:

'I am Lord Brigsley.'

Anne looked surprised and then burst out laughing. She realized what James had done and was flattered by the compliment.

They lunched together at the Empress, James's favourite eating place in town. He told Anne why it had been Lord Clarendon's favourite restaurant as well—'Ah,' he had declared, 'the millionaires are just a little fatter, and the mistresses are just a little thinner, than in any other restaurant in London.'

Anne was the first good thing that had happened to James for a long time. The next ten days shot by and James spent more time with Anne than he had bargained for. When Thursday came he had no plan to place in front of the Team. He only hoped they were in the same position and the whole exercise would be abandoned.

He travelled to Oxford in his Alfa Romeo and was again the last to arrive at Magdalen. Stephen, Adrian and Jean-Pierre greeted him with open arms. Oh hell, he thought, they all look very confident.

SEVEN

Stephen shook James warmly by the hand the way the Americans will and gave him a large whisky on the rocks. James took a gulp to give himself a bit of Dutch courage, and joined Adrian and Jean-Pierre. By unspoken mutual consent, the name of Harvey Metcalfe was not mentioned. They chattered inconsequentially of nothing in particular, each clutching his dossier, until Stephen summoned them to the table. Stephen had not, on this occasion, exercised the talents of the college chef and the butler to the Senior Common Room. Sandwiches, beer and coffee were stacked neatly on the table, and the college servants were not in evidence.

'This is a working supper,' said Stephen firmly, 'and as Harvey Metcalfe will eventually be footing the bill, I have cut down a bit on the hospitality. We don't want to make our task unnecessarily hard by eating our way through hundreds of dollars per meeting.'

The other three sat down quietly as Stephen took out some papers.

'I will start,' he said, 'with a general comment. I have been doing some further research into Harvey Metcalfe's movements over the next few months. He seems to spend every summer doing the same round of social and sporting events. Most of it is already in the file. My latest findings are summarized on this note, which should be added as page 38 of your dossiers. It reads:

Harvey Metcalfe will arrive in England on June 21st on the QE2, docking at Southampton. He has already reserved the Trafalgar Suite for his crossing and booked a Rolls Royce from Guy Salmon to take him to Claridge's. He will stay there for two weeks in the Royal Suite and he has debenture tickets for every day of the Wimbledon Championships. When they are over he flies to Monte Carlo to his yacht *Messenger Boy* for just over another two weeks. He then returns to London and Claridge's to see his filly, Rosalie, run in the King George VI and Queen Elizabeth Stakes. He has a private box at Ascot

74

for all five days of Ascot Week. He returns to America on a Pan American Jumbo jet from London Heathrow on July 29th, flight no. 009 at 11.15 to Logan International Airport, Boston.'

The others attached page 38 to their dossiers, aware once again how much detailed research Stephen had undertaken. James was beginning to feel ill and it certainly was not the sandwiches that were causing his discomfort.

'The next decision to be taken,' said Stephen, 'is to allocate the times during Metcalfe's trip to Europe when each plan will be put into operation. Adrian, which section would you like?'

'Monte Carlo,' said Adrian without hesitation. 'I need to catch the bastard off his home ground.'

'Anyone else want Monte Carlo?'

Nobody spoke.

'Which would you prefer, Jean-Pierre?'

'I would like Wimbledon fortnight.'

'Any objections?'

Again, nobody spoke. Stephen said:

'I am keen to have the Ascot slot and the short time before he returns to America. What about you, James?'

'It won't make any difference what period I have,' said James rather sheepishly.

'Right,' said Stephen. 'At the moment Jean-Pierre goes first, Adrian second and I am third. James will fit in according to how this discussion goes.'

Everybody, except James, seemed to be warming to the exercise.

'Now expenses. Have all of you brought cheques for $10,000? I think it wise to work in dollars as that was the currency Prospecta Oil shares were purchased in.'

Each member of the Team passed a cheque to Stephen. At least, thought James, this is something I can do as well as the others.

'Expenses to date?'

Each passed a chit to Stephen again and he began to work out figures on his stylish little HP 65 calculator, the digits glowing red in the dimly lit room.

'The shares cost us $1 million. Expenses to date are $142, so Mr Metcalfe is in debt to us to the tune of $1,000,142. Not a penny more and not a penny less,' he repeated. 'Now to our individual plans. We will take them in the order of execution.' Stephen was pleased with that word. 'Jean-Pierre, Adrian, myself and finally James. The floor is yours, Jean-Pierre.'

Jean-Pierre opened a large envelope and took out four sets of documents. He was determined to show that he had the measure of Stephen as well as of Harvey Metcalfe. He handed round photographs and road maps of the West End and Mayfair. Each street was marked with a figure, indicating how many minutes it took to walk. Jean-Pierre explained his plan in great detail, starting with the crucial meeting he had had with David Stein, and ending with instructions to the others.

'All of you will be needed on the day. Adrian will be the journalist and James the representative from Sotheby's. Stephen, you will act as the purchaser. You must practise speaking English with a German accent. I shall also require two tickets for the whole of Wimbledon fortnight on the Centre Court opposite Harvey Metcalfe's debenture box.'

Jean-Pierre consulted his notes.

'That is to say, opposite box no. 17. Can you arrange that, James?'

'No problem. I'll have a word with Mike Gibson, the Club referee, in the morning.'

'Good. Finally, then, you must all learn to operate these little boxes of tricks. They are called Pye Pocketfones and I had the devil of a job getting a licence from the Home Office and a registered wavelength, so treat them with respect.'

Jean-Pierre produced four miniature sets.

'Any questions?'

There was a general murmur of approval. There were going to be no loose ends in Jean-Pierre's plan.

'My congratulations,' said Stephen. 'That should get us off to a good start. How about you, Adrian?'

Adrian relayed the story of his fourteen days. He reported on his meeting with the specialist, and explained the toxic effects of anticholinesterase drugs.

'This one will be hard to pull off because we will have to wait for the right moment. However, we must be prepared at all times.'

'Where will we stay in Monte Carlo?' asked James. 'I usually go to the Metropole. Better not make it there.'

'No, it's all right, James, I have provisional reservations at the Hôtel de Paris from June 29th to July 4th. However, before that you are all to attend several training sessions at St Thomas's Hospital.'

76

Diaries were consulted, and a series of meetings arranged.

'Here is a copy of Houston's *Short Textbook of Medicine* for each of you. You must all read the chapter on first aid. I don't want any of you to stick out like sore thumbs when we are all dressed in white. You, Stephen, will be coming to Harley Street for an intensive course the week after next as you must be totally convincing as a doctor.'

Adrian had chosen Stephen because he felt that with his academic mind he would pick up the most in the short time available.

'Jean-Pierre, you must attend a gaming club every evening for the next month and learn exactly how baccarat and blackjack are played, and how to be able to play for several hours at a time without losing a great deal of money. James, you will learn to drive a small van through crowded streets, and you are also to come to Harley Street next week so that we can do a dry run together.'

All eyes were wide open. If they pulled that one off they could do anything. Adrian could see the anxiety in their faces.

'Don't worry,' he said, 'my profession has been carried out by witch-doctors for a thousand years. People never argue when they are confronted with a trained man, and you, Stephen, are going to be a trained man.'

Stephen nodded. Academics could be equally naïve. Hadn't that been exactly what had happened to all of them with Prospecta Oil?

'Remember,' said Adrian, 'Stephen's comment at the bottom of page 33 of the dossier ... "At all times we must think like Harvey Metcalfe".'

Adrian gave a few more details of how certain procedures were to be carried out. He then answered questions for twenty-eight minutes. Finally, Jean-Pierre softened:

'I thought none of you would beat me, but that is brilliant. If we get the timing right we will only need an ounce of luck.'

James was beginning to feel distinctly uneasy as his time drew nearer. He rather wished he had never accepted the invitation to the first dinner and urged the others to take up Stephen's challenge. At least the duties he had been given in the first two operations were well within his scope.

'Well, gentlemen,' said Stephen, 'you have both risen to the occasion, but my proposals will make more demands on you.'

He began to reveal the fruits of his research of the past two weeks and the substance of his plan. They all felt rather like students in the presence of a professor. Stephen did not lecture intentionally.

It was a manner he had developed and, like so many academics, he was unable to switch it off in private company. He produced a calendar for Trinity Term and outlined how the university term worked, the role of its Chancellor, Vice-Chancellor, the Registrar and the Secretary of the University Chest. Like Jean-Pierre, he supplied maps, this time of Oxford, to each member of the Team. He had carefully marked a route from the Sheldonian Theatre to Lincoln College, and from Lincoln to the Randolph Hotel with a contingency plan if Harvey Metcalfe insisted on using his car, despite the one-way system.

'Adrian, you must find out what the Vice-Chancellor does at Encaenia. I know it can't be like Cambridge; the two universities do everything the same but nothing identically. You must know the routes he is likely to take and his habits backwards. I have arranged a room at Lincoln to be at your disposal on the final day. Jean-Pierre, you will study and master the duties of the Registrar at Oxford and know the alternative route that is marked on your map. James, you must know how the Secretary of the University Chest goes about his work—the location of his office, which banks he deals with and how the cheques are cashed. You must also know the routes he is likely to take on the day of Encaenia as if they were part of your father's estate. I have the easiest role because I will be myself in all but name. You must all learn how to address each other correctly and we will have a dress rehearsal in the ninth week of term, on a Tuesday when the university is fairly quiet. Any questions?'

Silence ruled the day, but it was a silence of respect. All could see that Stephen's operation would demand split-second timing and that they would have to run through it two or three times, but if they were convincing they could hardly fail.

'Now, the Ascot part of my plan is simpler. I will only need Adrian and James in the Member's Enclosure. I shall need two Enclosure tickets which I am expecting you to acquire, James.'

'You mean badges, Stephen,' said James.

'Oh, do I?' said Stephen. 'I also require someone in London to send the necessary telegram. That will be you, Jean-Pierre.'

'Understood,' said Jean-Pierre.

For nearly an hour the others asked several questions of detail in order to be as familiar with the plan as Stephen was.

James's mind drifted again, hoping the earth would open up. He even began to wish that he had never met Anne, although she was hardly to blame. In fact, he would not wait to see her again. What was he going to say when they . . .

'James, wake up,' said Stephen sharply. 'We're all waiting.'

All eyes were now fixed on him. They had produced the ace of hearts, diamonds and spades. But had he the ace of trumps? James was flustered and took another drink.

'You bloody upper-class twit,' said Jean-Pierre, 'you haven't got an idea.'

'Well, actually, I have given it a lot of thought, but nothing came.'

'Useless—worse than useless,' said Adrian.

James was stammering helplessly. Stephen cut him short.

'Now listen, James, and listen carefully. We meet again in twenty-one days' time from tonight. By then we must know everybody else's plans by heart with no mistake. One error could blow the whole thing. Do you understand?'

James nodded—he was determined not to let them down in that.

'And what is more,' said Stephen firmly, 'you must have your own plan ready for scrutiny. Is that clear?'

'Yes,' mumbled James unhappily.

'Any other questions?' said Stephen.

There were none.

'Right. We go through the three individual operations again detail by detail.'

Stephen ignored muttered protests.

'Remember, we're up again a man who isn't used to being beaten. We won't get a second chance.'

For an hour and a half they went through the details of each operation in the order of action. First, Jean-Pierre during Wimbledon fortnight: second, Adrian in Monte Carlo: third, Stephen during and after Ascot.

It was late when they finally rose from the table. They departed wearily, each with several tasks to carry out before their next meeting. All went their separate ways, due to meet again the following Friday in the Jericho Theatre of St Thomas's Hospital.

EIGHT

The next twenty days turned out to be hard work for all four of them, for each had to master the other plans as well as organize his own. Friday brought them all together for the first of many sessions at St Thomas's Hospital, which would have been entirely successful if James had managed to stay on his feet—it was not even the sight of blood that daunted him, just the sight of the knife was enough. Its only virtue from James's standpoint was that he once again avoided having to explain why he had not come up with any ideas of his own.

The next week was almost full time, with Stephen in Harley Street taking a potted course in medicine on a fairly high level in one particular field.

James spent several hours driving an old van through heavy traffic from St Thomas's to Harley Street, preparing for his final test in Monte Carlo which he felt ought to be considerably easier. He spent some days in Oxford, learning how the Secretary of the University Chest's office operated, and also watching the movements of the Secretary himself, Mr Caston.

Jean-Pierre, at a cost to Mr Metcalfe of £5.25 and a 48-hour wait, became an overseas member of Crockford's, London's most distinguished gaming club, and spent his evenings watching the wealthy and lazy play baccarat and blackjack, the stakes often reaching £1,000. After three weeks he ventured to join the Golden Nugget casino in Soho, where the stakes rarely reached £5. At the end of the month he played 56 hours, but so conservatively that he was only showing a small loss.

James's overriding worry was still his personal contribution. The more he grappled with the problem, the less he came to grips with it. He turned it over and over in his mind, even when he was travelling through London at speed. After returning the van to Carnie's in Lots Road, Chelsea, he drove his Alfa Romeo over to Anne's flat by the river, wondering if he dared confide in her.

Anne was preparing a special meal for James. She was aware that he not only appreciated good food, but had taken it for granted all his life. The homemade gazpacho was smelling good and the *Coq au Vin* was all but ready. Lately she found herself avoiding modelling assignments out of London as she did not care to be away from James for any period of time. She was very conscious that he was the first man for some time she would have been willing to go to bed with, and to date he had been no more than gentle and attentive.

James arrived carrying a bottle of Beaune Montée Rouge 1971—even his wine cellar was fast disappearing. He only hoped it would last until the plans came to fruition. Not that he felt an automatic right to success after his own efforts.

James thought Anne looked very beautiful. She was wearing a long black dress of some soft material that tantalized him with the reticence with which it outlined her shape. She wore no make-up or jewellery, and her heavy nob of hair gleamed in the candlelight. The meal was a triumph for Anne and James started wanting her very badly. She seemed a little nervous, spilling ground coffee as she filtered two strong tiny cups. What was in her mind? He did not want to blunder with unwanted attentions. James had had much more practice at being loved than at being in love. He was used to adulation, to ending up in bed with girls who almost made him shudder in the cold clear light of morning. Anne affected him in an entirely new way. He wanted to be close to her, to hold her and to love her. Above all, he did want to find her there in the morning.

Anne cleared away the supper, avoiding James's eye, and they settled down to brandy and Billie Holiday singing 'I get along without you very well'. She sat, hands clasped round her knees on the floor at James's feet, staring into the fire. Tentatively, he put out a hand and stroked her hair. She sat unresponsive for a moment and then she bent her head back and stretched out her arm to bring his face down to hers. He responded, leaning forward and stroking her cheek and nose with his mouth, holding her head in his hands, his fingers gently exploring her ears and neck. Her skin smelled faintly of jasmine and her open mouth glinted in the firelight as she smiled up at him. He kissed her and slid his hands down on to her body. She felt soft and slight under his hands. He caressed her breasts gently, and moved down beside her, his body pressing against hers. Wordlessly, he reached behind her and unzipped her dress. He stood up, his eyes never leaving hers, and undressed quickly. She glanced at his body and smiled shyly,

81

'Darling James,' she said softly.

After they had made love, Anne settled her head on James's shoulder and stroked the hair on his chest with a fingertip. She sensed that something was wrong.

'What's the matter, James darling? I know I'm rather shy. Wasn't I very good?'

'You were fantastic. God knows, you were fantastic. That's not the problem . . . Anne, I have to tell you something, so just lie there and listen.'

'You're married.'

'No, it's much worse than that.' James thought for a moment, lit a cigarette and inhaled deeply. There are occasions in life when revelation is made easier by circumstance. 'Anne darling, I have made a bloody fool of myself by investing all my money with a bunch of crooks. I haven't even told my family as they would be terribly distressed if they knew the truth. Now I've got myself involved with three other people in the same predicament—we're all trying to get our money back. Nice chaps, full of bright ideas, but I haven't a clue where to begin and keep my part of the bargain. What with the worry of £150,000 down the drain and constantly racking my brain for a good idea, I'm half frantic. You're the only thing that's kept me sane.'

Thus James revealed the entire history of Prospecta Oil, from his meeting with David Kesler at Annabel's to his invitation to dine with Stephen Bradley at Magdalen through to the reason he had been driving a hired van in the rush hour like a maniac. The only detail James left out was the name of their intended victim as he felt that by withholding this fact he was not completely violating his bond of secrecy with the rest of the Team.

Anne breathed very deeply.

'I hardly know what to say. It's quite incredible. It's so unbelievable that I believe every word.'

'I feel better just for telling you, but it would be terrible if it ever got out.'

'James, you know I won't say a word to anyone. I'm so very sorry you're in such a mess. You must let me see if I can help in some way. Why don't we work together without letting the others know?'

She began stroking the inside of his leg. Twenty minutes later, they sank into a blissful sleep.

NINE

In Lincoln, Massachusetts, Harvey Metcalfe began to prepare for
his annual trip to England. He intended to enjoy himself thoroughly
and expensively. He had plans for transferring some money from his
numbered accounts in Zürich to Barclays Bank, Lombard Street,
ready for the purchase of another stallion from one of the Irish
stables to join his stud in Kentucky. Arlene had decided not to
accompany him on this trip: she did not care too much for Ascot
and even less for Monte Carlo. In any case, it gave her the chance
to spend some time with her ailing mother in Vermont, who still had
little time for her son-in-law.

Harvey checked with his secretary that all the arrangements for
his holiday had been made. There never was any need to check up
on Miss Fish, it was simply habit on Harvey's part. Miss Fish had
been with him for twenty-five years, from the days when he had first
taken over the Lincoln Trust. Most of the staff had walked out on
Harvey's arrival, or shortly afterwards, but Miss Fish had remained,
nursing in her unalluring bosom ever fainter hopes of marriage to
Harvey. By the time Arlene appeared on the scene, Miss Fish was an
able and completely discreet accomplice without whom Harvey could
hardly have operated. He paid her accordingly, so she swallowed her
chagrin at the creation of Mrs Metcalfe, and stayed put.

Miss Fish had already booked the short flight to New York and
the Trafalgar Suite on the QE2. The trip across the Atlantic was almost the only total break Harvey ever had from the telephone or
telex. The bank staff were instructed to contact the great liner only in
dire emergency. On arrival at Southampton it would be the usual
Rolls Royce to London and his private suite at Claridge's, which he
judged to be one of the last English hotels, along with the Connaught
and Browns, with a style money alone cannot reproduce.

Harvey flew to New York in high good humour, drinking rather
too many Manhattans on the way. The arrangements on board ship
were as impeccable as ever. The Captain, Peter Jackson, always

invited the occupant of the Trafalgar Suite or the Queen Anne Suite to join him on the first night out at the Captain's table. At $1,250 a day for the suites it was hardly an extravagant gesture on Cunard's part. On such occasions, Harvey was always on his best behaviour, although even that struck most onlookers as a little brash.

One of the Italian stewards was detailed to arrange a little diversion for Harvey, preferably in the shape of a tall blonde with a large bosom. The going rate for the night was $100, but the Italian could charge Harvey $150 and get away with it. At 5 ft 7 in. and 227 lb., Harvey's chances of picking up a young thing in the discotheque were not very good and by the time he had lashed out on drinks and dinner, he could have spent almost as much money to achieve absolutely nothing. Men in Harvey's position do not have time for that sort of failure and expect that everything will have its price. As the voyage was only five nights the steward was able to keep Harvey fully occupied, although he felt it just as well that Harvey had not booked a three-week Mediterranean cruise.

Harvey spent his days catching up with the latest novels and taking a little exercise, a swim in the morning and a painful session in the gymnasium in the afternoon. He could reckon to lose 10 lb. during the crossing, which was pleasing, but somehow Claridge's always managed to put it on again before he returned to the States. However, his suits were tailored by Bernard Weatherill of Dover Street, Mayfair, who managed by dint of near genius and impeccable skill to make him look well-built rather than distinctly fat. At £250 a time it was the least he could expect.

When the five days were drawing to a close, Harvey was more than ready for land again. The women, the exercise and the fresh air had quite revived him and he had lost all of 11 lb. this time. He felt a good deal of this must have come off the night before. She had made the *Kama Sutra* look like a Boy Scouts' handbook.

One of the advantages of real wealth is that menial tasks can always be left to someone else. Harvey could no longer remember when he last packed or unpacked a suitcase, and it came as no surprise to him when the ship docked at the Ocean Terminal to discover everything packed and ready for Customs—a $100 bill for the head steward seemed to bring men in little white coats from every direction.

Harvey always enjoyed disembarking at Southampton. The

English were a race he liked, though he feared he would never understand them. He found them so willing to be trodden on by the rest of the world. Since the Second World War, they had relinquished their colonial power in a way no American business man would have considered an exit from his own boardroom. Harvey had finally given up trying to understand the British way of business during the 1967 devaluation of the pound. Every jumped-up speculator on the face of the globe had taken advantage of it. Harvey knew on the Tuesday morning that Harold Wilson was going to devalue any time after Friday, 5 p.m. Greenwich Mean Time. On the Thursday even the junior clerk at the Lincoln Trust knew. It was no wonder that the Bank of England lost an estimated £1½ billion in four days. Harvey had often thought that if only the British could liven up their boardrooms and get their tax structure right, they could be the richest nation in the world instead of a nation, which, as *The Economist* had stated, could be bought by the Arabs with sixty days of oil revenue. While the British flirted with socialism and still retained a *folie de grandeur*, they seemed doomed to sink into insignificance.

Harvey strode down the gangplank like a man with a purpose. He had never learnt to relax completely, even when he was on vacation. He could just about spend four days away from the world, but if he had been left on the QE2 any longer he would have been negotiating to buy the Cunard Steamship Company. Harvey had met the Chairman of Cunard, Vic Matthews, at Ascot on one occasion and had been baffled by the emphasis he had put on the prestige and reputation of the company. Harvey had expected him to brag about his balance sheet. Prestige interested Harvey, of course, but he always let people know how much he was worth.

Customs clearance was given with the usual speed. Harvey never had anything of consequence to declare on his European trips, and after they had checked two of his Gucci suitcases, the other seven were allowed through without inspection. The chauffeur opened the door of the white Rolls Royce Corniche. It sped through Hampshire and into London in just over two hours, which gave Harvey time for a rest before dinner.

Albert, the head doorman at Claridge's, stood smartly to attention and saluted. He knew Harvey of old and was aware that he had come, as usual, for Wimbledon and Ascot. Albert would undoubtedly receive a 50 pence tip every time he opened the Rolls door. Harvey didn't know the difference between a 50 pence and 10 pence piece—

a difference which many head doormen had welcomed since the introduction of decimalization in Britain. Moreoever, Harvey always gave
Albert £5 at the end of Wimbledon fortnight if an American won the
singles title. An American invariably reached the finals, so Albert
would place a bet with Ladbrokes on the other finalists so that he
won either way. Gambling appealed to both Albert and Harvey: only
the sums involved were different.

Albert arranged for the luggage to be sent to the Royal Suite,
which during the year had already been occupied by King Con-
stantine of Greece, Princess Grace of Monaco and Emperor Haile
Selassie of Ethiopia, all with considerably more conviction than
Harvey. But Harvey thought (and subsequent events proved him
right) that his annual holiday at Claridge's was more assured than
theirs.

The Royal Suite is on the first floor at Claridge's and can be
reached by an elegant sweeping staircase from the ground floor,
or by a commodious lift. Harvey always took the lift up and walked
down. At least that way he convinced himself he was taking some
exercise. The suite itself consists of four rooms; a small dressing-
room, a bedroom, a bathroom, and an elegant drawing-room overlooking Brook Street. The furniture and pictures make it possible
for you to believe that you are still in Victorian England. Only the
telephone and television dispel the illusion. The room is large enough
to be used for cocktail parties or for visiting heads of state to entertain visitors. Henry Kissinger had received Harold Wilson there
only the week before. Harvey enjoyed the thought of that.

After a shower and change of clothes, Harvey glanced through
his waiting mail and telexes from the bank, which were all routine.
He took a short rest before going down to dine in the main restaurant.

There in the large foyer was the usual string quartet. Harvey
even recognized the four players. He had reached the time of life
when he did not like change—the management of Claridge's knew
that the average age of their customers was over fifty and they catered
accordingly. François, the head waiter, showed him to his usual table.

Harvey managed a little shrimp cocktail and a medium fillet
steak with a bottle of Mouton Cadet, and continued reading *The
Billion Dollar Killing*, which read not unlike his autobiography. He
did not notice the four young men eating in the alcove on the far side
of the room.

*

Stephen, Adrian, Jean-Pierre and James all had an excellent view of Harvey Metcalfe. He would have had to bend double and move slightly backwards to have any view of them.

'Not exactly what I expected,' commented Adrian.

'Put on a bit of weight since those photographs you supplied,' said Jean-Pierre.

'Hard to believe he's real after all this preparation,' remarked Stephen.

'He's real enough, the bastard, and a million dollars richer because of our stupidity,' said Jean-Pierre.

James said nothing. He was still in disgrace after his futile efforts and excuses at the last briefing, although the other three had to admit that they did receive good service wherever they went with him. Claridge's was no exception.

'Wimbledon tomorrow,' said Jean-Pierre. 'I wonder who will win the first round?'

'You will of course,' chipped in James, hoping to soften Jean-Pierre's acid comments about his own feeble efforts.

'We can only win your round, James, if we ever get an entry form.'

James sank back in silence.

'I must say looking at the size of him we ought to get away with your plan, Adrian,' said Stephen.

'If he doesn't die of cirrhosis of the liver before we get going,' replied Adrian. 'How do you feel about Oxford, Stephen?'

'I don't know yet. I'll feel better when I have belled the cat at Ascot. I want to hear him speak, watch him in his normal environment, get the feel of the man. You can't do all that from the other side of a dining-room.'

'You may not have to wait too long. This time tomorrow we may know everything we need to know, or we may all be in gaol,' said Adrian, 'maybe we won't pass go, let alone collect £200.'

'I can't even afford bail,' said Jean-Pierre.

When Harvey had downed a large glass of Remy Martin V.S.O.P. he left his table, slipping the head waiter a crisp new pound note.

'The bastard,' said Jean-Pierre with great feeling, 'it's bad enough knowing he's stolen our money, but it's humiliating having to watch him spend it.'

The four of them prepared to leave, the object of their outing achieved. Stephen paid the bill and carefully added it to the list of expenses against Harvey Metcalfe. Then they left the hotel separately and as inconspicuously as possible. Only James found this difficult as all the waiters and porters would insist on saying to him, 'Good night, my lord.'

Harvey took a stroll round Berkeley Square and did not even notice the tall young man slip into the doorway of Moyses Stevens, the florists, for fear of being spotted by him. Harvey never could resist asking a policeman the way to Buckingham Palace just to compare the reaction he would get with that of a New York cop, leaning on a lamp post, chewing gum, holster on hip. As Lenny Bruce had said on being deported from England. 'Your pigs is so much better than our pigs.' Yes, Harvey liked England.

He arrived back at Claridge's at about 11.15 p.m., showered and went to bed—a large double bed with that glorious feel of clean linen sheets. There would be no women for him at Claridge's or, if there were, it would be the last time he would find the Royal Suite available to him during Wimbledon or Ascot. The room moved just a little, but then after five days on an ocean liner it was unlikely to be still until the following night. He slept well despite it, without a worry on his mind.

TEN

Harvey rose at 7.30 a.m., a habit he could not break, but he did allow himself the holiday luxury of breakfast in bed. Ten minutes after he had called room service the waiter arrived with a trolley laden with half a grapefruit, bacon and eggs, toast, steaming black coffee, a copy of the previous day's *Wall Street Journal*, and the morning's edition of *The Times*, *Financial Times* and *International Herald Tribune*.

Harvey was not sure how he would have survived on a European trip without the *International Herald Tribune*, known in the trade as the 'Trib'. This unique paper, published in Paris, is jointly owned by the *New York Times* and the *Washington Post*. Although only one edition of 120,000 copies is printed, it does not go to press until the New York Stock Exchange has closed. Therefore, no American need wake up in Europe out of touch. When the *New York Herald Tribune* folded in 1966, Harvey had been among those who advised John H. Whitney to keep the *International Herald Tribune* going in Europe. Once again, Harvey's judgment had been proved sound. The *International Herald Tribune* went on to absorb its faltering rival, the *New York Times*, which had never been a success in Europe. From then on the paper has gone from strength to strength.

Harvey ran an experienced eye down the Stock Exchange lists in the *Wall Street Journal* and the *Financial Times*. His bank now held very few shares as he, like Jim Slater in England, had suspected that the Dow Jones Index would collapse and had therefore gone almost entirely liquid, holding only some South African gold shares and a few well-chosen stocks about which he had inside information. The only monetary transaction he cared to undertake with the market so shaky was selling the dollar short and buying gold so that he caught the dollar on the way down and gold on the way up. There were already rumours in Washington that the President of the United States had been advised by his Secretary to the Treasury,

George Shultz, to allow the American people to buy gold on the open market some time in 1975. Harvey had been buying gold for fifteen years: all the President was going to do was to stop him from breaking the law. Harvey was of the opinion that the moment the Americans were able to buy gold, the bubble would burst and the price of gold would recede—the real money would be made while the speculators anticipated the rise, and Harvey intended to be out of gold well before it came on to the American market.

Harvey checked the commodity market in Chicago. He had made a killing in copper a year ago. Inside information from an African Ambassador had made this possible—information the Ambassador had imparted to too many people. Harvey was not surprised to read that he had subsequently been recalled to his homeland and later shot.

He could not resist checking the price of Prospecta Oil, now at an all-time low of 18 cents: there would be no trading in the stock, simply because there would be only sellers and no buyers. The shares were virtually worthless. He smiled sardonically and turned to the sports pages of *The Times*.

Rex Bellamy's article on the forthcoming Wimbledon Championships tipped John Newcombe as favourite and Jim Connors, the new American star who had just won the Italian Open, as the best outside bet. The British Press wanted the 39-year-old Ken Rosewall to win. Harvey could well remember the epic final between Rosewall and Drobny in 1954, which had run to 58 games. Like most of the crowd, he had then supported the 33-year-old Drobny, who had finally won, after three hours of play, 13–11, 4–6, 6–2, 9–7. This time, Harvey wanted history to repeat itself and Rosewall to win, though he felt the popular Australian's chance had slipped by during the ten years when professionals did not compete at Wimbledon. Still, he saw no reason why the fortnight should not be a pleasant break, and perhaps there would be an American victor even if Rosewall couldn't manage it.

A quick glance at the art reviews and Harvey finished his breakfast, leaving the papers strewn over the floor. The quiet Regency furniture, the elegant service and the Royal Suite did nothing for Harvey's manners. He padded into the bathroom for a shave and shower. Arlene told him that most people did it the other way round—showered and then ate breakfast. But, as Harvey pointed out to her, most people did things the other way round from him, and look where it got them.

Harvey habitually spent the first morning of Wimbledon fortnight visiting the Summer Exhibition at the Royal Academy in Piccadilly. He would then follow this with visits to most of the West End's major galleries—Agnew's, Tooths, the Marlborough, O'Hana—all within easy walking distance of Claridge's. This morning would be no exception. If Harvey was anything, he was a creature of habit, which was something the Team were quickly learning.

After he had dressed and bawled out room service for not leaving enough whisky in his cabinet, he headed down the staircase, emerged through the swing door of the Davies Street entrance and surged towards Berkeley Square. Harvey did not notice a studious young man with a two-way radio on the other side of the road.

'He has left the hotel,' said Stephen quietly to his little Pye Pocketfone, 'and he's heading towards you, James.'

'I'll pick him up as he comes into Berkeley Square, Stephen. Adrian, can you hear me?'

'Yes.'

'I'll let you know when I spot him. You stay at the Royal Academy.'

'Right you are,' said Adrian.

Harvey strolled round Berkeley Square, down into Piccadilly and through the Palladian arches of Burlington House. With a bad grace, he stood and queued with the assorted humanity in the forecourt, shuffling past the Astronomical Society and the Society of Antiquaries. He did not see the young man opposite in the entrance of the Chemical Society, deep in a copy of *Chemistry in Britain*. (Adrian was a thorough man.) Finally, Harvey made it up the red-carpeted ramp into the Royal Academy itself. He handed the cashier £3.50 for a season ticket, realizing that he would probably come at least three or four times. He spent the entire morning studying the 1,182 pictures, none of which had been exhibited anywhere else in the world before the opening day, in accordance with the stringent rules of the Academy. Despite that ruling, the Hanging Committee still had to choose from over 5,000 pictures.

On the opening day of the exhibition the month before, Harvey had acquired, through his agent, a watercolour by Alfred Daniels of the House of Commons for £250 and two oils by Bernard Dunstan of English provincial scenes for £75 each. The Summer Exhibition was still the best value in the world. Even if he did not want to keep all the pictures himself, they made wonderful presents when he returned to the States. The Daniels reminded him of a Lowry he had bought some twenty years before at the Academy for £80: that had turned out to be a shrewd piece of judgment on his part.

Harvey made a special point of looking at the Bernard Dunstans in the Exhibition. Of course, they were all sold. Dunstan was one of the artists whose pictures always sold in the opening minutes of the opening day. Harvey had not been in London on that day; however he had had no difficulty in buying what he wanted. He had planted a man at the front of the queue, who obtained a catalogue and marked those artists he knew Harvey could resell easily if he had made a mistake and keep if his judgment were right. When the exhibition opened on the dot of 10 a.m. the agent had gone straight to the purchasing desk and acquired the five or six pictures he had marked in the catalogue before he had even seen them, or anyone else had seen them other than the Academicians. Harvey studied his vicarious purchases with care. On this occasion he was happy to keep them all. If there had been one that did not quite fit in with his collection he could have returned it for resale, undertaking to purchase it if nobody else showed interest. In twenty years he had acquired over a hundred pictures by this method and returned a mere dozen, never failing to secure a resale. Harvey had a system for everything.

At 1 p.m., after a thoroughly satisfactory morning, he left the Royal Academy. The white Rolls Royce was waiting for him in the forecourt.

'Wimbledon.'

'Shit.'

'What did you say?' queried Stephen.

'S.H.I.T. He's gone to Wimbledon, so today's down the drain.' said Adrian.

That meant Harvey would not return to Claridge's until at least seven or eight that evening. A rota had been fixed for watching him, and Adrian accordingly picked up his Rover 3500 V8 from St James's Square and headed for Wimbledon. James had obtained two tickets for every day of the Championships opposite Harvey Metcalfe's debenture box.

Adrian arrived at Wimbledon a few minutes after Harvey and took his seat in the Centre Court, far enough back in the sea of faces to be inconspicuous. The atmosphere was already building up for the opening match. Wimbledon seems to be getting more popular every year and the Centre Court was packed to capacity. Princess

Alexandra and the Prime Minister, Harold Wilson, were in the Royal Box awaiting the entrance of the gladiators. The little green scoreboards at the southern end of the court were flashing up the names of Kodes and Stewart as the umpire took his seat on the high chair in the middle of the court directly overlooking the net. The crowd began to applaud as the two athletes, both dressed in white, entered the court carrying four rackets each. Wimbledon did not allow its competitors to dress in any colour other than white, although they had relaxed a little by permitting the trimming of the ladies' dresses to be coloured.

Adrian enjoyed the opening match between the 1973 Champion, Kodes, and Stewart, an unseeded player from the United States, who gave the Czechoslovakian a hard time, Kodes winning 6–3, 6–4, 9–7. Adrian was sorry when Harvey decided to leave in the middle of an exciting doubles. Back to duty, he told himself, and followed the Rolls at a safe distance to Claridge's. On arriving, he telephoned James's flat, which was being used as the Team's headquarters in London, and briefed Stephen.

'May as well call it a day,' said Stephen. 'We'll try again tomorrow. Poor old Jean-Pierre's heart-beat reached 150 this morning. He may not last many days of false alarms.'

When Harvey left Claridge's the following morning he went through Berkeley Square into Bruton Street and on into Bond Street, only 50 yards from Jean-Pierre's gallery. But then he slipped into Agnew's where he had an appointment with Sir Geoffrey Agnew, the head of the family firm, to see if he had any news of Impressionist pictures on the market. Sir Geoffrey was anxious to get away to another meeting and could only spend a few minutes with Harvey. He had to disappoint him.

Harvey left Agnew's soon afterwards clutching a small consolation prize of a maquette by Rodin, a mere bagatelle at £400.

'He's coming out,' said Adrian, 'and heading in the right direction.' But again Harvey stopped, this time at the Marlborough Gallery to study their latest exhibition of Barbara Hepworth. He spent over an hour appreciating her beautiful work, but decided the prices were now mad. He had purchased two Hepworths only ten years ago for £800. The Marlborough was now asking between £7,000 and £10,000 for her work. So he left and continued up Bond Street.

'Jean-Pierre?'

'Yes,' replied a nervous voice.

'He's reached the corner of Conduit Street and is about 50 yards away from you.'

Jean-Pierre prepared his window, removing the Graham Sutherland watercolour of the Thames and the Boatman.

'He's turned left, the bastard,' said James, who was stationed opposite the gallery. 'He's walking down Bruton Street on the right-hand side.'

Jean-Pierre put the Sutherland back on the easel in the window and retired to the lavatory muttering to himself:

'I can't cope with two shits at once.'

Harvey meanwhile stepped into a little entrance in Bruton Street and climbed the stairs to Tooths. He was more hopeful of finding something in a gallery which had become so famous for its Impressionists. A Klee, a Picasso and two Salvador Dali—not what Harvey was looking for. The Klee was very well executed, but not as good as the one in his dining-room in Lincoln, Massachusetts. In any case, it might not fit in with any of Arlene's decorative schemes. Nicholas Tooth, the managing director, promised to keep his eyes open and ring Harvey at Claridge's should anything of interest crop up.

'He's on the move again, but I think it's back to Claridge's.'

James willed him to turn round and return in the direction of Jean-Pierre's gallery, but Harvey strode towards Berkeley Square, only making a detour to the O'Hana gallery. Albert, the head doorman, had told him there was a Renoir in the window, and indeed there was. But it was only a half-finished canvas which Renoir had obviously used for a practice run or had disliked and left unfinished. Harvey was curious as to the price and entered the gallery.

'£30,000,' said the assistant, as if it was £3 and a snip at that.

Harvey whistled through the gap between his front teeth. It never ceased to amaze him that an inferior picture by a first-rank name could fetch £30,000 and an outstanding picture by an artist with no particular reputation could only make a few hundred dollars. He thanked the assistant and left.

'A pleasure, Mr Metcalfe.'

Harvey was always flattered by people who remembered his name, but hell, they ought to remember, he had bought a Monet from them last year for $125,000.

'He's definitely on his way back to the hotel,' said James. Harvey spent only a few minutes in Claridge's, picking up one of their famous specially prepared luncheon hampers of caviar, beef, ham and cheese sandwiches and chocolate cake for later consumption at Wimbledon.

James was next on the rota for Wimbledon and decided to take Anne with him. Why not—she knew the truth. It was Ladies' Day and the turn of Billie Jean King, the vivacious American champion, to take the court. She was up against the unseeded American, Kathy May, who looked as if she was in for a rough time. The applause Billie Jean received was not worthy of her abilities, but somehow she had never become a Wimbledon favourite. Harvey had a guest with him who James thought had a faintly mid-European look.

'Which one is your victim?'

'He's almost exactly opposite us with the man in the grey suit who looks like a government official from Brussels.'

'The short fat one?' inquired Anne.

'Yes,' said James.

Whatever comments Anne might have made were interrupted by the umpire's call of 'Service' and everyone's attention was focused on Billie Jean. It was exactly 2 p.m.

'Kind of you to invite me to Wimbledon, Harvey,' said Jörg Birrer. 'I never seem to have the chance for much pleasure nowadays. You can't leave the market for more than a few hours without some panic or other.'

'If you feel that way it's time for you to retire,' said Harvey.

'No one to take my place,' said Birrer. 'I've been Chairman of the bank for ten years now and finding a successor is turning out to be my hardest task.'

'First game to Mrs King. Mrs King leads by one game to love in the first set.'

'I know you too well, Harvey, to expect this invitation to have been just for pleasure.'

'What an evil mind you have, Jörg.'

'You have to have in my profession.'

'I just wanted to check how my three accounts stand and brief you on my plans for the next few months.'

'Game to Mrs King. Mrs King leads two games to love in the first set.'

'Your no. 1 official account is a few thousand dollars in credit.

95

Your numbered commodity account,' at this point Birrer unfolded a small piece of unidentifiable paper with a set of neat figures on it, 'is short by $3,726,000, but you are holding 37,000 ounces of gold at today's selling price of $135 an ounce.'

'What's your advice on that?'

'Hold on, Harvey. I still think your President is either going to announce a new gold standard or allow your fellow-countrymen to buy gold on the open market some time next year.'

'That's my view too, but I think we want to sell a few weeks before the masses come in. I have a theory about that.'

'I expect you are right, as usual, Harvey.'

'Game to Mrs King. Mrs King leads by three games to love in the first set.'

'What are your charges on my overdraft?'

'$1\frac{1}{2}$ per cent above inter-bank rate, which at present is 13.25, and therefore we are charging you 14.75 per cent per annum, while gold is rising in price at nearly 70 per cent per annum. It can't go on, but there are still a few months left in it.'

'O.K.,' said Harvey, 'hold on until November 1st and we'll discuss it again. Coded telex as usual. I don't know what the rest of the world would do without the Swiss.'

'Just take care, Harvey. Do you know there are more specialists in our police force on fraud than there are on murder?'

'You worry about your end, Jörg, and I'll worry about mine. The day I get uptight about bureaucrats from Zürich who haven't got any balls, I'll let you know. Now, enjoy your lunch and watch the game. We'll have a talk about the other account later.'

'Game to Mrs King. Mrs King leads by four games to love in the first set.'

'They are very deep in conversation,' said Anne. 'I cannot believe they are enjoying the game.'

'He's probably trying to buy Wimbledon at cost price,' laughed James. 'The trouble with seeing the man every day is that I begin to have a certain admiration for him. He's the most organized man I have ever come across. If he's like this on holiday, what the hell is he like at work?'

'I can't imagine,' said Anne.

'Game to Miss May. Mrs King leads by four games to one in the first set.'

'No wonder he's so overweight. Just look at him stuffing that cake down.' James lifted his Zeiss binoculars. 'Which reminds me to ask, darling, what have you brought for my lunch?'

Anne dug into her hamper and unpacked a crisp salad in French bread for James. She contented herself with nibbling a stick of celery.

'Getting far too fat,' she explained. 'I'll never get into the swimwear I'm supposed to be modelling next week.' She touched James's knee and smiled. 'It must be because I'm so happy.'

'Well, don't get too happy. I prefer you thin.'

'Game to Mrs King, Mrs King leads by five games to one in the first set.'

'This is going to be a walkover,' said James, 'which it so often is in the opening match. People only come to see if the champion's in good form, but I think she'll be very hard to beat this year. She's after Helen Moody's record of eight Wimbledon championships.'

'Game and first set to Mrs King by six games to one. Mrs King leads one set to love. New balls, please. Miss May to serve.'

'Do we have to watch him all day?' asked Anne.

'No, we must make sure he returns to the hotel and doesn't change his plans suddenly or anything silly like that. If we miss our chance when he walks past Jean-Pierre's gallery, we won't get another one.'

'What do you do if he does change his plans?'

'God knows, or to be more accurate, Stephen knows—he's the mastermind.'

'Game to Mrs King. Mrs King leads by one game to love in the second set.'

'Poor Miss May, she's about as successful as you. How is the Jean-Pierre operation going?'

'Awful, he just won't go anywhere near the gallery. He was within 30 yards of it today. Poor Jean-Pierre nearly had heart failure. But we are more hopeful of tomorrow. He seems to have covered Piccadilly and the top end of Bond Street and the one thing we can be sure of about Harvey Metcalfe is that he's thorough, so he's almost bound to cover our bit of territory at one time or another.'

'You should all have taken out life insurances for $1 million, naming the other three as beneficiaries,' said Anne, 'and then when one of you had a heart attack you could have got your money back.'

'It's not a laughing matter, Anne. It's bloody nerve-racking while you are waiting, especially when you have to allow him to make all the moves.'

'Game to Mrs King. Mrs King leads by two games to love in the second set and one set to love.'

'How about your own plan?'

'Nothing. Useless, and now we have started with the others I seem to have less time to concentrate on it.'

'Why don't I seduce him?'

'Not a bad idea, but it would have to be some night to get £100,000 out of him when he can stand outside the Hilton or in Shepherd Market and get it for £20. If there's one thing we have learnt about that gentleman it's that he expects value for money. At £20 a night it would take you just under fifteen years to repay my share, and I'm not sure the other three would be willing to wait that long. In fact, I'm not sure they will wait fifteen days.'

'We'll think of something,' said Anne.

'Game to Miss May. Mrs King leads by two games to one and by one set to love.'

'Well, well. Miss May has managed another game. Excellent lunch, Harvey.'

'A Claridge's special,' said Harvey, 'so much better than getting caught up with everybody in the restaurant where you can't even watch the tennis.'

'Billie Jean is making mincemeat of her.'

'Much as I expected,' said Harvey. 'Now, Jörg, to my second numbered account.'

Once again the unidentifiable piece of paper that bore a few numbers appeared. It is this discretion of the Swiss that leads half the world, from heads of state to Arab sheiks, to trust them with their money. In return the Swiss maintain one of the healthiest economies in the world because the system works. So why go anywhere else? Birrer spent a few seconds studying the figures.

'On April 1st—only you could have chosen that day, Harvey—you transferred $7,486,000 to your no. 2 account, which was already in credit $2,791,428. On April 2nd, on your instructions, we placed $1 million in the Banco do Minas Gerais in the names of Mr Silverman and Mr Elliott. We covered the bill with Reading & Bates for the hire of the rig for $420,000 and several other bills amounting to $104,112, leaving your present no. 2 account standing at $8,753,316.'

'Game to Mrs King. Mrs King leads three games to one in the second set and by one set to love.'

'Very good,' said Harvey.

'The tennis or the money?' said Birrer.

'Both. Now, Jörg, I anticipate needing about $2 million over the next six weeks. I want to purchase one or two pictures in London. I have seen a Klee that I quite like and I still have a few galleries to visit. If I had known that the Prospecta Oil venture was going to be such a success, I would have outbid Armand Hammer at the Sotheby Parke Bernet for that Van Gogh last year. I shall also need ready cash for the purchase of some new horses at the Ascot Blood Stock Auctions. My stud is running down and it's still one of my greatest ambitions to win the King George and Elizabeth Stakes. (James would have winced if he could have heard Harvey describe such a famous race so inaccurately.) My best result so far, as you know, was third place and that is not good enough. This year I have entered Rosalie, my best chance for some considerable time. If I lose I must build up the stud again, but I am damn well going to win this year.'

'Game to Mrs King. Mrs King leads four games to one and one set to love.'

'So is Mrs King, it seems,' said Birrer. 'I will brief my senior cashier that you are likely to be drawing large amounts over the next few weeks.'

'Now I don't want the remainder to lie idle so I want you to purchase more gold carefully over the next few months, with a view to off-loading in the New Year. If the market does take a turn, I'll phone you in Zürich. At the close of business each day you are to loan the outstanding balance on an overnight basis to first-class banks and triple "A" commercial names.'

'What are you going to do with it all, Harvey, if those cigars don't get you first?'

'Oh, lay off, Jörg. You are sounding like my doctor. I have told you a hundred times, next year I retire, I quit, finito.'

'I can't see you dropping out of the rat race voluntarily, Harvey. It pains me to wonder how much you are worth now.'

Harvey laughed.

'I can't tell you that, Jörg. It's like Aristotle Onassis says—if you can count it, you haven't got any.'

'Game to Mrs King. Mrs King leads by five games to one and by one set to love.'

'How's Rosalie? We still have instructions to pass the accounts on to her if anything should happen to you.'

'She's well. Phoned me this morning to tell me she was unable to join me at Wimbledon because she's tied up with her work. I expect she'll marry some rich American in any case and then she won't need it. Enough of them have asked her. Can't be easy for her to decide if they like her or my money. I'm afraid we had a row about that a couple of years back and she still hasn't forgiven me.'

'Game, set and match to Mrs King: 6–1, 6–1.'

Harvey, Jörg, James and Anne joined in the applause while the two girls left the court, curtseying in front of the Royal Box to the President of the All England Club, His Royal Highness The Duke of Kent. Harvey and Jörg Birrer stayed for the next match, a doubles, and then returned to Claridge's together for dinner.

James and Anne had enjoyed their afternoon at Wimbledon and when they had seen Harvey safely back to Claridge's, accompanied by his mid-European friend, they returned to Anne's flat.

'Stephen, I'm back. Metcalfe is settled in for the night. On parade at 8.30 a.m.'

'Well done, James. Maybe he will bite tomorrow.'

'Let's hope so.'

The sound of running water led James to the kitchen in search of Anne. She was elbow-deep in suds, attacking a soufflé dish with a scourer. She turned and brandished it at him.

'Darling, I don't want to be offensive about your daily, but this is the only kitchen I've ever been in where you have to do the washing up before you make the dinner.'

'I know. She only cleans the clean bits of the flat. As a result her work load is getting lighter by the week.'

He sat on the kitchen table, admiring the slenderness of her arms and body.

'Will you scrub my back like that if I go and have a bath before dinner?'

The water was deep and comfortably hot. James lay back in it luxuriously, letting Anne wash him. Then he stepped dripping out of the bath.

'You're a bit overdressed for a bathroom attendant, darling,' he said. 'I think you ought to do something about it.'

Anne slipped out of her clothes while James dried himself. Later, he smiled down at her.

'You know, you're getting quite good.'

'With such a fine teacher, how can I do other than improve? Out you get. The baked cheese will be ready and I want to remake the bed.'

'No need to bother about that, you silly woman.'

'Yes there is. Last night I didn't sleep at all. You pulled all the blankets over to your side and I just watched you huddled up like a self-satisfied cat while I froze to death. Making love to you is not at all like Harold Robbins promised it was going to be.'

'When you have finished chattering, set the alarm for 7 a.m.'

'7 a.m.? You don't have to be at Claridge's until 8.30.'

'I know, but I want to go to work on an egg.'

'James, you really must get rid of your undergraduate sense of humour.'

'Oh, I thought it was rather funny.'

'Yes, darling. Why don't you get dressed before the dinner is burnt to a cinder?'

James arrived at Claridge's at 8.29 a.m. He was determined, despite his own inadequacies, not to fail the others in their plans. He tuned in to check that Stephen was in Berkeley Square and Adrian in Bond Street.

'Morning,' said Stephen. 'Had a good night?'

'Bloody good,' said James.

'Sleep well, did you?' said Stephen.

'Hardly a wink.'

'Stop making us jealous,' said Adrian, 'and concentrate on Harvey Metcalfe.'

James stood in the doorway of Slater's the furriers watching the early morning cleaners leave for home and the first of the office staff arriving.

Harvey Metcalfe was going through his normal routine of breakfast and the papers. He had had a telephone call from his wife in Boston the night before and another from his daughter during breakfast, which started his day well. He decided to pursue the hunt for an Impressionist picture in some of the other galleries in Cork Street and Bond Street. Perhaps Sotheby's would be able to help him.

He left the hotel at 9.47 a.m. at his usual brisk pace.

'Action stations.'

Stephen and Adrian snapped out of their day-dreaming.

'He's just entered Bruton Street. Now he's heading for Bond Street.'

Harvey walked briskly down Bond Street, past the territory he had already covered.

'Only 50 yards off now,' said James. '40 yards, 30 yards, 20 yards . . . Oh no, damn it, he's gone into Sotheby's. There's a sale of medieval painted panels. Hell, I didn't know he was interested in them.'

He glanced up the road at Stephen, padded out and aged to the condition of a wealthy, middle-aged business man. The cut of the collar and the rimless glasses proclaimed him as West German. Stephen's voice came over the speaker:

'I am going into Jean-Pierre's gallery. James, you stay upstream from Sotheby's on the far side of the street and report every fifteen minutes. Adrian, you go inside and dangle the bait under Harvey's nose.'

'But that's not in the plan, Stephen,' stammered Adrian.

'Use your iniative and get on with it otherwise all you will be doing is taking care of Jean-Pierre's heart condition. O.K.?'

'O.K.' said Adrian nervously.

Adrian went into Sotheby's and made a surreptitious bee-line for the nearest mirror. Yes, he was still unrecognizable. Upstairs, he located Harvey near the back of the sale room, and inserted himself in a nearby seat in the row behind.

The sale of medieval painted panels was well under way. Harvey knew he ought to like them, but could not bring himself to condone the Gothic partiality for jewellery and bright, gilded colours. Behind him, Adrian thought quickly, then struck up a quiet-voiced conversation with his neighbour.

'Looks very fine to me, but I've no knowledge. I am happier with the modern era. Still, I must think of something appropriate to say for my paper.'

Adrian's neighbour smiled politely.

'Do you cover all the auctions?'

'Almost all—especially where there may be surprises. Actually I'm really on my way to the Lamanns Gallery up the road. One of the assistants here gave me a tip that they may have something special in the Impressionist field.'

Adrian beamed the whispered information carefully at Harvey's right ear. Shortly afterwards, he was rewarded by the sight of Harvey squeezing out of his row to leave. Adrian waited for three more lots to be auctioned, then followed him.

Outside, James had been keeping a patient vigil.

'10.30—no sign of him.'

'Roger.'

'10.45—still no sign of him.'

'Roger.'

'11.00—he's still inside.'

'Roger.'

'11.12—action stations, action stations.'

James slipped quickly into the Lamanns Gallery as Jean-Pierre once again removed the Sutherland watercolour of the Thames and the Boatman, and placed in the window a picture by Van Gogh, as magnificent an example of the master's work as a London gallery had ever seen. Now came its acid test: the litmus paper walked purposefully down Bond Street towards it.

The picture had been painted by David Stein, who was notorious in the art world for faking 300 paintings and drawings by well known Impressionists, for which he received a total of $864,000 and later four years. He was exposed when he put on a Chagall exhibition at the Niveaie Gallery in Madison Avenue in 1969. Unknown to Stein, Chagall was in New York at the time for an exhibition at the New Metropolitan Museum at the Lincoln Center where two of his most famous works were on display. When Chagall was informed of the Niveaie exhibition he furiously reported the pictures as fakes to the District Attorney's office. Stein had sold one of the imitation Chagalls to Louis D. Cohen at a price of nearly $100,000, and to this day there is a Stein Chagall and a Stein Picasso at the Galleria d'Arte Moderna in Milan. Jean-Pierre was confident that what Stein had achieved in the past in New York he could repeat in London.

Stein continued to paint Impressionist pictures, but signed them with his own name, and because of his indubitable talent he was still making a handsome living. He had known and admired Jean-Pierre for several years and when he heard the story of Metcalfe and Prospecta Oil, he agreed to produce the Van Gogh for $10,000 and to sign the painting with the master's famous 'Vincent'.

Jean-Pierre had gone to great trouble to identify a Van Gogh, vanished in mysterious circumstances, that Stein could resurrect to tempt Harvey. He started with de la Faille's comprehensive *œuvres* catalogue *The Works of Vincent Van Gogh* and selected from it three pictures that had hung in the National Gallery in Berlin prior to the Second World War. In de la Faille, they were entered under nos. 485 *Les Amoureux* (*The Lovers*), 628, *La Moisson* (*The Harvest*) and 776 *Le Jardin de Daubigny* (*The Garden of Daubigny*). The last two were known to have been bought in 1929 by the Berlin Gallery, and *Les Amoureux* probably around the same time. At the start of the war, they had all three disappeared.

Jean-Pierre had contacted Professor Wormit of the Preussischer Kulturbesitz. The Professor, a world authority on missing works of art, ruled out one of the possibilities. *Le Jardin de Daubigny* had after the war apparently reappeared in the collection of Siegfried Kramarsky in New York, though how it got there was a mystery. Kramarsky had subsequently sold it to the Nichido Gallery in Tokyo, where it now hangs. Of the fate of the other two Van Goghs, the Professor had no knowledge.

Next, Jean-Pierre turned to Madame Tellegen-Hoogendoorm of the Dutch Rijksbureau voor Kunsthistorische Documentatie. Madame Tellegen was the acknowledged authority on Van Gogh and gradually, with her expert help, Jean-Pierre pieced together the story of the missing paintings. They had been removed, with many others, from the Berlin National Gallery in 1937 by the Nazis, despite vigorous protests from the Director, Dr Hanfstaengl, and the Keeper of Paintings, Dr Hentzen. The paintings, stigmatized by the philistinism of the National Socialists as degenerate art, were stored in a depot in the Köpenickerstrasse in Berlin. Hitler himself visited the depot in January 1938, after which these illegal proceedings had been legalized by an official confiscation.

What happened to the two Van Goghs is simply not known. Many of the confiscated works were quietly sold abroad by Joseph Angerer, an agent of Hermann Goering, to obtain much-needed foreign currency. Some were disposed of in a sale organized by the Fischer Art Gallery of Lucerne on June 30th, 1939. But many of the works in the depot in the Köpenickerstrasse were simply burned or stolen.

Jean-Pierre managed to obtain black-and-white reproductions of *Les Amoureux* and *La Moisson*: no colour positives survive, even if they were ever made. It seemed to Jean-Pierre unlikely that any colour reproductions of two paintings last seen in 1938 would exist anywhere. He therefore settled down to choose between the two.

Les Amoureux was the larger of the two, at 76 x 91 cm. However Van Gogh did not seem to have been satisfied with it. In October 1889 (letter no. 556) he referred to 'a very poor sketch of my last canvas'. Moreover, it was impossible to guess the colour of the background. *La Moisson*, in contrast, had pleased Van Gogh. He had painted it in September 1889 and written of it, 'I feel very much inclined to do the reaper once more for my mother' (letter no. 604). He had in fact already painted three other very similar pictures of a reaper at harvest time. Jean-Pierre obtained colour transparencies of two of them from the Louvre and the Rijksmuseum, where they now hang, and studied the sequence. The position of the sun, and the play of light on the scene, were practically the only points of difference. Jean-Pierre saw in his mind's eye what *La Moisson* had looked like in colour.

Stein agreed with Jean-Pierre's final choice and he studied the black-and-white reproduction of *La Moisson* and the colour transparencies of its sister paintings long and minutely before he set to work. Then he found an insignificant late-nineteenth-century French work, and removed the paint from it, leaving a clean canvas. He marked upon it the exact size of the picture, 48.5 x 53 cm. and selected a palette knife and brush of the type that Van Gogh had favoured. Six weeks later *La Moisson* was finished. Stein varnished it, and baked it for four days in an oven at a gentle 85°F to age it. Jean-Pierre provided a heavy gilt Impressionist frame. Finally he showed the picture to Vincent, Van Gogh's grandson and a connoisseur of his illustrious forebear's work. Vincent had been entirely take in, which gave Jean-Pierre confidence that the picture would pass Harvey Metcalfe's scrutiny.

Harvey, acting on his overheard tip, could see no harm in dropping into the Lamanns Gallery. When he was about five paces away, he caught sight of the picture being taken out of the window and could not believe his eyes. A Van Gogh, without a doubt, and a superlative one at that. It had actually been on display for only two minutes.

Harvey walked into the gallery to discover Jean-Pierre deep in conversation with Stephen and James. None of them took any notice of him. Stephen was addressing Jean-Pierre in a guttural accent.

'170,000 guineas is high, but it is a fine example. Can you be sure that it is the picture that disappeared from Berlin in 1937?'

'You can never be sure of anything, but you can see on the back of the canvas the stamp of the Berlin National Gallery, and the Bernheim Jeune have confirmed they sold it to the Germans in 1927. The rest of its history is chronicled back to 1890. It seems certain that it was looted from the museum in the upheaval of the war.'

'How did you obtain it?'

'From the collection of a member of the British aristocracy who wishes it to be sold privately.'

'Excellent,' said Stephen. 'I would like to reserve it until 4 p.m. when I will bring round my cheque for 170,000 guineas from the Dresdner Bank A.G. Will that be acceptable?'

'Of course, sir,' replied Jean-Pierre. 'I will put a green dot on it.'

James, in the sharpest of suits and a dashing trilby, hovered knowledgeably behind Stephen.

'It certainly is a marvellous example of the master's work,' he remarked ingratiatingly.

'Yes. I took it round to Julian Barron at Sotheby's and he seemed to like it.'

James retreated mincingly to the end of the gallery, relishing his role as a connoisseur. At that moment Adrian walked in, a copy of the *Guardian* sticking out of his pocket.

'Hello, Mr Lamanns. I heard a rumour about a Van Gogh, which I thought was in Russia, and I would like to write a few paragraphs about it for tomorrow's paper. Is that O.K. by you?'

'I should be delighted,' said Jean-Pierre, 'although actually I have just reserved the picture for Herr Drosser, a distinguished German dealer, at 170,000 guineas.'

'Very reasonable,' said James knowingly from the end of the gallery. 'I think it's the best Van Gogh I have seen in London and I'm only sorry my firm will not be auctioning it. You're a lucky man, Mr Drosser. If you ever want to auction it don't hesitate to contact me.' James handed Stephen a card and smiled at Jean-Pierre.

Jean-Pierre watched James. It was a fine performance. Adrian began to take notes in what he hoped looked like shorthand and addressed Jean-Pierre.

'Do you have a photograph of the picture?'

'Of course.'

Jean-Pierre opened a drawer and took out a colour photograph of the picture with a typewritten description attached. He handed it to Adrian.

'Do watch the spelling of Lamanns, won't you? I get so tired of being confused with a French motor race.'

He turned to Stephen.

'So sorry to keep you waiting, Herr Drosser. How would you like us to dispatch the picture?'

'You can send it to the Dorchester tomorrow morning, room 120.'

'Certainly, sir.'

With that, Stephen started to leave.

'Excuse me, sir,' said Adrian, 'can I take the spelling of your name?'

'DROSSER.'

'And may I have your permission to quote you in my article?'

'Yes, you may. I am with my purchase very pleased. Good day, gentlemen.'

Stephen bowed his head smartly, and departed. He stepped into Bond Street and to the horror of Jean-Pierre, Adrian and James, Harvey, without a moment's hesitation, followed him.

Jean-Pierre sat down heavily on his Georgian mahogany desk and looked despairingly at Adrian and James.

'God Almighty, the whole thing's a fiasco. Six weeks of preparation and three days of agony and he walks out on us.' Jean-Pierre looked at *La Moisson* angrily.

'I thought Stephen told us that Harvey would be bound to stay and bargain with Jean-Pierre,' said James plaintively. 'He shouldn't have let the picture out of his sight.'

'Who the hell thought of this bloody silly enterprise?' muttered Adrian.

'Stephen,' they call cried together, and rushed to the window.

'What an interesting piece by Henry Moore,' said an impeccably corseted middle-aged lady, her hand on the bronze loin of a naked acrobat. She had slipped unnoticed into the gallery while the three had been grumbling. 'How much are you asking for it?'

'I will be with you in a minute, madam,' said Jean-Pierre. 'Oh hell, Metcalfe's following Stephen. Get him on the pocket radio, Adrian.'

'Stephen, can you hear me? Whatever you do, don't look back. We think Harvey's a few yards behind you.'

'What the hell do you mean he's a few yards behind me? He's with you in the gallery buying the Van Gogh, isn't he? What are you all playing at?'

'Harvey didn't give us a chance. He walked straight out after you before any of us could get a word in.'

'Very clever. Now what am I meant to do?'

Jean-Pierre took over:

'You'd better go to the Dorchester just in case he is actually following you.'

'Where in hell's name is the Dorchester?' yelped Stephen.

Adrian came to his rescue:

'Take the first right, Stephen, and that will take you into Bruton Street, keep walking as straight as you can until you reach Berkeley Square. Stay on the line, but don't look back or you may turn into a pillar of salt.'

'James,' said Jean-Pierre, thinking on his feet for not the first time in his life. 'You take a taxi immediately for the Dorchester and book room 120 in the name of Drosser. Have the key ready for Stephen the moment he arrives through the door, then make yourself scarce. Stephen, are you still there?'

'Yes.'

'Did you hear all that?'

'Yes. Tell James to book 119 or 121 if 120 is not available.'

'Roger,' replied Jean-Pierre. 'Get going, James.'

James bolted and barged in front of a woman who had just hailed a taxi, a thing he had never done before.

'The Dorchester,' he hollered, 'as fast as you can go.'

The taxi shot off.

'Stephen, James has gone and I am sending Adrian to follow Harvey so he can keep you briefed and guide you to the Dorchester. I am staying here. Everything else O.K.?'

'No,' said Stephen, 'start praying. I've reached Berkeley Square. Where now?'

'Across the garden then continue down Hill Street.'

Adrian ran all the way to Bruton Street until he was 50 yards behind Harvey.

'Now about that Henry Moore,' said the well-corseted lady.

'Screw Henry Moore!'

The steel-reinforced bosom heaved.

'Young man, I have never been spoken to in . . .'

But it was pointless. Jean-Pierre had already reached the lavatory, retching with nervousness.

*

108

'You're crossing South Audley Street now, then continue into Deanery Street. Keep going, don't turn right or left and don't look back. Harvey is about 50 yards behind you. I'm a little more than 50 yards behind him,' said Adrian.

'Is Room 120 free?'

'Yes sir, they checked out this morning, but I am not sure if it is ready for occupancy yet, I think the maid is still clearing the room. I'll have to check, sir,' said the tall receptionist in the morning suit, which indicated that he was a senior member of the floor staff.

'Oh, don't worry about that,' said James. 'I always have that room. Can you book me in for one night. Name's Drosser, Herr—um—Helmut Drosser.'

He slipped a pound over the counter.

'Certainly, sir.'

'That's Park Lane, Stephen. Look right—the big hotel on the corner straight in front of you is the Dorchester. The semi-circle facing you is the main entrance. Go up the steps and through the revolving door and you'll find the reception on your right. James ought to be there.'

Adrian was grateful that the annual dinner of the Royal Society for Medicine had been held at the Dorchester last year.

'Where's Harvey?' bleated Stephen.

'Only 40 yards behind you.'

Stephen quickened his pace, ran up the steps of the Dorchester and pushed through the revolving door so hard that the other residents going round found themselves on the street faster than they had originally planned. Thank God, James was there holding a key.

'The lift's over there,' said James, pointing. 'You've only chosen one of the most expensive suites in the hotel.'

Stephen glanced in the direction James had indicated and turned back to thank him. But James was already heading off to the American Bar to be sure he was well out of sight when Harvey arrived.

Stephen left the lift and found room 120 on the first floor. The Dorchester, which he had never entered before, was as traditional as Claridge's and its thick royal blue and golden carpets led to a magnificently appointed corner suite which overlooked Hyde Park.

He collapsed into an easy chair, not quite sure what to expect. Nothing had gone as planned.

Jean-Pierre waited at the gallery, James sat in the American Bar and Adrian loitered by the side of Barclays Bank, Park Lane, a mock-Tudor building 50 yards from the entrance of the Dorchester.

'Have you a Mr Drosser staying at this hotel? I think it's room 120,' barked Harvey.

The receptionist looked up the name.

'Yes, sir. Is he expecting you?'

'No, but I want a word with him on the house phone.'

'Of course, sir. Would you be kind enough to go through the small archway on your left and you will find five telephones. One of them is the house phone.'

Harvey marched through the archway as directed.

'Room 120,' he instructed the operator, who sat in his own little section, wearing the green Dorchester uniform with golden castles on the lapels.

'Cubicle no. 1, please sir.'

'Mr Drosser?'

'Speaking,' said Stephen, summoning up his German accent for a sustained effort.

'I wonder if I could come up and have a word with you? My name is Harvey Metcalfe. It's about the Van Gogh you bought this morning.'

'Well, it's a little inconvenient at the moment. I am about to take a shower and I do have a lunch appointment.'

'I won't keep you more than a few minutes.'

Before Stephen could reply, the telephone had clicked. A few moments later there was a knock on the door. Stephen answered it nervously. He was dressed in a white Dorchester dressing-gown and his brown hair was somewhat dishevelled and darker than normal. It was the only disguise he could think of at such short notice as the original plan had not allowed for a face-to-face meeting with Harvey.

'Sorry to intrude, Mr Drosser, but I had to see you immediately. I know you have just obtained a Van Gogh from the Lamanns Gallery and I was hoping that, as you are a dealer, you might be willing to re-sell it for a quick profit.'

110

'No, thank you,' said Stephen, relaxing for the first time. 'I've wanted a Van Gogh for my gallery in Munich for many years. I'm sorry, it's not for sale.'

'Listen, you paid 170,000 guineas for it. What's that in dollars?' Stephen paused.

'Oh, about $435,000.'

'I will give you $15,000 if you release the picture to me. All you have to do is ring the gallery and say that the picture is mine and that I will cover the bill.'

Stephen sat silent, not sure how to deal with the situation without blowing it. Think like Harvey Metcalfe, he told himself.

'$20,000 in cash and it's a deal.'

Harvey hesitated. Stephen felt weak.

'Done,' said Harvey. 'Ring the gallery immediately.'

Stephen picked up the telephone.

'Can you get me the Lamanns Gallery in Bond Street as quickly as possible—I have a lunch appointment.'

A few seconds later the call came through.

'Lamanns Gallery.'

'I would like to speak to Mr Lamanns.'

'At last, Stephen. What the hell happened your end?'

'Ah, Mr Lamanns, this is Herr Drosser. You remember, I was in your gallery earlier this morning.'

'Of course I remember, you fool. What are you going on about, Stephen? It's me—Jean-Pierre.'

'I have a Mr Metcalfe with me.'

'Christ, I'm sorry, Stephen. I hadn't . . .'

'And you can expect him in the next few minutes.'

Stephen looked towards Harvey who nodded his assent.

'You are to release the Van Gogh I purchased this morning to him and he will give you a cheque for the full amount, 170,000 guineas.'

'Out of disaster, triumph,' said Jean-Pierre quietly.

'I'm very sorry I shall not be the owner of the picture myself, but I have, as the Americans would say, had an offer I can't refuse. Thank you for the part you played,' said Stephen and put the telephone down.

Harvey was writing out a cheque to cash for $20,000.

'Thank you, Mr Drosser. You have made me a happy man.'

'I am not complaining myself,' said Stephen honestly. He escorted Harvey to the door and they shook hands.

111

'Goodbye, sir.'

'Goodbye, Mr Metcalfe.'

Stephen closed the door and tottered to the chair, almost too weak to move.

Adrian and James saw Harvey leave the Dorchester. Adrian followed him in the direction of the gallery, his hopes rising with each stride. James took the lift to the first floor and nearly ran to Room 120. He banged on the door. Stephen jumped at the noise. He didn't feel he could face Harvey again.

'James, it's you. Cancel the room, pay for one night and then join me in the cocktail bar.'

'Why? What for?'

'A bottle of Krug 1964 Privée Cuvée.'

One down and three to go.

ELEVEN

Jean-Pierre was the last to arrive at Lord Brigsley's King's Road flat. He felt he had the right to make an entrance. Harvey's cheques were cleared and the Lamanns Gallery account was for the moment $447,560 the better for it. The painting was in Harvey's possession and the heavens had not fallen in. Jean-Pierre had cleared more money in two months of crime than he had in ten years of legitimate trading.

The other three greeted him with acclaim and a glass of James's last bottle of Veuve Clicquot 1959.

'We were lucky to pull it off,' said Adrian.

'We weren't lucky,' said Stephen. 'We kept our cool under pressure. What we have learnt is that Harvey can change the rules in the middle of the game.'

'He almost changed the game, Stephen.'

'Agreed, and we must remember that we shall fail unless we can be as successful, not once, but four times. We must not underestimate our opponent because we have won the first round.'

'Relax, Professor,' said James. 'We can get down to business again after dinner. Anne came in this afternoon especially to make the salmon mousse, and it won't go well with Harvey Metcalfe.'

'When are we going to meet this fabulous creature?' asked Jean-Pierre.

'When this is all over and behind us.'

'Don't marry her, James. She's only after our money.'

They all laughed. James hoped the day would come when he could tell them she had known all along. He produced the *Boeuf en Croûte* and two bottles of Echezeaux 1970. Jean-Pierre sniffed the sauce appreciatively.

'On second thoughts, she ought to be seriously considered if her touch in bed is half as deft as it is in the kitchen.'

'You're not going to get the chance to be the judge of that, Jean-Pierre. Content yourself with admiring her French dressing.'

'You were outstanding this morning, James,' said Stephen, steering the conversation away from Jean-Pierre's pet subject. 'You should go on the stage. As a member of the English aristocracy, your talent is simply wasted.'

'I have always wanted to, but my old pa is against it. Those who live in expectation of a large inheritance have to toe the filial line.'

'Why don't we let him play all four parts in Monte Carlo?' suggested Adrian.

The mention of Monte Carlo sobered them up.

'Back to work,' said Stephen. 'We have so far received $447,560. Expenses with the picture and an unexpected night at the Dorchester were $11,142 so Metcalfe still owes us $563,582. Think of what we have lost, not of what we have won. Now for the Monte Carlo operation, which depends upon split-second timing and our ability to sustain our roles. Adrian will bring us up to date.'

Adrian retrieved the green dossier from the briefcase by his side and studied his notes for a few moments.

'Jean-Pierre, you must grow a beard starting today, so that in three weeks' time you will be unrecognizable. You must also cut your hair very short.' Adrian grinned unsympathetically at Jean-Pierre's grimace. 'Yes, you will look absolutely revolting.'

'That,' said Jean-Pierre, 'will not be possible.'

'How are the baccarat and blackjack coming on?' continued Adrian.

'I have lost $37 in five weeks, including my member's fee at Crockford's.'

'It all goes on expenses,' said Stephen. 'That puts the bill up to $563,619.'

The others laughed. Only Stephen's lips did not move. He was in sober earnest.

'James, how is your handling of the van going?'

'I can get to Harley Street from St Thomas's in 14 minutes. I should be able to do the actual run in Monte Carlo in about 11 minutes, though naturally I shall do some practice runs the day before. I must master driving on the wrong side of the road.'

'Strange how everybody except the British drives on the wrong side of the road,' observed Jean-Pierre.

James ignored him.

'I'm not sure of all the Continental road signs either.'

'They are all in the Michelin guide that I gave you as part of my dossier.'

'I know, but I will still feel easier when I have experienced the actual run and not just studied maps. There are quite a few one-way streets in Monaco and I want to be going down them in the right direction.'

'Don't worry. You will have ample time when we are there. So, that just leaves Stephen, who is about the most able medical student I have ever had. You're happy with your newly acquired knowledge, I hope?'

'About as happy as I am with your American accent, Adrian. Anyway, I trust that Harvey Metcalfe will be in no state to size us up by the time we meet.'

'Don't worry. Believe me, he wouldn't even register if you introduced yourself as Herr Drosser with a Van Gogh under each arm.'

Adrian handed round the final schedule of rehearsals at Harley Street and St Thomas's, and consulted the green file again.

'I have booked four single rooms on different floors at the Hôtel de Paris and confirmed all the arrangement with the Centre Hospitalier Princesse Grace. The hotel is reputed to be one of the best in the world—it's certainly expensive enough—but it is very near the Casino. We fly to Nice on Monday, the day after Harvey is due to arrive on his yacht.'

'What do we do for the rest of the week?' inquired James innocently.

Stephen resumed control:

'We master the green dossier—backwards, frontwards and sideways for a full dress rehearsal on Friday. The most important thing for you, James, is to get a grip of yourself and let us know what you intend to do.'

James sunk back into gloom.

Stephen closed his file briskly.

'That seems to be all we can do tonight.'

'Hang on, Stephen,' said Adrian. 'Let's strip you off once more. I'd like to see if we can do it in 90 seconds.'

Stephen lay down slightly reluctantly in the middle of the room, and James and Jean-Pierre swiftly and carefully removed his clothes.

'87 seconds. Excellent,' said Adrian, looking down at Stephen, naked except for his watch. 'Hell, look at the time. I must get back to Newbury. My wife will think I have a mistress and I don't fancy any of you.'

Stephen dressed himself quickly while the others prepared to

115

leave. A few minutes later, James stood by the front door, watching them depart one by one. As soon as Stephen was out of sight, he bounded downstairs into the kitchen.

'Did you listen?'

'Yes, darling. They're rather nice and I don't blame them for being cross with you. They are being very professional about the whole venture. Frankly, you sounded like the only amateur. We'll have to think up something good for you to match them. We've over a week before Mr Metcalfe goes to Monte Carlo.'

James sighed: 'Well, let's enjoy tonight. At least this morning was a triumph.'

'Yes, but not yours. Tomorrow we work.'

TWELVE

'Passengers for flight 017 to Nice are now requested to check in at gate no. 7,' boomed the loudspeaker at Heathrow Airport.

'That's us,' said Stephen.

The four of them ascended the escalator to the first floor, and walked down the long corridor. After being searched for guns, bombs, or whatever terrorists are searched for, they boarded the aircraft.

They sat separately, neither looking at nor speaking to one another. Stephen had warned them that the flight could well be sprinkled with Harvey's friends, and each imagined himself to be sitting next to the closest of them.

James gazed moodily at the cloudless sky and brooded. He and Anne had read every book they could lay their hands on that even hinted at stolen money or successful duplicity, but they had found nothing they could plagiarize. Even Stephen, in the intervals of being undressed and practised upon at St Thomas's, was becoming daunted by the task of finding a winning plan for James.

The Trident touched down at Nice at 13.40, and the train journey from Nice to Monte Carlo took them a further twenty minutes. Each member of the team made his separate way to the elegant Hôtel de Paris in the Place du Casino. At 7 p.m. they were all present in room 217.

'All settled into your rooms?'

The other three nodded. 'So far, so good,' said Adrian. 'Right, let's get down to it. Jean-Pierre, you will go to the Casino tonight and play a few hands of baccarat and blackjack. Try to acclimatize to the place and learn your way round. In particular, master any variations there might be from Crockford's. Do you foresee any problems?'

'No, can't say I do, Adrian. In fact I may as well go now and start rehearsing.'

'Don't lose too much of our money,' said Stephen.

Jean-Pierre, resplendent in beard and dinner-jacket, grinned and slipped out of room 217 and down the staircase, avoiding the lift. He walked the short distance from the hotel to the famous Casino.

Adrian continued:

'James, you take a taxi from the Casino to the hospital. On arriving at the hospital leave the meter running for a few minutes and then return to the Casino. You can normally rely on a taxi taking the shortest route, but to be sure, tell the driver it's an emergency. That will give you the opportunity of seeing which traffic lanes he uses under pressure. When he has returned you to the Casino, walk the route from there to the hospital and back. Then you can assimilate it in your own time. After you have mastered that repeat the same procedure for the route between the hospital and Harvey's yacht. Don't ever enter the Casino or even get close enough to the boat to be recognized.'

'What about my knowledge of the Casino on the night of the operation?'

'Jean-Pierre will take care of that. He'll meet you at the door because Stephen won't be able to leave Harvey. I don't think they will charge you the 12 franc entrance fee because of your white coat and the stretcher. When you have completed the walk, go to your room and stay there till the meeting at 11 a.m. tomorrow. Stephen and I will be going to the hospital to check that all the arrangements have been carried out as cabled from London.'

Just as James left room 217, Jean-Pierre arrived at the Casino.

It stands in the heart of Monte Carlo, surrounded by beautiful gardens looking over the sea. The present building has several wings, the oldest of which was designed by Charles Garnier, the architect of the Paris Opera House. The gambling rooms, which were added in 1910, are linked by an atrium to the Salle Garnier in which operas and ballets are performed.

Jean-Pierre marched up the marble staircase to the entrance and paid his 12 francs. The gambling rooms are vast and display the decadence and grandeur of Europe at the turn of the century. Massive red carpets, statues, paintings and tapestries give the building an almost royal appearance and the portraits lend an air of a country home still lived in. The clientele were of all nationalities—Arabs and Jews played next to each other at the roulette wheel and it looked more like a gathering of the United Nations than a casino. Jean-Pierre was totally at ease in the unreal world of the wealthy. Adrian had summed up his character very quickly and given him a role he would master with aplomb.

Jean-Pierre spent over three hours studying the layout of the Casino—its gambling rooms, bars and restaurants, the telephones, the entrances and exits. Then he turned his attention to the gambling itself. Two shoes of baccarat are played in the Salons Privés at 3 p.m. and 11 p.m., and Jean-Pierre discovered from Pierre Cattalano, the head of the public relations department of the Casino, which of the private rooms Harvey Metcalfe played in.

Blackjack is played in the Salon des Amériques from 11 a.m. daily. There are three tables, and Jean-Pierre's informant told him that Harvey always played on table no. 2 at seat no. 3. Jean-Pierre played a little blackjack and baccarat, to discover any slight variations there might be from Crockford's. There were in fact none, as Crockford's still adhere to French rules.

Harvey Metcalfe arrived noisily at the Casino just after 11 p.m., and blazed a trail of cigar ash to his baccarat table. Jean-Pierre, inconspicuous at the bar, watched as the head croupier first showed Harvey politely to a reserved seat, and then walked through to the Salon des Amériques to the no. 2 blackjack table and placed a discreet white card marked 'Reservée' on one of the chairs. Harvey was clearly a favoured client. The management knew as well as Jean-Pierre which games Harvey Metcalfe played. At 11.27 p.m. Jean-Pierre left quietly and returned to the solitude of his hotel room where he remained until 11 a.m. the next day.

James's evening went well. The taxi-driver was superb. The word 'emergency' brought out the Walter Mitty in him: he travelled through Monte Carlo as if it were the Rally. When James arrived at the hospital in 8 minutes 44 seconds, he genuinely felt a little sick and rested for a few minutes in the Entrée des Patients before returning to the taxi.

'Back to the Casino, but much slower, please.'

The journey back along the Rue Grimaldi took just over eleven minutes and James decided he would settle for trying to master it in about ten. He paid off the taxi-driver and carried out the second part of his instructions.

Walking to the hospital and back took just over an hour. The night air was gentle on his face, and the streets crowded with lively people. Tourism is the chief source of income for the Principality, and the Monégasques take the welfare of their visitors very seriously. James passed innumerable little pavement restaurants and souvenir shops stocked with expensive trinkets of no significance. Noisy groups of holiday-makers strolled along the pavements, their multi-lingual chatter forming a meaningless chorus to James's thoughts of Anne. James then took a taxi to the harbour to locate the *Messenger Boy*, Harvey's yacht, and from there once more to the hospital. Like Jean-Pierre, he was safely in his room before midnight, having completed his first task.

Adrian and Stephen found the walk to the hospital from their hotel took just over 40 minutes. On arrival Adrian asked the receptionist if he could see the superintendent.

'The night superintendent is now on,' said a freshly starched French nurse. 'Who shall I say is asking him for?'

Her English pronunciation was excellent and they both avoided a smile at her slight mistake.

'Doctor Wiley Barker of the University of California.'

Adrian began to pray that the French superintendent would not happen to know that Wiley Barker, President Nixon's physician and one of the most respected surgeons in the world, was actually touring Australia at the time lecturing to the major universities.

'Bon soir, Docteur Barker. M. Bartise à votre service. Votre visite fait grand honneur à notre humble hôpital.'

Adrian's newly acquired American accent stopped any further conversation in French.

'I would like to check the layout of the theatre,' said Adrian, 'and confirm that we have it booked for tomorrow from 11 p.m. to 4 a.m. for the next five days.'

'That is quite correct, Docteur Barker. The theatre is off the next corridor. Will you follow me please?'

The theatre was not unlike the one the four of them had been practising in at St Thomas's, two rooms with a rubber swing door dividing them. The main theatre was well equipped and a nod from Adrian showed Stephen that he had all the instruments he needed. Adrian was impressed. Although the hospital had only some 200 beds, the theatre was of the highest standard. Rich men had obviously been ill there before.

'Will you be requiring an anaesthetist or any nurses to assist you, Docteur Barker?'

'No,' said Adrian. 'I have my own anaesthetist and staff, but I will require a tray of laparotomy instruments to be laid out every night. However, I will be able to give you at least an hour's warning.'

'That's plenty of time. Is there anything else, sir?'

'Yes, the special vehicle I ordered. Can it be picked up by my driver at 12 p.m. tomorrow?'

'Yes, Docteur Barker. I will leave it in the small car park behind the hospital and your driver will be able to pick up the keys from reception.'

'Can you recommend an agency from which I can get an experienced nurse for post-operative care?'

'Bien sûr, the Auxiliaire Medical of Nice will be happy to oblige—at a certain price, of course.'

'No problem,' said Adrian. 'And that reminds me to ask, have all the expenses been dealt with?'

'Yes, Docteur. We received a cheque from California last Thursday for $7,000.'

Adrian had been very pleased with that touch. It had been so simple. Stephen had contacted his bank at Harvard and asked them to send a draft from the First National City Bank in San Francisco to the hospital secretary at Monte Carlo.

'Thank you for all your help, M. Bartise. You have been most obliging. Now you understand I am not quite sure which night I shall bring my patient in. He's a sick man, although he doesn't know it, and I have to prepare him for the operation.'

'Of course, mon cher Docteur.'

'Finally, I would appreciate it if you would let as few people as possible know that I am in Monte Carlo as I am trying to snatch a holiday at the same time as working.'

'I understand, Docteur Barker. I can assure you of my discretion.'

Adrian and Stephen bade farewell to M. Bartise and took a taxi back to the hotel.

'I'm always slightly humiliated by how well the French speak our language compared with our grasp of theirs,' said Stephen.

'It's all the fault of you bloody Americans,' said Adrian.

'No, it isn't. If France had conquered America your French would be excellent. Blame it on the Pilgrim Fathers.'

Adrian laughed. For fear of being overheard, neither of them spoke again until they reached room 217. Stephen had no doubts about the risk and responsibility they were taking this time.

*

Harvey Metcalfe was on the deck of his yacht, sunbathing and reading the morning papers. *Nice-Matin*, irritatingly enough, was in French. He read it laboriously, with the aid of a dictionary, to see if there were any social events to which he ought to get himself invited. He had gambled late into the night, and was enjoying the sun's rays on his fleshy back. If money could have obtained it, he would have been 6 ft and 170 lb. with a handsome head of hair, but no amount of suntan oil would stop his balding dome from burning, so he covered it with a cap inscribed 'I'm sexy'. If Miss Fish could see him now . . .

At 11 a.m., as Harvey turned over and allowed the sun to see his massive stomach, James strolled into room 127 to find the rest of the team waiting for him.

Jean-Pierre reported on the layout of the Casino and Harvey Metcalfe's habits. James brought them up to date on the result of his run the night before and confirmed that he thought he could cover the distance in just under eleven minutes.

'Perfect,' said Adrian. 'Stephen and I took 15 minutes by taxi from the hospital to the hotel and if Jean-Pierre warns me immediately the balloon goes up in the Casino, I should have enough time to see that everything is ready before you all arrive.'

'I do hope the balloon is going to go down, not up, in the Casino,' remarked Jean-Pierre.

'I have booked an agency nurse to be on call from tomorrow night. The hospital has all the facilities I require. It will take about 2 minutes to get a stretcher from the front door to the theatre so from the moment James leaves the car park, I should have at least 16 minutes to prepare myself. James, you will be able to pick up the vehicle from the hospital car park at 12 p.m. The keys have been left in reception in the name of Dr Barker. Do a couple of practice runs and no more. I don't want you causing interest or looking conspicuous. And could you put this parcel in the back, please.'

'What is it?'

'Three long white laboratory coats and a stethoscope for Stephen. While you're at it, better check that you can unfold the stretcher easily. When you have finished the two runs, put the vehicle back in the car park and return to your room until 11 p.m. From then through to 4 a.m. you will have to wait in the car park until you get the message from Jean-Pierre of "action stations" or "all clear". Everybody buy new batteries for your transmitters. We can't have the whole plan collapse for the sake of a tenpenny battery. I am afraid there is nothing much for you to do, Jean-Pierre, until this evening, except relax. I hope you have some books in your room.'

'Can't I go to the Princes Cinema and see François Truffaut's *La nuit américaine*? I just adore Jacqueline Bisset. Vive la France!'

'My dear Jean-Pierre, Miss Bisset's from Reading,' said James.

'I don't care. I still want to see her.'

'A frog he would a-wooing go,' said Adrian mockingly.

'But why not? The last thing Harvey will do is take in an intellectual French film with no sub-titles. Hope you enjoy it—and good luck tonight, Jean-Pierre.'

Jean-Pierre left for his room as quietly as he had come, leaving the rest of them together in room 217.

'Right, James. You can do your practice runs any time you like now. Just make sure you are fully awake tonight.'

'Fine. I'll go and pick up the keys from the hospital reception. Let's just hope nobody stops me for a real emergency.'

'Now, Stephen, let's go over it again. There is more than money to lose if we get this one wrong. We will start from the top. What do you do if the nitrous oxide falls below five litres . . .'

'Station check—station check—operation Metcalfe. This is Jean-Pierre. I am on the steps of the Casino. Can you hear me, James?'

'Yes. I am in the car park of the hospital. Out.'

'Adrian here. I am on the balcony of room 217. Is Stephen with you, Jean-Pierre?'

'Yes. He's drinking on his own at the bar.'

'Good luck and out.'

Jean-Pierre carried out a station check every hour on the hour from 7 p.m. until 11 p.m., merely to inform Adrian and James that Harvey had not arrived.

Eventually, at 11.16, he did show up, and took his reserved place at the baccarat table. Stephen stopped sipping his tomato juice and Jean-Pierre moved over and waited patiently by the table for one of the men seated on the left or right of Harvey to leave. An hour passed by. Harvey was losing a little, but remained playing. So did the tall thin American on his right and the Frenchman on his left. Another hour and still no movement. Then suddenly the Frenchman on the left of Metcalfe had a particularly bad run, gathered his few remaining chips and left the table. Jean-Pierre moved forward.

'I am afraid, Monsieur, that that seat is reserved for another gentleman,' said the banker. 'We do have an unreserved place on the other side of the table.'

'It's not important,' said Jean-Pierre and retreated, cursing the deference with which the Monégasques treat the wealthy. Stephen could see from the bar what had happened and made furtive signs to leave. They were all back in room 217 just after 2 a.m.

'What a bloody silly mistake. Merde, merde, merde. I should have thought of it.'

'No, it was my fault. I don't know how casinos work and I should have queried it during rehearsals,' said Adrian, stroking his newly acquired moustache.

'No one is to blame,' chipped in Stephen. 'We still have three nights and we mustn't panic. We will have to work out how to overcome the seating problem, but for now we'll all get some sleep and meet again in this room at 10 a.m.

They left, a little depressed. Adrian had sat waiting in the hotel on edge for four hours, James was cold and bored in the hospital car park, Stephen was sick of tomato juice and Jean-Pierre had been on his feet by the baccarat table waiting for a seat that wasn't even available.

Once again Harvey lounged in the sun. He was now a light pink and was hoping to be a better colour towards the end of the week. The *New York Times* informed him that gold was still going up and the Deutschmark and the Swiss franc were firm, while the dollar was on the retreat against every currency except sterling. Sterling stood at $2.42. Harvey thought a more realistic price was $1.80 and the sooner it reached that the better.

'Nothing new in that,' he thought, when the sharp ring of a French telephone roused him. He never could get used to the sound of another country's telephones. The attentive steward bustled out on deck with the instrument on an extension lead.

'Hi, Lloyd. Didn't know you were in Monte . . . why don't we get together? . . . 8 p.m. . . . me too . . . I'm even getting brown . . . must be getting old . . . what? . . . great, I'll see you then.'

Harvey replaced the receiver and asked the steward for a large whisky on the rocks. He settled down happily once again to the morning's financial bad news.

'That seems to be the obvious solution,' said Stephen.

They all nodded their approval.

'Jean-Pierre will give up the baccarat table and book a place next to Harvey Metcalfe on his blackjack table in the Salon des Amériques and wait for him to change games. We know both the seat numbers Harvey plays at and we will alter our plans accordingly.'

Jean-Pierre dialled the number of the Casino and asked to speak to Pierre Cattalano:

'Réservez-moi la deuxième place sur la table 2 pour le vingt-et-un ce soir et demain soir, s'il vous plaît.'

'Je pense que cette place est déjà reservée, Monsieur. Un instant, s'il vous plaît, je vais vérifier.'

'Peut-être que 100 francs la rendra libre,' replied Jean-Pierre.

'Mais certainement, Monsieur, présentez-vous à moi dés votre arrivée, et le nécessaire sera fait.'

'Merci,' said Jean-Pierre and replaced the receiver. 'That's under control.'

Jean-Pierre was visibly sweating, though had the outcome of his call been of no significance, not a drop of perspiration would have appeared for such a simple request. They all returned to their rooms.

Just after midnight Adrian was waiting quietly in room 217, James stood in the car park humming 'I get along without you very well', Stephen was at the bar of the Salon des Amériques toying with yet another tomato juice and Jean-Pierre was at seat no. 2 on table no. 2 playing blackjack. Both Stephen and Jean-Pierre saw Harvey come through the door chatting to a man in a loud, checked jacket which only a Texan could have worn outside his own front garden. Harvey and his friend sat down together at the baccarat table. Jean-Pierre beat a hasty retreat to the bar.

'Oh no! I give up.'

'No, you don't,' whispered Stephen. 'Back to the hotel.'

Spirits were very low when they were all assembled in room 217, but it was agreed that Stephen had made the right decision. They could not risk the whole operation being carefully watched by a friend of Harvey's.

'The first operation is beginning to look a bit too good to be true,' said Jean-Pierre.

'Don't be silly,' said Stephen. 'We had two false alarms then, and the entire plan had to be changed at the last minute. We can't expect him just to walk in and hand over his money. Now snap out of it, all of you, and get some sleep.'

They returned to their separate rooms, but not to much sleep. The strain was beginning to tell.

'That's enough I think, Lloyd. A goodish evening.'

'For you, you mean, Harvey, not for me. You are one of nature's winners.'

Harvey patted the checked shoulder expansively. If anything pleased him more than his own success, it was other people's failure.

'Do you want to spend the night on my yacht, Lloyd?'

'No thanks. I must get back to Nice. I have a meeting in Paris, France, tomorrow lunch. See you soon, Harvey—take care of yourself.' He dug Harvey in the ribs jocularly. 'That's a fair-sized job.'

'Goodnight, Lloyd,' said Harvey a little stiffly.

The next evening Jean-Pierre did not arrive at the Casino until 11 p.m. Harvey Metcalfe was already at the baccarat table minus Lloyd. Stephen was at the bar looking angry and Jean-Pierre glanced at him apologetically as he took his seat at the blackjack table. He played a few hands to get the feel, trying to keep his losses fairly limited without drawing attention to the modesty of his stakes. Suddenly Harvey left the baccarat table and walked into the Salon des Amériques, glancing at the roulette tables as he passed more out of curiosity than interest. He detested games of pure chance, and considered baccarat and blackjack games of skill. He headed to table no. 2 seat no. 3, on the left of Jean-Pierre. The adrenalin started pumping round again and the heart-beat was back up to 120. Stephen left the Casino for a few minutes to warn James and Adrian that Harvey was now sitting next to Jean-Pierre. He then returned to the bar and waited.

There were now seven punters at the blackjack table. On box no. 1, a middle-aged lady, smothered in diamonds, who looked as if she was passing time while her husband played roulette or perhaps baccarat. On box no. 2, Jean-Pierre. On box no. 3, Harvey. On box no. 4, a dissipated young man with the world-weariness that goes with a large unearned income. On box no. 5, an Arab in full robes. On box no. 6, a not-unattractive actress who was clearly resting with, Jean-Pierre suspected, the occupier of box no. 5; and on box no. 7, an elderly, straight-backed, aristocratic Frenchman.

'A large black coffee,' Harvey drawled to the slim waiter in his smart brown jacket.

Monte Carlo does not allow hard liquor to be sold at the tables or girls to serve the customers. The Casino's business is gambling, not booze or women, in direct contrast to Las Vegas. Harvey had enjoyed Vegas when he was younger, but the older he became the more he appreciated the sophistication of the French. He had grown to prefer the formal atmosphere and decorum of the Casino. Although at the no. 3 table only he and Jean-Pierre were in dinner-jackets, it was frowned upon to be dressed in any way that might be described as casual.

A moment later, piping hot coffee in a large golden cup arrived at Harvey's side. Jean-Pierre eyed it nervously while Harvey placed 100 francs on the table next to Jean-Pierre's 3 franc chip, the minimum stake allowed. The dealer, a tall young man not more than thirty who was proud of the fact that he could deal a hundred hands in an hour, slipped the cards out of the shoe. A king for Jean-Pierre, a four for Harvey, a five for the young man on Harvey's left and a six for the dealer. Jean-Pierre's second card was a seven. He stuck. Harvey drew a ten and also stuck. The young man on Harvey's left also drew a ten and asked the dealer to twist again. It was an eight—bust.

Harvey despised amateurs in any field and even fools know you don't twist if you have twelve or more when the dealer's card face up is a three, four, five or six. He grimaced slightly. The dealer dealt himself a ten and a six. Harvey and Jean-Pierre were winners. Jean-Pierre ignored the fate of the other players.

The next round was unwinnable. Jean-Pierre stuck at eighteen, two nines which he did not split as the dealer had an ace. Harvey stuck on eighteen, an eight and a jack, and the young man on the left bust again. The bank drew a queen—'Black Jack'—and took the table.

The next hand gave Jean-Pierre a three, Harvey a seven and the young man a ten. The dealer drew himself a seven. Jean-Pierre drew an eight and doubled his stake to 6 francs and then drew a ten—vingt-et-un. Jean-Pierre did not blink. He realized he was playing well and that he must not draw attention to it, but let Harvey take it for granted. In fact Harvey hadn't even noticed him: his attention was riveted on the young man on his left who seemed anxious to make a gift to the management on every hand. The dealer continued, giving Harvey a ten and the young man an eight, leaving them both no choice but to stick. The dealer drew a ten, giving himself seventeen. He paid Jean-Pierre, left Harvey's stake and paid the young man.

There were no more cards left in the shoe. The dealer made a great show of re-shuffling the four packs and invited Harvey to cut the cards before replacing them in the shoe. They slipped out again: a ten for Jean-Pierre, a five for Harvey, a six for the young man and a four for the dealer. Jean-Pierre drew an eight. The cards were running well. Harvey drew a ten and stuck at fifteen. The young man drew a ten and asked for another card. Harvey could not believe his eyes and whistled through the gap in his front teeth. Sure enough, the next card was a king. The young man was bust. The dealer dealt himself a jack and then an eight, making twenty-two, but the young man did not take the lesson in. Harvey stared at him. When would he discover that, of the fifty-two cards in a pack, no less than sixteen have a face value of ten?

Harvey's distraction gave Jean-Pierre the opportunity he had been waiting for. He slipped his hand into his pocket and took the prostigmin tablet Adrian had given him into the palm of his left hand. He sneezed, pulling his handkerchief from his breast pocket in a well-rehearsed gesture with his right hand. At the same time, he quickly and unobtrusively dropped the tablet into Harvey's coffee. It would, Adrian had assured him, be an hour before it took effect. To begin with Harvey would just feel a little sick, then it would get rapidly worse until the pain was too much to bear and he would finally collapse in absolute agony.

Jean-Pierre turned to the bar, gripped his right hand fist three times and then placed it in his pocket. Stephen left immediately and warned Adrian and James from the steps of the Casino that the prostigmin tablet was in Metcalfe's drink. It was now Adrian's turn for a test under pressure. He rang the hospital and asked the sister on duty to have the theatre in preparation. Then he rang the nursing agency and asked that the nurse he had booked should be waiting in the hospital reception in exactly ninety minutes' time. He then sat nervously waiting for another call from the Casino.

Stephen returned to the bar. Harvey had started to feel ill, but was loath to leave. Despite the growing pain, he found greed the greater incentive. He drank the rest of his coffee and ordered another one, hoping it would clear his head. The coffee did not help and Harvey began to feel steadily worse. An ace and a king followed by a seven, a four and a ten, and then two queens helped him to stay at the table. Jean-Pierre forced himself not to look at his watch. The dealer gave Jean-Pierre a seven, Harvey another ace and the young man a two. Quite suddenly, almost exactly on the hour, Harvey could not bear it any longer. He tried to stand up and leave the table.

'Le jeu a commencé, Monsieur,' the dealer said formally.

'Go fuck yourself,' said Harvey and collapsed to the ground, gripping his stomach in agony. Jean-Pierre sat motionless while the croupiers and gamblers milled around helplessly. Stephen fought his way through the circle which had gathered round Harvey.

'Stand back, please. I am a doctor.'

The crowd moved back quickly at the relief of having a professional man available.

'What is it, Doctor?' gasped Harvey, who now felt the end of the world was about to come.

'I don't know yet,' replied Stephen. Adrian had warned him that from collapse to passing out might be as short a time as ten minutes so he set to work fast. He loosened Harvey's tie and took his pulse. He then undid his shirt and started feeling his abdomen.

'Have you a pain in the stomach?'

'Yes,' groaned Harvey.

'Did it come on suddenly?'

'Yes.'

'Can you try and describe the quality of the pain? Is it stabbing, burning or gripping?'

'Gripping.'

'Where is it most painful?'

Harvey touched the right side of his stomach. Stephen pressed down the tip of the ninth rib, making Harvey bellow with pain.

'Ah,' said Stephen, 'a positive Murphy's sign. You probably have an acutely inflamed gall-bladder and I am afraid that may mean gall-stones.' He continued to palpate the massive abdomen gently. 'It looks as if a stone has come out of your gall-bladder and is passing down the tube to your intestine and it's the squeezing of that tube that is giving you the dreadful pain. Your gall-bladder and the stone

129

must be removed at once. I can only hope there is someone at the hospital who can perform an emergency operation.'

Jean-Pierre came in bang on cue:

'Doctor Wiley Barker is staying at my hotel.'

'Wiley Barker, the American surgeon?'

'Yes, yes,' said Jean-Pierre. 'The chap who's been taking care of Nixon.'

'My God, what a piece of luck. We couldn't have anyone better, but he's very expensive.'

'I don't give a damn about the expense,' wailed Harvey.

'Well, it might be as high as $50,000.'

'I don't care if it's $100,000,' screamed Harvey. At that moment he would have been willing to part with his entire fortune.

'Right,' said Stephen. 'You, sir,' looking at Jean-Pierre, 'ring for an ambulance and then contact Doctor Barker and ask if he can get to the hospital immediately. Tell him it's an emergency. This gentleman requires a surgeon of the highest qualifications.'

'You're damn right I do,' said Harvey as he passed out.

Jean-Pierre left the Casino and called over his transmitter:

'Action stations! Action stations!'

Adrian left the Hôtel de Paris and took a taxi. He would have given $100,000 to change places with the driver, but the car was moving relentlessly towards the hospital. It was too late to turn back now.

James smashed the ambulance into first gear and rushed to the Casino, siren blaring. He was luckier than Adrian. With so much to concentrate on he didn't have time to worry.

Eleven minutes and forty-one seconds later he arrived, leapt out of the driver's seat and opened the back door, gathered the stretcher and rushed up the Casino steps in his long white coat. Jean-Pierre was standing expectantly on the top step. No words passed between them as he guided James quickly through the Salon des Amériques where Stephen was bending over Harvey. The stretcher was placed on the floor. It took all three of them to put the 227 lb. of Harvey Metcalfe on to the canvas. Stephen and James picked him up and took him quickly through to the ambulance, followed by Jean-Pierre.

'Where are you going with my employer?' demanded a voice. Startled, the three of them turned round. It was Harvey's chauffeur Mellor standing by the white Rolls Royce. After a moment's hesitation, Jean-Pierre took over.

130

'Mr Metcalfe has collapsed and has to go to hospital for an emergency operation. You must return to the yacht immediately, inform the staff to have his cabin ready and await instructions.'

The chauffeur touched his cap and ran to the Rolls Royce. James leapt behind the wheel, while Stephen and Jean-Pierre joined Harvey in the back of the vehicle.

'Hell, that was close. Well done, Jean-Pierre. I was speechless,' admitted Stephen.

'It was nothing,' said Jean-Pierre, sweat pouring down his face.

The ambulance shot off like a scalded cat. Stephen and Jean-Pierre both replaced their jackets with the long white laboratory coats left on the seat and Stephen placed the stethoscope round his neck.

'It looks as if he's dead,' said Jean-Pierre.

'Adrian says he isn't,' said Stephen.

'How can he tell four miles away?'

'I don't know. We'll just have to take his word for it.'

James screeched to a halt outside the entrance to the hospital. Stephen and Jean-Pierre hurried their patient through to the operating theatre. James returned the ambulance to the car park and quickly joined the others in the theatre.

Adrian, scrubbed up and gowned, was there to meet them and while they were strapping Harvey Metcalfe to the operating table in the small room next to the theatre, he spoke for the first time:

'All of you, change your clothes. And Jean-Pierre, you scrub up as instructed.'

All three of them changed and Jean-Pierre started to wash immediately—a long, laborious process which Adrian had firmly taught him must never be cut short. Post-operative septicaemia formed no part of his plans. Jean-Pierre appeared from the scrubbing-up room ready for action.

'Now, relax. We have done this nine times already. Just carry on exactly as if we were still at St Thomas's.'

Stephen moved behind the mobile Boyles machine. For four weeks he had been training as an anaesthetist: he had rendered James and a faintly protesting Jean-Pierre unconscious twice each in practice runs at St Thomas's. Now was his chance to exercise his new powers over Harvey Metcalfe.

Adrian removed a syringe from a plastic packet and injected 250 mg. of thiopentone into Harvey's arm. The patient sank back into a deep sleep. Jean-Pierre and James quickly and efficiently undressed Harvey and then covered him in a sheet. Stephen placed the mask from the Boyles machine over Metcalfe's nose. The two flow-meters on the back of the machine showed 5 litres nitrous oxide and 3 litres of oxygen.

'Take his pulse,' said Adrian.

Stephen placed a finger in front of the ear just above the lobe to check the pre-auricular pulse. It was 70.

'Wheel him through into the theatre,' instructed Adrian.

James pushed the operating trolley into the next room until it was just under the operating lights. Stephen trundled the Boyles machine along behind them.

The operating theatre was windowless and coldly sterile. Gleaming white tiles covered every wall from floor to ceiling, and it contained only the equipment needed for one operation. Jean-Pierre had covered Harvey with a sterile green sheet, leaving only his head and left arm exposed. One trolley of sterile instruments, drapes and towels had been carefully laid out by the theatre nurse, and stood covered with a sterile sheet. Adrian hung a bottle of intravenous fluid from a standard near the head of the table and taped the end of the tubing to Harvey's left arm to complete the preparation. Stephen sat at the head of the table with the Boyles machine and adjusted the face-mask over Harvey's mouth and nose. Only one of the three massive operating lights hanging directly over Harvey had been turned on, causing a spot-light effect on the protruding bulge of the abdomen.

Eight eyes stared down on their victim. Adrian continued:

'I shall give exactly the same instructions as I did in all our rehearsals, so just concentrate. First, I shall clean the abdomen with a skin preparation of iodine.'

Adrian had all the instruments ready on the side of the table next to Harvey's feet. James lifted the sheet and folded it back over Harvey's legs, then he carefully removed the sterile sheet covering the trolley of instruments and poured iodine into one of the small basins. Adrian picked up a swab in a pair of forceps and dipped it in the iodine solution. With a swift action up and down over the abdomen, he cleaned about 1 sq. ft of Harvey's massive body. He threw the swab into a bin and repeated the action with a fresh one. Next he placed a sterile towel below Harvey's chin, covering his chest, and another one over his hips and thighs. A third one was placed lengthways along the left-hand side of his body and a further one along the right-hand side, leaving a 9 in. square of flabby belly exposed. He put a towel clip on each corner to secure them and then placed the laparotomy drapes over the prepared site. He was now ready.

'Scalpel.'

Jean-Pierre placed what he would have called a knife firmly in Adrian's outstretched palm. James's apprehensive eyes met Jean-Pierre's across the operating table, and Stephen concentrated on Harvey's breathing as Adrian made a 10 cm. paramedian incision, reaching about 3 cm. into the fat. Adrian had rarely seen a larger stomach and thought he could probably have gone as far as 8 cm. without reaching the muscle. Blood started flowing everywhere, which Adrian stopped with diathermy. No sooner had he finished the incision and staunched the flow of blood than he began to stitch up the patient's wound with a 3/0 interrupted plain catgut for ten stitches.

'That will dissolve within a week,' he explained.

He then closed the skin with a 2/0 interrupted plain silk using an atraumatic needle. Then he cleaned the wound, removing the patches of blood that still remained. Finally, he placed a medium self-adhesive wound dressing over his handiwork.

James removed the drapes and sterile towels and placed them in the bin while Adrian and Jean-Pierre put Metcalfe into a hospital gown and carefully packed his clothes in a grey plastic bag.

'He's coming round,' said Stephen.

Adrian took another syringe and injected 10 mg. of diazepan.

'That will keep him asleep for at least 30 minutes,' he said, 'and, in any case, he'll be ga-ga for about three hours and he won't remember much of what has happened. James, get the ambulance immediately and bring it round to the front of the hospital.'

James left the theatre and changed back into his clothes, a procedure which he could now perform in 90 seconds. He disappeared to the car park.

'Now, you two, get changed, and then place Harvey very carefully in the ambulance and you, Jean-Pierre, wait in the back with him. Stephen, you carry out your next job.'

Stephen and Jean-Pierre changed quickly, donned their long white coats again, and wheeled the slumbering Harvey Metcalfe gently to the ambulance. Stephen ran to the public telephone by the hospital entrance, checked a piece of paper in his top pocket and dialled.

'Hello, *Nice-Matin*? My name's Terry Robards of the *New York Times*. I'm here on holiday, and I have a great little story for you . . .'

Adrian returned to the operating theatre and wheeled the trolley of instruments he had used to the sterilizing room, and left them there to be dealt with by the hospital theatre staff in the morning. He picked up the plastic bag which contained Harvey's clothes and, going through to the changing room, quickly removed his operating gown, cap and mask and put on his own clothes. He went in search of the theatre sister, and smiled charmingly at her.

'All finished, ma soeur. I have left the instruments by the sterilizer. Please thank M. Bartise for me once again.'

'Oui Monsieur. Notre plaisir. Je suis heureuse d'être à même de vous aider. Votre infirmière de l'Auxiliaire Medical est arrivée.' A few moments later, Adrian arrived at the ambulance, accompanied by the agency nurse. He helped her into the back.

'Drive very slowly and carefully to the harbour.'

James nodded and set off at funeral pace.

'Nurse Faubert.'

'Yes, Docteur Barker.' Her hands were tucked primly under her blue cape, and her French accent was enchanting. Adrian thought Harvey would not find her ministrations unwelcome.

'My patient has just had an operation for the removal of a gall-stone and will need plenty of rest.'

With that Adrian took out of his pocket a gall-stone the size of an orange with a hospital tag on it which read 'Harvey Metcalfe'. Adrian had in fact acquired the huge stone from St Thomas's Hospital, the original owner being a 6 ft 6 in. West Indian bus conductor on the no. 14 route. Stephen and Jean-Pierre stared at it in disbelief. The nurse checked her new charge's pulse and respiration.

'Were I your patient, Nurse Faubert,' said Jean-Pierre, 'I should take good care never to recover.'

By the time they arrived at the yacht Adrian had briefed the nurse on diet and rest, and told her that he would be round to see his patient at 11 a.m. the next day. They left him sleeping soundly in his large cabin, stewards and staff clucking attentively.

James drove the other three back to the hospital, deposited the ambulance in the car park and the keys with reception. The four of them headed back to the hotel by separate routes. Adrian was the last to arrive at room 217, just after 3.30 a.m. He fell into an armchair.

'Will you allow me a whisky, Stephen?'

'Yes, of course.'

'Good God, he meant it,' said Adrian, and downed a large Johnnie Walker before handing the bottle to Jean-Pierre.

'He will be all right?' said James.

'You sound quite concerned for him. Yes, he can have his ten stitches out in a week's time and all he'll have is a nasty scar to brag about to his friends. I must get to bed. I have to see him at 11 a.m. tomorrow and the confrontation may well be harder than the operation. You were all great tonight. My God, am I glad we had those sessions at St Thomas's. If you are ever out of work and I need a croupier, a driver and an anaesthetist, I will ring for you.'

The others left and Adrian collapsed on his bed, exhausted. He fell into a deep sleep and woke just after 8 a.m. to discover he was still fully dressed. That had not happened to him since his days as a young houseman, when he had been on night duty after a fourteen-hour day without a break. Adrian had a long, soothing bath in very hot water. He dressed and put on a new shirt and suit, ready for his face-to-face meeting with Harvey Metcalfe. His newly acquired moustache and rimless glasses and the success of the operation made him feel a little like the famous surgeon he was impersonating.

The other three all appeared during the next hour to wish him luck and elected to wait in room 217 for his return. Stephen booked them all out of the hotel and arranged the flight to London for late that afternoon. Adrian left, again taking the staircase rather than the lift. Once outside the hotel, he walked a little way before hailing a taxi to take him to the harbour.

It was not hard to find the *Messenger Boy*. She was a gleaming, newly painted 100-footer lying at the east end of the harbour. She sported a massive Panamanian flag on her stern mast, which Adrian assumed must be for tax purposes. He ascended the gangplank and was met by Nurse Faubert.

'Bonjour, Docteur Barker.'

'Good morning, Nurse. How is Mr Metcalfe?'

'He has had a very peaceful night and is having a light breakfast and making a few telephone calls. Would you like to see him now?'

'Yes, please.'

Adrian entered the magnificent cabin and faced the man he had spent eight weeks plotting and planning against. He was talking into the telephone:

'Yes, I'm fine, dear. But it was an A1 emergency at the time all right. Don't worry, I'll live,' and he put the telephone down. 'Doctor Barker, I have just spoken to my wife in Massachusetts and told her that I owe you my life. Even at 5 a.m. she seemed pleased. I understand that I had private surgery, a private ambulance and that you saved my life. Or that's what it says in *Nice-Matin*.'

There was the old picture of Harvey in Bermuda shorts on the deck of the *Messenger Boy*, familiar to Adrian from his dossier. The headline read 'Millionnaire s'évanouit au Casino' over 'La Vie d'un Millionnaire Américain a été Sauvé par une Opération Urgente Dramatique!' Stephen would be pleased.

'Tell me, Doctor,' said Harvey with relish, 'was I really in danger?'

'Well, you were on the critical list, and the consequences might have been serious if we hadn't got this out of you.' Adrian removed the inscribed gall-stone from his pocket with a flourish.

Harvey's eyes grew as large as saucers.

'Gee, have I really been walking round with that inside me all this time? Isn't that something? I can't thank you enough. If I ever can do anything for you, don't hesitate to call on me.' He offered Adrian a grape. 'Look, you're going to see me through this thing, aren't you? I don't think the nurse fully appreciates the gravity of my case.'

Adrian thought fast.

'I'm afraid I can't do that, Mr Metcalfe. My holiday finishes today. I have to get back to California. Nothing urgent: just a few elective surgeries and a rather heavy lecture schedule.' He shrugged deprecatingly. 'Nothing very earth-shattering about it, but it helps me keep up a way of life I have grown accustomed to.'

Harvey sat bolt upright, tenderly holding his stomach.

'Now you listen to me, Doctor Barker. I don't give a damn about a few hernias. I'm a sick man and I need you here. I'll make it worth your while to stay, don't you worry. I never grudge the money where my health is concerned, and what's more I'll make the cheque cash. The last thing I want Uncle Sam to know is how much I'm worth.'

Adrian coughed delicately, wondering how American doctors approached the ticklish subject of fees with their patients.

'It would cost you a lot of money if I'm not to be out of pocket by staying. Say $80,000.'

Harvey didn't blink.

'Sure. You're the best. That's not a lot of money to be alive.'

'Very well. I'll get back to my hotel and see if I can rearrange my schedule for you.'

Adrian retreated from the sick-room and the white Rolls Royce took him back to the hotel. In room 217 they sat staring at Adrian.

'Stephen, for Christ's sake, the man's a raving hypochondriac. He wants me to stay on here for his convalescence.'

He recounted his conversation with Harvey Metcalfe verbatim.

'We hadn't planned for this. What the hell shall we do?'

Stephen looked up coolly:

'You'll stay here and play ball. Why not give him value for money —at his own expense, of course. Go on, get on the blower and tell him you'll be round to hold his hand every day at 11 a.m. We'll just have to go back without you. And keep the hotel bill down, won't you.'

Adrian picked up the telephone . . .

Three young men left the Hôtel de Paris after a long lunch in room 217, returned to Nice Airport in a taxi and caught BA flight 012 at 16.10 to London Heathrow. They were once again in separate seats. One sentence remained on Stephen's mind from Adrian's reported conversation with Harvey Metcalfe.

'If ever I can do anything for you, don't hesitate to call on me at any time.'

Adrian visited his patient once a day, borne in the white Corniche with white-walled tyres and a chauffeur in a white uniform. Only Harvey could be quite so brash, he thought. On the third day, Nurse Faubert asked for a private word with him.

'My patient,' she said plaintively, 'is making improper advances when I change his dressing.'

Adrian allowed Dr Wiley Barker the liberty of an unprofessional remark.

'Can't say I altogether blame him. Still, be firm, Nurse. I'm sure you must have encountered that sort of thing before.'

'Naturellement, but never from a patient only three days after

137

major surgery. His constitution, it must be formidable.'

'I tell you what, let's catheterize him for a couple of days. That'll cramp his style. Look, it must be pretty boring for you cooped up here all day. Why don't you come and have a spot of supper with me after Mr Metcalfe has gone to sleep tonight?'

'I should love to, Docteur. Where shall I meet you?'

'Room 217, Hôtel de Paris,' said Adrian unblushingly. '9 p.m.'

'I'll look forward to it, Docteur.'

'A little more Chablis, Angeline?'

'No more, thank you, Wiley. That was a memorable meal. I think, maybe, you have not yet had everything you want?'

She got up, lit two cigarettes and put one in his mouth. Then she moved away, her long skirt swinging slightly from the hips. She wore no bra under her pink shirt. She exhaled smokily and watched him.

Adrian thought of the blameless Dr Barker in Australia, of his wife and children in Newbury, and the rest of the Team in London. Then he put them out of his mind.

'Will you complain to Mr Metcalfe if I make improper advances to you?'

'From you, Wiley,' she smiled, 'they will not be improper.'

Harvey made a talkative recovery, and Adrian removed the stitches gravely on the sixth day.

'That seems to have healed very cleanly, Mr Metcalfe. Take it easy, and you should be back to normal by the middle of next week.'

'Great. I have to get over to England right away for Ascot week. You know, my horse Rosalie is favourite this year. I suppose you can't join me as my guest? What if I had a relapse?'

Adrian suppressed a smile.

'Don't worry. You're getting along fine. Sorry I can't stay to see how you do at Ascot.'

'So am I, Doc. Thanks again, anyway. I've never met a surgeon like you before.'

And you're not likely to again, thought Adrian, his American accent beginning to fray at the edges. He bid his adieus to Harvey with relief and to Angeline with regret, and sent the chauffeur back from the hotel with a copper-plate bill:

Dr Wiley Franklin Barker
presents his Compliments to
Mr Harvey Metcalfe
and begs to inform him that the bill for
professional services rendered is
$80,000
in respect of surgery and post-operative treatment.

The chauffeur was back within the hour with a cash cheque for $80,000. Adrian bore it back to London in triumph.

Two down and two to go.

THIRTEEN

The following day, Friday, Stephen sat on Adrian's examination couch in Harley Street and addressed his troops.

'The Monte Carlo operation was totally successful in every way, thanks to Adrian keeping his cool. The expenses were fairly high, though. The hospital and hotel bills totalled $11,351 and we received $80,000. Therefore, we have had $527,560 returned to us, and expenses so far have come to $22,530. So Mr Metcalfe still owes us $494,970. Does everyone agree with that?'

There was a general murmur of approval. Their confidence in Stephen's arithmetic was unbounded, although in fact, like all algebraists, he found working with figures tedious.

'Incidentally, Adrian, however did you manage to spend $73.50 on dinner on Wednesday night? What did you have, caviar and champagne?'

'Something a little out of the ordinary,' said Adrian. 'It seemed to be called for at the time.'

'I would bet more than I laid out in Monte Carlo that I know who answered that call,' said Jean-Pierre, taking his wallet out of his pocket. 'Here you are, Stephen, 219 francs—my winnings from the Casino on Wednesday night. If you had left me there in peace, we needn't have bothered with Adrian's butchery. I could have won it all back on my own. I think the least I deserve is Nurse Faubert's telephone number.'

Jean-Pierre's remarks went straight over Stephen's head.

'Well done, Jean-Pierre, it will come off expenses. At today's exchange rate, your 219 francs,' he paused for a moment and tapped out on his calculator, 'is $46.76. That brings expenses down to $22,483.24.

'Now, my plans for Ascot are simple. James has acquired two badges for the Members' Enclosure at a cost of £8. We know that Harvey Metcalfe also has a badge, as all owners do, so as long as we get our timing right and make it appear natural, he should once again fall into our trap. James will control the walkie-talkie, watching the movements of Metcalfe from start to finish. Adrian will wait by the entrance of the Members' Enclosure and follow him in. Jean-Pierre will send the telegram from London at 1 p.m., so Harvey ought to receive it during lunch in his private box. That part of the plan is simple. It's when we lure him to Oxford we all have to be at our best. I must confess it would be a pleasant change if Ascot were to work first time.'

Stephen grinned widely.

'That would give us extra time to go over the Oxford plan again and again. Any questions?'

'You don't need us for part (a) of the Oxford plan, only (b)?' asked Adrian.

'That's correct, I can manage part (a) on my own. In fact, it will be better if you all remain in London on that night. Our next priority must be to think up some ideas for James or he might, heaven preserve us, think up something for himself. I am very concerned about this,' continued Stephen, 'for once Harvey returns to America we will have to deal with him on his own territory. To date he has always been at the venue of our choosing and James could stick out like a sore thumb in Boston, even though he is the best actor of the four of us. In Harvey's own words, "It's a whole different ball game".'

James sighed lugubriously and studied the Axminster carpet.

'Poor old James—don't worry, you drove that ambulance like a trooper,' said Adrian.

'Perhaps you could learn to fly a plane and then we could hijack him,' suggested Jean-Pierre.

Miss Meikle did not approve of the laughter coming from Dr Tryner's room and she was glad to see the strange trio leave. When she had closed the door on them she returned to Adrian's room.

'Will you take patients now, Dr Tryner?'

'Yes, if I must, Miss Meikle.'

Miss Meikle pursed her lips. Whatever had come over him? It must be those dreadful types he had started mixing with lately. He had become so unreliable.

'Mrs Wentworth-Brewster—Dr Tryner will see you now.'

Stephen returned for a few days' rest to Magdalen College. He had started the entire exercise eight weeks before and two of the Team had succeeded far beyond his expectations. He was conscious that he must crown their efforts with something that would live on in the legends of Oxford long after his departure.

Jean-Pierre returned to work in his gallery in Bond Street. Sending a telegram was not going to overtax him, although part (b) of Stephen's Oxford plan kept him nightly in front of the mirror rehearsing his role.

James took Anne down to Stratford-upon-Avon for the weekend. The Royal Shakespeare Company obliged with a sparkling performance of *Much Ado about Nothing* and afterwards, walking along the banks of the Avon, James proposed. Only the royal swans could have heard her reply. The diamond ring James had noticed in the window of Cartier while he had been waiting for Harvey Metcalfe to join Jean-Pierre in the gallery, looked even more beautiful on her slim finger. James's happiness seemed complete. If only he could come up with a plan and shock them all, then he would want for nothing. He discussed it with Anne again that night, considering new ideas and old ones, but getting nowhere.

FOURTEEN

On Monday morning James drove Anne back to London and changed into the most debonair of his suits. Anne was returning to work, despite James's suggestion that she should accompany him to Ascot. She felt the others would not approve of her presence and would realize that James had confided in her.

Although James had not told her the details of the Monte Carlo exercise, Anne knew every step of what was to take place at Ascot and she could tell that James was nervous. Still, she would be seeing him that night and would know the worst by then. James looked lost. Anne was very thankful that Stephen, Adrian and Jean-Pierre held the baton most of the time in the relay team—but an idea was forming in her mind that just might work out for him.

Stephen rose early and admired his grey hair in the mirror. The result had been expensively achieved the previous day in the hairdressing salon of Debenhams. He dressed carefully, putting on his one respectable grey suit and blue checked tie. These were brought out for all special occasions, ranging from a talk to students at Sussex to dinner with the American Ambassador. The suit was no longer fashionable and it sagged slightly at elbow and knee, but by Stephen's standards it was sheer elegance. He travelled from Oxford to Ascot by train, while Adrian came from Newbury by car. They met up with James at the Belvedere Arms, almost a mile from the course, at 11 a.m.

Stephen immediately telephoned Jean-Pierre to confirm that all three of them had arrived and asked for the telegram to be read over to him.

'That's right, Jean-Pierre. Now travel to Heathrow and send it at exactly 1 p.m.'

'Good luck, Stephen. Grind the bastard into the dust.'

Stephen returned to the others and confirmed that Jean-Pierre had the London end under control.

'Off you go, James, and let us know immediately Harvey arrives.'

James downed a bottle of Carlsberg and departed. The problem was he kept bumping into friends and he could hardly explain what he was up to.

Harvey arrived at the members' car park just after midday, his white Rolls Royce shining like a Persil advertisement. It was being stared at by all the racegoers with English disdain which Harvey mistook for admiration. He led his party to his box. His newly tailored suit had taxed the ingenuity of Bernard Weatherill to the utmost. A red carnation in his buttonhole and a hat to cover his bald head left him nearly unrecognizable to James, who followed the little group at a careful distance until he saw Harvey enter a door marked 'Mr Harvey Metcalfe and Guests'.

'He's in his private box,' said James.

'Where are you?' inquired Adrian.

'Directly below him on the ground level by a course bookmaker called Sam O'Flaherty.'

'Now don't be rude about the Irish, James,' said Adrian. 'We'll be with you in a few minutes.'

James stared up at the vast white stand which accommodated 10,000 spectators with comfort and gave them an excellent view of the course. He was finding it hard to concentrate on the job in hand as once again he had to avoid relations and friends. First was the Earl of Halifax and then the frightful girl he had so unwisely agreed to take to Queen Charlotte's Ball in the spring. What was the creature's name? Ah yes. The Hon. Selina Wallop. How appropriate. She was wearing a mini-skirt a good four years out of fashion and a hat which didn't look as if it could ever come into fashion. James jammed his trilby over his ears, looked the other way and passed the time chatting to Sam O'Flaherty about the King George VI and Queen Elizabeth Stakes at 3.20. O'Flaherty quoted the latest odds on the favourite.

'Rosalie at 6:4, owned by that American, Harvey Metcalfe, and ridden by Pat Eddery.'

Eddery was heading towards being the youngest-ever champion jockey and Harvey always liked winners.

Stephen and Adrian joined James at the side of Sam O'Flaherty's bag. His tick-tack man was standing on an upturned orange box beside him and swinging his arms like a semaphore sailor aboard a sinking ship.

'What do you fancy, gentlemen?' Sam asked the three of them.

James ignored Stephen's slight frown of disapproval.

'£5 each way on Rosalie,' he said, and handed over a crisp £10 note, receiving in return a little green card with the series number and 'Sam O'Flaherty' stamped right across the middle.

'I suppose, James, this is an integral part of your as yet undisclosed plan,' said Stephen. 'What I should like to know is, if it works, how much do we stand to make?'

'£9.10 after tax if Rosalie wins,' chipped in Sam O'Flaherty, his large cigar bobbing up and down in his mouth as he spoke.

'A great contribution towards $1 million, James. Well, we're off to the Members' Enclosure. Let us know the moment Harvey leaves his box. My guess is that it will be about 1.45 when he will come to look at the runners and riders for the 2 o'clock, so that gives us a clear hour.'

The waiter opened another bottle of Krug 1964 champagne and began pouring it for Harvey's guests, three bankers, two economists, a couple of ship-owners and an influential City journalist.

Harvey always liked his guests to be famous and influential, and so he invited people who would find it almost impossible to refuse him because of the business he might put their way. He was pleased with the company he had assembled for his big day. Senior among them was Sir Howard Dodd, the ageing chairman of the merchant bank that bore his name, but referred to his great-grandfather. Sir Howard was 6 ft 2 in. and as straight as a ramrod. He looked more like a Grenadier Guard than a respectable banker. The only thing he had in common with Harvey was the amount of hair, or lack of hair, on his balding head. His young assistant, Jamie Clark, accompanied him. Just over thirty and extremely bright, he was there to be sure his chairman did not commit the bank to anything he would later regret. Clark, although he had a sneaking admiration for Harvey, did not think him the sort of customer the bank should do business with. Nevertheless, he was far from averse to a day at the races.

The two economists, Mr Colin Emson and Dr Michael Hogan from the Hudson Institute, were there to brief Harvey on the parlous state of the British economy. They could not have been more different. Emson was a totally self-made man who had left school at fifteen and educated himself. Using his social contacts, he had built up a company that specialized in taxation which had been very successful, thanks to the British Government's putting through a new Finance Act every few weeks. Emson was 6 ft, solid and genial, game to help the party along whether Harvey lost or won. Hogan, in contrast, had

145

been to all the right places—Winchester, Trinity College, Oxford and Wharton Business School in Pennsylvania. A spell with McKinsey, the management consultants, in London had made him one of the best-informed economists in Europe. Those who observed his slim, sinewy body would not have been surprised to learn that he had been an international squash player. Dark-haired, with brown eyes that rarely left Harvey, he found it hard not to show contempt, but this was the fifth invitation to Ascot and it seemed Harvey would not take no for an answer.

The Kundas brothers, second-generation Greeks who loved racing almost as much as ships, could hardly be told apart, with their black hair, swarthy skins and heavy eyebrows. It was difficult to guess how old they were, and nobody knew how much they were worth. They probably did not know themselves. Harvey's final guest, Nick Lloyd of the *News of the World*, had come along to pick up any dirt he could about his host. He had come near to exposing Metcalfe in the mid-'sixties, but another scandal had kept less juicy stories off the front page for several weeks, and by then Harvey had escaped. Lloyd, hunched over the inevitable triple gin with a faint suggestion of tonic, watched the motley bunch with interest.

'Telegram for you, sir.'

Harvey ripped it open. He was never neat about anything.

'It's from my daughter Rosalie. That's cute of her to remember, but damn it all, I named the horse after her.'

They took their seats for lunch—cold vichyssoise, pheasant and strawberries. Harvey was even more loquacious than usual, but his guests dismissed it, knowing he was nervous about the race he had always wanted to win. He would rather be a winner of this trophy than any he could be offered in America. Harvey never could understand why he felt this way. Perhaps it was the special atmosphere of Ascot which appealed to him so strongly—a combination of lush green grass and gracious surroundings, of elegant crowds and an efficiency of organization which made Ascot the envy of the racing world.

'You must have a better chance this year than ever before, Harvey,' said the senior banker.

'Well, you know, Sir Howard, Lester Piggott is riding the Duke of Devonshire's horse, Crown Princess, and the Queen's horse, Highclere, is the joint favourite. When you have been third twice before, even favourite and not placed, you begin to wonder when one of your horses is going to make it.'

146

'Another telegram, sir.'

Once again Harvey's fat little finger ripped it open.

' "All best wishes and good luck for the King George VI and Queen Elizabeth Stakes." It's from the staff of your bank, Sir Howard. Jolly good show.'

Harvey's Polish American accent made the English expression sound slightly grotesque.

'More champagne, everybody.'

Another telegram arrived.

'At this rate, Harvey, you will need a special room at the Post Office.' They all laughed at Sir Howard's feeble joke. Once again Harvey read it out loud:

' "Regret unable to join you Ascot. Heading soonest California. Grateful look out for Professor Rodney Porter, Oxford Nobel Prize Winner. Don't let English bookies stitch you up. Wiley B., Heathrow Airport." It's from Wiley Barker. He's the guy who did stitch me up in Monte Carlo. He saved my life. He took out a gall-stone the size of that bread roll you're eating, Dr Hogan. Now how the hell am I supposed to find this Professor Porter.' Harvey turned to the head waiter. 'Get my chauffeur.'

A few seconds later the smartly clad Guy Salmon flunkey appeared.

'There's a Professor Rodney Porter of Oxford here today. Go find him.'

'What does he look like, sir?'

'How the hell do I know,' said Harvey. 'Like a professor.'

The chauffeur regretfully abandoned his plans for an afternoon at the railings and departed.

Harvey's guests were enjoying the strawberries, the champagne and the string of telegrams that were arriving.

'You know if you win, the cup will be presented by the Queen,' said Nick Lloyd.

'You bet. It will be the crowning moment of my life to win the King George and Elizabeth Stakes and meet Her Majesty The Queen. If Rosalie wins, I will suggest my daughter marries Prince Charles—they're about the same age.'

'I don't think even you will be able to fix that, Harvey.'

'What will you do with the odd £81,000 prize money, Mr Metcalfe?' asked Jamie Clark.

'Give it to some charity,' said Harvey, pleased with the impression the remark made on his guests.

'Very generous, Harvey. Typical of your reputation.' Nick Lloyd gave Michael Hogan a knowing look. Even if the others didn't they both knew what was typical of his reputation.

The chauffeur returned to report that there was no trace of a solitary professor anywhere in the champagne bar, balcony luncheon room or the paddock buffet, and he'd been unable to gain access to the Members' Enclosure.

'Naturally not,' said Harvey in a rather pompous manner. 'I shall have to find him myself. Drink up and enjoy yourselves.'

Harvey rose and walked to the door with the chauffeur. Once he was out of earshot of his guests, he said: 'Get your ass out of here and don't give me any crap about not being able to find him.'

The chauffeur bolted. Harvey turned to his guests and smiled.

'I'm going to look at the runners and riders for the 2 o'clock.'

'He's leaving the box now,' said James.

'What's that you're saying?' asked an authoritative voice he recognized. 'Are you talking to yourself, James?'

James stared at the noble lord 6 ft 1 in. and still able to stand his full height, an M.C. and a D.S.O. in the First World War. Although the lines on his face suggested that he had passed the age at which the Maker had fulfilled his contract, he still exuded enthusiastic energy.

'Oh hell. No, sir, I was just . . . em . . . coughing.'

'What do you fancy in the King George VI and Queen Elizabeth Stakes?' inquired the nobleman.

'Well, I have put £5 each way on Rosalie, sir.'

'He seems to have cut himself off,' said Stephen.

'Well, buzz him again,' said Adrian.

'What's that noise, James? Have you got a hearing-aid or something?'

'No, sir. It's . . . it's . . . it's a transistor radio.'

'Those things ought to be banned. Bloody invasion of one's privacy.'

'Absolutely right, sir.'

'What's he playing at, Stephen?'

'I don't know—I think something must have happened.'

'Oh my God, it's Harvey heading straight for us. You go into the Members' Enclosure, Stephen, and I'll follow you. Take a deep

148

breath and relax. He hasn't seen us.'

Harvey marched up to the official blocking the entrance to the Members' Enclosure.

'I'm Harvey Metcalfe, the owner of Rosalie and this is my badge.'

The official let Harvey through. Thirty years ago, he thought, they would not have let him in if he'd owned every horse in the race. Then racing at Ascot was only held on four days a year, jolly, social occasions. Now it was twenty-four days a year and big business. Times had changed. Adrian followed closely, showing his pass without speaking to the official.

A photographer broke away from stalking outrageous hats, for which Ascot has such a reputation, to take a picture of Harvey just in case Rosalie won the King George VI Stakes. As soon as his bulb flashed he rushed over to the other entrance. Linda Lovelace, the star of *Deep Throat*, the film running to packed houses in New York but banned in England, was trying to enter the Members' Enclosure. She was not succeeding, despite having been introduced to a well-known London banker, Richard Szpiro, just as he was entering the Enclosure. She wore a top hat and morning suit with nothing under the top coat. No one was going to bother with Harvey while she was around. When she was quite certain that every photographer had taken a picture of her attempting to enter the Enclosure she left, swearing at the top of her voice, her publicity stunt completed.

Harvey returned to studying the horses as Stephen moved up to within a few feet of him.

'Here we go again,' said Adrian to himself and went smartly over to Stephen and, standing directly between the two of them, shook Stephen's hand warmly and declared in a voice intended to carry:

'How are you, Professor Porter? I didn't know you were interested in racing.'

'I'm not really, but I have just been to a seminar in London and thought it a good opportunity to see how . . .'

'Professor Porter,' cried Harvey. 'I am honoured to make your acquaintance. Sir, my name is Harvey Metcalfe from Boston, Massachusetts. My good friend, Dr Wiley Barker, who saved my life, told me you would be here today and I am going to make sure you have a wonderful afternoon.'

Adrian slipped away. He could not believe how easy it had been. The telegram had worked like a charm.

'Her Majesty The Queen; His Royal Highness The Duke of

Edinburgh; Her Royal Highness Queen Elizabeth The Queen Mother; and Her Royal Highness The Princess Anne are now entering the Royal Box.'

The massed bands of the Brigade of Guards struck up the National Anthem:

'God Save The Queen.'

The crowd of 25,000 rose and sang loyally out of tune.

'We should have someone like that in America,' said Harvey to Stephen, 'to take the place of Richard Nixon, then we would not have any of our problems.'

Stephen thought his fellow American was being just a little unfair. Richard Nixon was almost a saint by Harvey Metcalfe's standards.

'Come and join me in my box, Professor, and meet my other guests. The damned box cost me £750, we may as well fill it. Have you had some lunch?'

'Yes, I had an excellent lunch,' Stephen lied—something else Harvey had taught him. He had stood by the Members' Enclosure for an hour, nervous and pensive, unable even to manage a sandwich, and by now he was starving.

'Well, come and enjoy my champagne,' roared Harvey.

On an empty stomach, thought Stephen.

'Thank you, Mr Metcalfe. I am a little lost. This is my first Royal Ascot.'

'This isn't Royal Ascot, Professor. It's the last day of Ascot Week, but the Royal Family always comes to see the King George and Elizabeth Stakes so everybody dresses up.'

'I see,' said Stephen timidly, pleased with his deliberate error.

Harvey collared his find and took him back to the box.

'Everybody, I want you to meet my distinguished friend, Rodney Porter. He's a Nobel Prize Winner, you know. By the way, what's your subject, Rod?'

'Biochemistry.'

Stephen was getting the measure of Harvey. As long as he played it straight, the bankers and shippers, and even the journalist, were not going to realize that he was not the cleverest thing since Einstein. He relaxed a little and even found time to fill himself with smoked salmon sandwiches when the others were not looking.

Lester Piggott won the 2 o'clock on Olympic Casino and the 2.30 on Roussalka, achieving his 3000th win. Harvey was getting steadily more nervous. He talked incessantly without making much sense. He had sat through the 2.30 without showing any interest in the result and consumed more and more champagne. At 2.50 he called for them all to join him in the Members' Enclosure to look at his famous filly. Stephen, like the others, trailed behind him in a little pseudo-royal entourage.

Adrian and James watched the procession from a distance.

'He's too far in to back out now,' said Adrian.

'He looks happy enough to me,' replied James. 'Let's make ourselves scarce. We can only get under his feet now.'

They headed into the champagne bar where a considerable number of red-faced men looked as if they spent more time there than they did watching the racing.

'Isn't she beautiful, Professor? Almost as beautiful as my daughter. If she doesn't win today I am never going to make it.'

Harvey left his little crowd to have a word with Pat Eddery, the jockey, to wish him luck. Peter Walwyn, the trainer, was giving final instructions before the jockey mounted and left the Enclosure. The ten horses were paraded in front of the stand before the race, a custom at Ascot that is only carried out for the King George VI and Queen Elizabeth Stakes. The gold, purple and scarlet colours of Her Majesty the Queen's horse Highclere led the procession, followed by Crown Princess, who was giving her jockey a little trouble. Directly behind her came Rosalie who was very relaxed and looked fresh and ready to go. Buoy and Dankaro came behind Rosalie, with the outsiders Messipatania, Ropey and Minnow bringing up the rear. The crowd rose to cheer the horses and Harvey beamed with as much pride as if he owned every horse in the face.

'. . . and I have with me today the distinguished American owner, Harvey Metcalfe,' said Julian Wilson into the BBC TV outside-broadcast camera. 'I'm going to ask him if he'd be kind enough to give me his views on the King George VI and Queen Elizabeth Stakes, for which he has the joint favourite, Rosalie. Welcome to England, Mr Metcalfe. How do you feel about the big race?'

'It's a thrill to be here, just to participate in the race again. Rosalie's got a great chance. Still, it's not winning that matters. It's taking part.'

Stephen flinched. Baron de Coubertin, who had first made that remark about the 1896 Olympics, must have turned in his grave.

'The latest betting shows Rosalie joint favourite with Her Majesty The Queen's horse, Highclere. How do you react to that?'

'I am just as worried about the Duke of Devonshire's Crown Princess. Lester Piggott is always hard to beat on a great occasion. He won the first two races and will be all set for this one and Crown Princess is a fine little filly.'

'Is a mile and a half a good distance for Rosalie?'

'Results this season show it's definitely her best distance.'

'What will you do with the $81,240 prize money?'

'The money is not important, it hasn't even entered my mind.'

It had certainly entered Stephen's mind.

'Thank you, Mr Metcalfe, and the best of luck. And now over to the latest news on the betting.'

Harvey moved back to his group of admirers and suggested that they return to watch the race from the balcony just outside his box.

Stephen was fascinated to be able to observe Harvey at such close quarters. He had become nervous and even more mendacious than usual under pressure—not at all the icy operator they had feared him to be. This man was human, susceptible and could be beaten.

They all leant over the rails watching the horses being put into the stalls. Crown Princess was still giving a little trouble while all the others waited. The tension was becoming unbearable.

'They're off,' boomed the loudspeaker.

Twenty-five thousand people raised glasses to their eyes and Harvey said, 'She's got a good start and she's well placed.'

He continued to give everybody a running commentary until the last mile, when he became silent. The others waited also in silence, intent on the loudspeaker.

'They're into the straight mile—Minnow leads the field round the bend—with Buoy and Dankaro, looking relaxed, just tucked in behind him—followed by Crown Princess, Rosalie and Highclere . . .

'As they approach the six-furlong marker—Rosalie and Crown Princess come up on the stand side with Highclere making a bid . . .

'Five furlongs to go—Minnow still sets the pace, but is beginning to tire as Crown Princess and Buoy make up ground . . .

'Half a mile to go—Minnow still just ahead of Buoy, who has moved up into second place, perhaps making her move too early . . .

'Three furlongs from home—they are quickening up just a little— Minnow sets the pace on the rails—Buoy and Dankaro about a length behind—followed by Rosalie, Crown Princess and the Queen's filly Highclere all making ground . . .

'Inside the two-furlong marker—Highclere and Rosalie move up to challenge Buoy—Crown Princess is right out of it now . . .

'A furlong to go . . .'

The commentator's voice rose in pitch and volume.

'It's Joe Mercer riding Highclere who hits the front, just ahead of Pat Eddery on Rosalie—two hundred yards to go—they're neck and neck—one hundred yards to go—it's anybody's race and on the line it's a photo finish between the gold, purple and scarlet colours of Her Majesty the Queen and the black-and-green check colours of the American owner, Harvey Metcalfe—M. Moussac's Dankaro was third.'

Harvey stood paralysed, waiting for the result. Even Stephen felt some sympathy for him. None of Harvey's guests dared to speak for fear they would get it wrong.

'The result of The King George VI and The Queen Elizabeth Stakes.' Once again the loudspeaker boomed out and silence fell over the whole course:

'The winner is no. 5, Rosalie.'

The rest of the result was lost in the roar of the crowd and the bellow of triumph from Harvey. Pursued by his guests, he raced to the nearest lift, pressed a pound note into the lift-girl's hand and shouted, 'Get this thing moving.' Only half of his guests managed to jump in with him. Stephen was one of them. Once they reached the ground floor, the lift gates opened and Harvey came out like a thoroughbred, past the champagne bar, through the rear of the Members' Enclosure into the Winners' Enclosure, and flung his arms round the horse's neck, almost unseating the jockey. A few minutes later he triumphantly led Rosalie to the little post marked 'FIRST'. The crowd thronged around him, offering their congratulations.

The Clerk of the Course, Captain Beaumont, was briefing Harvey on the procedure that would be followed when he was presented. Lord Abergavenny, the Queen's Representative at Ascot, accompanied Her Majesty to the Winners' Enclosure.

'The winner of The King George VI and The Queen Elizabeth Stakes—Mr Harvey Metcalfe's Rosalie.'

Harvey was in a dream world—flash-bulbs popped and film cameras followed him as he walked towards the Queen. He bowed and received the trophy. The Queen, resplendent in a turquoise silk suit and matching turban that could only have been designed by Hardy Amies, said a few words, but Harvey was speechless for the first time in his life. Taking a pace backwards, he bowed again and returned to his place accompanied by loud applause.

Back in his box the champagne flowed and everybody was Harvey's friend. Stephen realized this was not the moment to try anything clever. He must bide his time and watch his quarry's reaction to these circumstances. He stayed quietly in a corner, letting the excitement subside, and observed Harvey carefully.

It took another race before Harvey was half back to normal and Stephen decided the time had come to act. He made as if to leave.

'Are you going already, Professor?'

'Yes, Mr Metcalfe. I must get some scripts marked before tomorrow morning.'

'I always admire the work you boys put in. I hope you enjoyed yourself?' Stephen avoided the famous George Bernard Shaw riposte, 'I had to, there was nothing else to enjoy.'

'Yes, thank you, Mr Metcalfe. An amazing achievement. You must be a very proud man.'

'Well, I guess so. It's been a long time coming, but it all seems worth it now . . . Rod, it's too bad you have to leave us. Can't you stay on a little longer and join my party at Claridge's tonight?'

'I should have liked that, Mr Metcalfe, but you must visit me at my college at Oxford and allow me to show you the university.'

'That's swell. I have a couple of days after Ascot and I've always wanted to see Oxford, but I never seem to have had the time.'

'It's the university Garden Party on Wednesday. Why don't you join me for dinner at my college next Tuesday evening and then we can spend the following day looking at the university and go on to the Garden Party?' He scribbled a few directions on a card.

'Fantastic. This is turning out to be the best vacation I have ever had in Europe. How are you getting back to Oxford, Professor?'

'By train.'

'No, no,' said Harvey. 'My Rolls Royce will take you. It will be back well in time for the last race.'

And before Stephen could protest, the chauffeur was called for.

'Take Professor Porter back to Oxford and then return here. Have a good trip, Professor. I'll look forward to seeing you next Tuesday at 8 p.m. Great meeting you.'

'Thank you for a wonderful day, and congratulations on your splendid victory.'

Seated in the back of the white Rolls Royce on his way to Oxford, the car which Adrian had boasted he and he alone would travel in,

Stephen relaxed and smiled to himself. Taking a small notebook from his pocket he made an entry:

'Deduct 98p from expenses, the price of a single second-class ticket from Ascot to Oxford.'

FIFTEEN

'Bradley,' said the Senior Tutor. 'You're looking a bit grey these days, dear boy. Is the office of Junior Dean proving too much for you?'

Stephen had wondered whether any of the Senior Common Room would think his hair worthy of comment. Dons are seldom surprised by anything their colleagues do.

'My father went grey at an early age, Senior Tutor, and there seems to be no way of defying heredity . . .'

'Ah well, dear boy, there is the Garden Party for you to look forward to next week.'

'Oh yes. I'd quite forgotten about that.'

Stephen returned to his rooms where the rest of the team were assembled for their next briefing.

'Wednesday is the day of the Encaenia and the Garden Party. One thing we have learnt about our millionaire friend is that even if we take him away from his own environment he continues to act as if he knows everything. But his bluff can be called as long as we remember that we know what is going to happen next and he doesn't. Just in the way he did us over Prospecta Oil, keeping one step ahead the whole time. Now, we will have a rehearsal today and tomorrow a full dress-rehearsal.'

'Time spent on reconnaissance is seldom wasted,' muttered James. It was about the only sentiment he could recall from his Army Cadet days at school.

'Haven't had to spend much time on reconnaissance for your plan, have we?' said Jean-Pierre.

Stephen ignored the interruptions.

'Now, the whole process on the day takes about seven hours for me and four hours for you, including the time spent on make-up, and we will need an extra session of tuition from James before the day.'

'How often will you need my two sons?' asked Adrian.

'Only once, on the Wednesday. Too many runs at it will make them stiff and awkward.'

'When do you think Harvey will want to return to London?' inquired Jean-Pierre.

'I rang Guy Salmon to check the Rolls and they have been instructed to have him back at Claridge's by 7 p.m., so I assume we have only until 5.30.'

'Clever,' said Adrian.

'It's awful,' said Stephen. 'I even think like him now. Right, let's run through the whole plan once again. We'll take it from the red dossier, page 16. When I leave All Souls . . .'

On Sunday and Monday they carried out full rehearsals. By the Tuesday they knew every route Harvey could take and where he would be at any given moment of the day from 9 a.m. to 5.30 p.m. Stephen had covered everything. He had little choice. They were only going to be allowed one crack at this one. Any mistakes like Monte Carlo and there would be no second chance. The dress rehearsal went to a second.

'I haven't worn clothes like this since I was six years old and going to a fancy-dress party,' said Jean-Pierre. 'We are going to be anything but inconspicuous.'

'There will be red and blue and black all round you on the day,' said Stephen. 'It's such a circus. No one will look twice, not even at you, Jean-Pierre.'

They were all nervous again, waiting for the curtain to go up. Stephen was glad they were edgy: he had no doubt that they were lost the moment they relaxed with Harvey Metcalfe.

The Team spent a quiet weekend. Stephen watched the College Dramatic Society's annual effort in the gardens, Adrian took his wife to Glyndebourne and was uncommonly attentive, Jean-Pierre read the latest art book, *Goodbye Picasso* by David Douglas Duncan, and James took Anne to Tathwell Hall, near Louth in Lincolnshire, to meet his father, the fifth earl. Even Anne was nervous that weekend.

'Harry?'

'Dr Bradley.'

'I have an American guest dining with me in my rooms tonight. His name is Harvey Metcalfe. When he arrives, will you bring him over, please.'

157

'Certainly, sir.'

'And one more thing. He seems to have mistaken me for Professor Porter of Trinity College. Don't correct the mistake, will you? Just humour him.'

'Certainly, sir.'

Harry retreated into the Porter's Lodge shaking his head sadly. Of course, all academics went dotty in the end, but Dr Bradley had been afflicted at an unusually tender age.

Harvey arrived at eight. He was always on time in England. The head porter guided him through the cloisters and up the old stone staircase to Stephen's rooms.

'Mr Metcalfe, sir.'

'How are you, Professor?'

'I'm well, Mr Metcalfe. Good of you to be so punctual.'

'Punctuality is the politeness of princes.'

'I think you will find it is the politeness of kings, and, in this instance, of Louis XVIII.' For a moment Stephen forgot that Harvey wasn't a pupil.

'I'm sure you're right, Professor.'

Stephen mixed him a large Manhattan. His guest's eyes took in the room and settled on the desk.

'Gee—what a wonderful set of photographs. You with the late President Kennedy, another with the Queen and even the Pope.'

That touch was due to Jean-Pierre, who had put Stephen in contact with a photographer who had been in jail with his artist friend David Stein. Stephen was already looking forward to burning the photographs and pretending they never existed.

'Let me give you another to add to your collection.'

Harvey pulled out of his pocket a large photograph of himself receiving the trophy for the King George VI and Queen Elizabeth Stakes from the Queen.

'I'll sign it for you, if you like.'

He scribbled an exuberant signature diagonally across the Queen.

'Thank you,' said Stephen. 'I can assure you I will treasure it as much as my other photographs, and I do appreciate you sparing the time to visit me here, Mr Metcalfe.'

'It's an honour for me to come to Oxford and this is such a lovely old college.'

Stephen really believed he meant it, and he suppressed an inclination to tell Harvey the story of the late Lord Nuffield's dinner at Magdalen. For all Nuffield's munificence to the university, the two were never on entirely easy terms. When a manservant assisted the guest's departure after a college feast, Nuffield took the proffered hat ungraciously. 'Is this mine?' he said. 'I don't know, my lord,' was the rejoinder, 'but it's the one you came with.'

Harvey was gazing a little blankly at the books on Stephen's shelves. The disparity between their subject matter, pure mathematics, and the putative Professor Porter's discipline, biochemistry, happily failed to strike him.

'Do brief me on tomorrow.'

'Surely,' said Stephen. 'Let's have dinner and I'll go through what I have planned for you and see if it meets with your approval.'

'I'm game for anything. I feel ten years younger since this trip to Europe and I'm thrilled about being at Oxford University.'

Stephen wondered if he really could stand seven hours of Harvey Metcalfe, but for another $250,000 and his reputation with the rest of the team . . .

The college servants brought in shrimp cocktail.

'My favourite,' said Harvey. 'How did you know?'

Stephen would have liked to say, 'There's nothing I don't know about you,' but he satisfied himself with, 'Just a lucky guess. Now, if we meet at 10 a.m. tomorrow we can join in with what is thought to be the most interesting day in the university calendar. It is called Encaenia.'

'What's that?'

'Well, once a year at the end of Trinity Term, which is the equivalent to the summer term in an American university, we celebrate the ending of the university year. There are several ceremonies and a big Garden Party, attended by the Chancellor and Vice-Chancellor of the university. The Chancellor is the ex-British Prime Minister, Harold Macmillan, and the Vice-Chancellor is Mr Habakkuk. I am hoping it will be possible for you to meet them both, and we should manage to cover everything in time for you to be back in London by 7 p.m.'

'How did you know I had to be back by 7 p.m.?'

'You told me at Ascot.' Stephen could lie very quickly now. He thought that if they did not get their million very soon he would end up a hardened criminal.

Harvey enjoyed his meal, which Stephen had been almost too clever about, as each course was one of Harvey's favourites. After

Harvey had drunk a good deal of after-dinner brandy (price £7.25 per bottle, thought Stephen), they strolled through the quiet Magdalen Cloisters past the Song School. The sound of the choristers rehearsing a Gabrieli mass hung gently in the air.

'Gee, I'm surprised you allow record players on that loud,' said Harvey.

Stephen escorted his guest to the Randolph Hotel, pointing out the iron cross set in Broad Street outside Balliol College, said to mark the spot on which Archbishop Cranmer had been burnt to death for heresy in 1556. Harvey forbore to say that he had never heard of the reverend gentleman.

Stephen and Harvey parted on the steps of the Randolph.

'See you in the morning, Professor. Thanks for a great evening.'

'My pleasure. I'll pick you up at 10 a.m. Goodnight.'

Stephen returned to Magdalen and immediately called Adrian.

'All's well, though I nearly went too far. The meal was altogether too carefully chosen and I even had his favourite brandy. Still, it will keep me on my toes tomorrow. One must remember to avoid overkill. See you then, Adrian. Have a good night's sleep.'

Stephen repeated the same message to Jean-Pierre and James before falling gratefully into his bed. The same time tomorrow he would be a wiser man, but would he be a richer one?

SIXTEEN

At 5 a.m. the sun rose over the Cherwell, and those few Oxonians who were about that early would have been left in no doubt why the connoisseurs consider Magdalen to be the most beautiful college at either Oxford or Cambridge. Nestling on the banks of the river, its perpendicular architecture is easy on the eye. It has educated King Edward VII, Prince Henry, Cardinal Wolsey, Edward Gibbon and Oscar Wilde. Not that such thoughts were passing through Stephen's mind as he lay awake.

He could hear his heart-beat and for the first time he knew what Adrian and Jean-Pierre had been through. It seemed a lifetime since their first meeting only three months before. He smiled to himself at the thought of how close they had been brought by the common aim of defeating Harvey Metcalfe. Stephen, like James, was beginning to have a sneaking admiration for the man, although he was now even more convinced that he could be out-manoeuvred when he was not on his own territory. For over two hours Stephen lay motionless in bed, deep in thought, and when the sun had risen from behind the tallest tree, he rose, showered, shaved and dressed slowly and deliberately, his mind concentrating on the day ahead.

He made his face up carefully to age himself by fifteen years. It took him a long time, and he wondered whether women had to struggle as long in front of the mirror to achieve the reverse effect. He put on his gown, a magnificent scarlet that proclaimed him a Doctor of Philosophy of the University of Oxford. It amused him that Oxford had to be different. Every other university abbreviated this, the ubiquitous award for research work, to Ph.D. In Oxford, it was D.Phil. He studied himself in the mirror.

'If that doesn't impress Harvey Metcalfe, nothing ever will.'

And what's more, he had the right to wear it. He sat down to read his red dossier for the last time. He had studied it so often that he practically had it by heart.

He avoided breakfast. Looking nearly fifty, he would have caused an undoubted stir amongst his colleagues, though the older dons would probably have failed to notice anything unusual in his appearance.

Stephen headed out of the college into the High unnoticed, joining the thousand other graduates all dressed like fourteenth-century archbishops. Anonymity on that day was easy. That, and the fact Harvey would be bemused by the strange traditions of the ancient university, were the two reasons why Stephen had chosen Encaenia for his battle-ground.

He arrived at the Randolph at 9.55 a.m. and informed one of the younger bell-boys that his name was Professor Porter and that he was awaiting Mr Metcalfe. The young man scurried away and returned moments later with Harvey.

'Mr Metcalfe—Professor Porter.'

'Thank you,' said Stephen. He made a note to return and tip the bell-boy. That touch had been useful, even if it was only part of his job.

'Good morning, Professor. Where do we start?'

'Well,' said Stephen. 'Encaenia starts with Lord Nathaniel Crewe's Benefaction at Jesus College, which is champagne, strawberries and cream for all the notabilities of the university. They then form a procession to the Sheldonian Theatre.'

'What happens then?'

'The most exciting event is the presentation of the Honorands for degrees.'

'The what?' said Harvey.

'The Honorands,' said Stephen. 'They are the distinguished men and women who have been chosen by the senior members of the university to be awarded honorary degrees.'

'Who's this Lord Crewe guy?'

'Ah well, that's most interesting. Lord Nathaniel Crewe was a Doctor of the university and the Bishop of Durham. He died in the seventeenth century, but he left £200 a year to the university as a Benefaction to provide the entertainment I told you about and an oration which we shall hear later. Of course, the money he left does not cover expenses nowadays with rising prices and inflation, so they have to dip into the university pocket.' Stephen rose and guided his guest out of the Randolph Hotel. 'We must leave now to secure a good position on the route from which to watch the procession.'

They strolled down the Broad and found an excellent spot just in front of the Sheldonian Theatre, the police clearing a little space for

Stephen because of his scarlet gown. A few minutes later the procession wound into sight round the corner from the Turl. The police held up all the traffic and kept the public on the pavement.

'Who are the guys in front carrying those clubs?' inquired Harvey.

'They are the University Marshal and the Bedels. They are carrying maces to safeguard the Chancellor's procession.'

'Hell, of course it's safe. This isn't Central Park, New York.'

'I agree,' said Stephen, 'but it hasn't always been safe over the past three hundred years and tradition dies hard in England.'

'And who's that behind the Bedel fellows?'

'The one wearing the black gown with gold trimmings is the Chancellor of the university, accompanied by his page. The Chancellor is the Right Honourable Harold Macmillan, who was Prime Minister of Great Britain in the late '50s and early '60s.'

'Oh yes, I remember the guy. Tried to get the British into Europe and De Gaulle wouldn't have it.'

'Well, I suppose that's one way of remembering him. Now, he's followed by the Vice-Chancellor, Mr Habakkuk, who is also the Principal of Jesus College.'

'You're losing me, Professor.'

'Well, the Chancellor is always a distinguished Englishman who was educated at Oxford, but the Vice-Chancellor is a leading member of the university itself and is usually chosen from the heads of one of the colleges.'

'Got it.'

'Now, after him, we have the University Registrar, Mr Caston, who is a fellow of Merton College. He is the senior administrator of the university, or you might look on him as the university's top civil servant. He's directly responsible to the Vice-Chancellor and Hebdomadal Council, who are the sort of cabinet for the university. Behind them we have the Senior Proctor, Mr Campbell of Worcester College, and the Junior Proctor, the Reverend Doctor Bennett of New College.'

'What is a Proctor?'

'For over 700 years men like them have been responsible for decency and discipline in the university.'

'What? Those two old men take care of 9000 rowdy youths?'

'Well, they are helped by the bulldogs,' said Stephen.

'Ah, that's better, I suppose. A couple of bites from an old English bulldog will keep anyone in order.'

'No, no,' protested Stephen, trying desperately not to laugh. 'The name bulldog is only a term for the men who help the Proctors keep order. Now, finally in the procession you can see that tiny crocodile of colour: it consists of heads of colleges who are Doctors of the university, Doctors of the university who are not heads of colleges and the heads of colleges who are not doctors of the university, in that order.'

'Listen, Rod, all doctors mean to me is money.'

'They are not that sort of doctor,' replied Stephen.

'Forget it. You beat me. I only know about making millions.'

Stephen watched Harvey's face carefully. He was drinking it in and had already become quieter.

'The long line will proceed into the Sheldonian Theatre and all the people in the procession will take their places in the hemicycle.'

'Excuse me, sir, what type of cycle is that?'

'The hemicycle is a round bank of seats, the most uncomfortable in Europe. But don't you worry. I have managed to arrange special seats for us because of your well-known interest in education at Harvard and there will be just time for us to take them ahead of the procession.'

'Well, lead the way, Rod. Do they really know what goes on in Harvard here?'

'Why yes, Mr Metcalfe. You have a reputation in university circles as a generous man interested in financing the pursuit of academic excellence.'

'Well, what do you know.'

Very little, thought Stephen.

He guided Harvey to his reserved seat in the balcony. He did not want his guest to be able to see the individual men and women too clearly. The truth of the matter was that the senior members of the university in the hemicycle were so covered from head to toe in gowns and caps and bow-ties and bands, that even their mothers would not have recognized them. The organist played his final chord while the guests settled.

'The organist,' said Stephen, 'is from my own college and is the Choragus, the leader of the chorus, and Deputy Professor of Music.'

Harvey could not take his eyes off the hemicycle and the scarlet-clad figures. He had never seen a sight like it in his life. The music stopped and the Chancellor rose to address the assembled company in vernacular Latin.

164

'Causa hujus convocationis est ut . . .'

'What the hell's he saying?'

'He's telling us why we are here,' explained Stephen. 'I will try and guide you through it.'

'Ite Bedelli,' said the Chancellor, and the great doors opened for the Bedels to go and fetch the Honorands from the Divinity School. There was a hush as they were led in by the Public Orator, Mr J. G. Griffith, and one by one he presented them to the Chancellor, enshrining the careers and achievements of each in polished and witty Latin prose.

Stephen's translation, however, followed a rather more liberal line and was embellished with suggestions that their doctorates were as much the result of financial generosity as of academic prowess.

'That's Lord Amory. They're praising him for all the work he has done in the field of education.'

'How much did he give?'

'Well, he was Chancellor of the Exchequer. And there's Lord Hailsham. He has held eight Cabinet positions, including Secretary of State for Education and finally Lord Chancellor. Both he and Lord Amory are receiving the degree of Doctor of Civil Law.'

Harvey recognized Dame Flora Robson, the actress, who was being honoured for a distinguished lifetime in the theatre and Stephen explained that she was receiving the degree of Doctor of Letters, as was the Poet Laureate, Sir John Betjeman. Each was given his scroll by the Chancellor, shaken by the hand and then shown to a seat in the front row of the hemicycle.

The final Honorand was Sir George Porter, Director of the Royal Institution and Nobel Laureate. He received his honorary degree of Doctor of Science.

'My namesake, but no relation. Oh well, nearly through,' said Stephen. 'Just a little prose from the Professor of Poetry, John Wain, about the benefactors of the university.'

Mr Wain delivered the Crewian Oration, which took him some twelve minutes, and Stephen was grateful for something so lively in a language he could understand. He was only vaguely aware of the recitations of undergraduate prize winners which concluded the proceedings.

The Chancellor of the university rose and led the procession out of the hall.

'Where are they off to now?' said Harvey.

'They are going to have lunch at All Souls, where they will be joined by other distinguished guests.'

'I would love to have gone to that,' said Harvey.

'I have arranged it,' replied Stephen.

Harvey was quite overwhelmed.

'How did you fix it, Professor?'

'The Registrar is most impressed by the interest you have shown in Harvard and I think they hope you may be able to assist Oxford in some small way, especially after your wonderful win at Ascot.'

'What a great idea.'

Stephen tried to show little interest. The time had not yet come to move in for the kill. The truth was that the Registrar had never heard of Harvey Metcalfe, and Stephen, because it was his last term at Oxford, had been put on the list of invitations by a friend who was a Fellow of All Souls.

They walked over to All Souls, just across the road from the Sheldonian Theatre. Stephen attempted, without much success, to explain the nature of All Souls to Harvey. Indeed, many Oxford people themselves find the college something of an enigma. Its corporate name, the College of All Souls of the Faithful Departed of Oxford, resonantly commemorates the victors of Agincourt. It was intended that masses should for ever be said there for the repose of their souls. Its modern role is unique in academic life. All Souls is a society of graduates distinguished either by promise or achievement, mostly academic, from home and abroad, with a sprinkling of men who have made their mark in other fields. The college has no under-graduates, admits no female Fellows, and generally appears to the outside world to do much as it pleases with its massive financial and intellectual resources.

Stephen and Harvey took their places among the hundred or more guests at the long tables in the noble Codrington Library. Stephen spent the entire time ensuring that Harvey was kept occupied and was not too obvious. He was thankfully aware that on such occasions people never remembered whom they met or what they said, and he happily introduced Harvey to everyone around as a distinguished American philanthropist. He was fortunately some way from the Vice-Chancellor, the Registrar and the Secretary of the University Chest.

Harvey was quite overcome by the new experience and enjoyed listening to the distinguished men around him—something that had rarely happened to him before. When the meal was over and the guests had risen, Stephen drew a deep breath and played one of his riskier cards. He deliberately took Harvey up to the Chancellor.

'Chancellor,' he said to Harold Macmillan.

'Yes, young man.'

'May I introduce Mr Harvey Metcalfe from Boston. Mr Metcalfe, as you will know, Chancellor, is a great benefactor of Harvard.'

'Yes, of course. Capital, capital. What brings you to England, Mr Metcalfe?'

Harvey was nearly speechless.

'Well, sir, I mean Chancellor, I came to see my horse Rosalie run in the King George and Elizabeth Stakes.'

Stephen was now standing behind Harvey and made signs to the Chancellor that Harvey's horse had won the race. Harold Macmillan, as game as ever and never one to miss a trick, replied:

'Well, you must have been very pleased with the result, Mr Metcalfe.'

Harvey turned as red as a beetroot.

'Well, sir, I guess I was lucky.'

'You don't look to me the type of man who depends on luck.'

Stephen took his career firmly in both hands.

'I am trying to interest Mr Metcalfe in some of the research we are doing at Oxford, Chancellor.'

'What a good idea.' No one knew better than Harold Macmillan, after seven years of leading a political party, about flattery on such occasions. 'Keep in touch, young man. Boston was it, Mr Metcalfe? Do give my regards to the Kennedys.'

Macmillan swept off, resplendent in his academic dress. Harvey stood dumbfounded.

'What a great man. What an occasion. I feel I'm part of history. I just wish I deserved to be here.'

Stephen had completed his task and was determined to get out before any mistakes could be made. He knew Harold Macmillan would shake hands with and talk to over a thousand people by the time the day was over and his chances of remembering Harvey were minimal. In any case, it would not much matter if he did. Harvey was, after all, a genuine benefactor of Harvard.

'We ought to leave before the senior people, Mr Metcalfe.'

'Of course, Rod. You're the boss.'

'I think that would be wise.'

Once they were out on the street Harvey glanced at his Jaeger le Coultre watch. It was 2.30 p.m.

'Excellent,' said Stephen, who was running three minutes late for the next rendezvous. 'We have just over an hour before the Garden Party. Let's take a look at one or two of the colleges.'

They walked slowly up past Brasenose College and Stephen explained that the name really meant brass nose and the famous original brass nose, a sanctuary knocker of the thirteenth century, was still mounted in the hall. One hundred yards further on Stephen directed Harvey to the right.

'He's turned right, Adrian, and is heading towards Lincoln College,' said James, hidden in the entrance to Jesus College.

'Fine,' said Adrian and turned to his two sons. They stood awkwardly, aged seven and nine, in unfamiliar Eton suits, ready to play their part as pages—not that they could understand what Daddy was up to.

'Are you ready?'

'Yes, Daddy.'

Stephen continued slowly towards Lincoln and when they were a few paces away Adrian appeared from the main entrance of the college in the official dress of the Vice-Chancellor, bands, collar, white tie and all. He looked fifteen years older and as much like Mr Habakkuk as possible. Perhaps not quite so bald, thought Stephen.

'Would you like to meet the Vice-Chancellor?' asked Stephen.

'That would be something,' said Harvey.

'Good afternoon, Vice-Chancellor, may I introduce Mr Harvey Metcalfe.'

Adrian doffed his academic cap and bowed. He spoke before Stephen could continue:

'Not the benefactor of Harvard University?'

Harvey blushed and looked at the two little boys who were holding the Vice-Chancellor's train. Adrian continued:

'This is a pleasure, Mr Metcalfe. I do hope you are enjoying your visit to Oxford. Mind you, it's not everybody who's shown around by a Nobel Laureate.'

'I have enjoyed it immensely, Vice-Chancellor, and I'd like to feel I could help this university in some way.'

'Well, that's excellent news.'

'Look, gentlemen, I'm staying here at the Randolph Hotel. It would be my great pleasure to have tea with you all later this afternoon.'

Adrian and Stephen were thrown for a moment. Surely the man realized that on the day of Encaenia the Vice-Chancellor did not have a moment free to attend tea parties.

Adrian recovered first.

'I'm afraid that is impossible. One has so many responsibilities on a day like this, you understand. Perhaps you could join me in my rooms at the Clarendon Building which will give us the chance for a private discussion?'

Stephen immediately followed suit:

'Excellent. Will 4.30 p.m. be convenient for you, Vice-Chancellor?'

Adrian tried not to look as if he wanted to run a mile. They had only been standing there for about two minutes, but it seemed to him a lifetime. He had not objected to being a journalist, or an American surgeon, but he genuinely hated being a Vice-Chancellor. Surely someone would appear at any moment and recognize him for the fraud he was. Thank God most of the undergraduates had gone home the week before.

Stephen thought of Jean-Pierre and of James, the finest string to their dramatic bow, now loitering uselessly in fancy dress behind the tea tent at the Garden Party in the grounds of Trinity College.

'Perhaps it would be wise, Vice-Chancellor, if we were to ask the Registrar and the Secretary of the University Chest to join us?'

'First class idea, Professor. I will ask them to be there. It isn't every day we have a distinguished philanthropist to visit us. I must take my leave of you now, sir, and go to my Garden Party. Nice to have made your acquaintance, Mr Metcalfe, and I look forward to seeing you again at 4.30 p.m.'

They shook hands warmly, and Stephen guided Harvey towards Exeter College while Adrian darted back into the little room in Lincoln that had been arranged for him. He sank into a seat.

'Are you all right, Daddy?' asked his elder son, William.

'Yes, I'm fine. Let's go and have some ice-cream and Coca-Cola.'

Both boys were transformed—ice-cream and Coca-Cola were much more important than helping with that silly gown.

Adrian slipped off all the paraphernalia—the gown, hood, bow-tie and bands—and placed them in a suitcase. He returned to the street just in time to watch the real Vice-Chancellor, Mr Habakkuk, leave

Jesus College on the opposite side of the road, obviously making his way towards the Garden Party. Adrian glanced at his watch. If they had run five minutes late the whole plan would have struck disaster.

Meanwhile, Stephen had gone full circle and was heading towards Shepherd & Woodward, the tailor's shop which supplies academic dress for the university. He was preoccupied with the thought of getting a message through to James. Stephen and Harvey came to a halt in front of the shop window.

'What magnificent robes.'

'That's the gown of a Doctor of Letters. Would you like to try it on and see how you look?'

'That would be great. But would they allow it?' said Harvey.

'I'm sure they will have no objection.'

They entered the shop, Stephen still in his full academic dress as a Doctor of Philosophy.

'My friend would like to see the gown of a Doctor of Letters.'

'Certainly, sir,' said the assistant, who was not going to argue with a Fellow of the university.

He vanished to the back of the shop and returned with a magnificent red gown with grey facing and a black, floppy velvet cap. Stephen plunged on, brazen-faced.

'Why don't you try it on, Mr Metcalfe? Let's see what you would look like as an academic.'

The assistant looked somewhat surprised. He wished Mr Venables would return from his lunch break.

'Would you like to come through to the fitting-room, sir?'

Harvey disappeared. Stephen slipped out on to the road.

'James, can you hear me? Oh hell, for God's sake answer, James.'

'Cool down, old fellow. I'm having a deuce of a time putting on this ridiculous gown, and in any case, our rendezvous isn't for seventeen minutes.'

'Cancel it.'

'Cancel it?'

'Yes, and tell Jean-Pierre as well. Both of you report to Adrian on the speaker and meet as quickly as possible. He will brief you on the new plans.'

'New plans. Is everything all right, Stephen?'

'Yes, better than I could have hoped for.'

Stephen clicked off his speaker and rushed back into the tailor's shop.

Harvey was just coming out of the cubicle dressed as a Doctor of Letters; a more grotesque sight Stephen had not seen for many years.

'You look magnificent.'

'What do they cost?'

'About £100, I think.'

'No, no. How much would I have to give . . .?'

'I have no idea. You would have to discuss that with the Vice-Chancellor after the Garden Party.'

After a long look at himself in the mirror, Harvey returned to the dressing-room while Stephen thanked the assistant, asking him to wrap up the gown and cap and send them to the Clarendon building to be left with the porter in the name of Sir John Betjeman. He paid cash. The assistant looked even more bewildered.

'Yes, sir.'

He was not sure what to do, except pray for Mr Venables's arrival. His prayers were answered some ten minutes later, but by then Stephen and Harvey were well on the way to Trinity College for the Garden Party.

'Mr Venables, I have just been asked to send the D.Litt. dress to Sir John Betjeman at the Clarendon Building.'

'Strange. We kitted him out for this morning's ceremony weeks ago. I wonder why he wants another outfit.'

'He paid cash.'

'Well, send it round to the Clarendon, but be sure it's in his name.'

Stephen and Harvey arrived at Trinity College shortly after 3.30 p.m. The elegant green lawns, the croquet hoops removed, were already crowded with over a thousand people. The members of the university wore an odd hybrid dress—best lounge suits or silk dresses topped with their gowns, hoods and caps. Cups of tea and crates of straw-berries and cucumber sandwiches were disappearing with alacrity.

'What a swell party this is,' said Harvey, unintentionally mimicking Frank Sinatra. 'You certainly do things in style here, Professor.'

'Yes, the Garden Party is always rather fun. It's the main social event of the university year, which is just ending, of course. Half the senior members here will be snatching an afternoon off from reading examination scripts. Exams for the final-year undergraduates have only just come to an end.'

Stephen staked out the Vice-Chancellor, the Registrar and the Secretary of the University Chest with a firm eye, and led Harvey well clear of them, introducing him to as many of the older members of the university as possible, hoping they would not find the encounter too memorable. They spent just over three-quarters of an hour moving from person to person. Stephen felt rather like an aide-de-camp to an incompetent dignitary whose mouth must be kept shut for fear of a diplomatic incident if he opens it. Despite Stephen's anxious approach, Harvey was clearly having the time of his life.

'Adrian, Adrian, can you hear me?'

'Yes, James.'

'Where are you?'

'I'm in the Eastgate Restaurant: come and join me here with Jean-Pierre.'

'Fine. We will be there in five minutes. No, make it ten. With my disguise, I'd better go slowly.'

Adrian rose. The children had finished their treat and he took them out of the Eastgate to a waiting car and instructed the driver, who had been hired especially for the day, to return them to Newbury. They had played their part and could now only be in the way.

'Aren't you coming, Dad?' demanded Jamie.

'No, I'll be home later tonight. Tell your mother to expect me about 7 p.m.'

Adrian returned to the Eastgate to find Jean-Pierre and James hobbling towards him.

'Why the change of plan?' asked Jean-Pierre. 'It's taken me over an hour to get dressed and ready.'

'Never mind. You're still in the right gear. We had a stroke of luck. I chatted up Harvey in the street and the cocky bastard invited me to tea with him at the Randolph Hotel. I said that was impossible, but asked him to join me at the Clarendon. Stephen suggested that you two should be invited as well.'

'Clever,' said James. 'No need for the build-up at the Garden Party.'

'Let's hope it's not too clever,' said Jean-Pierre.

'Well, at least we can do the whole damn charade behind closed doors,' said Adrian, 'which ought to make it easier. I never did like the idea of walking through the streets with him.'

'Nothing with Harvey Metcalfe is easy,' said Jean-Pierre.

'I will get myself into the Clarendon Building by 4.15 p.m.,' continued Adrian. 'You will appear a few minutes after 4.30 p.m.,

172

Jean-Pierre, and then you, James, about 4.45 p.m. But keep exactly to the same routine as if the meeting had taken place, as originally planned, at the Garden Party and we had all walked over to the Clarendon together.'

Stephen suggested to Harvey that they should return to the Clarendon Building as it would be discourteous to be late for the Vice-Chancellor.

'Sure. Jesus, it's 4.20 p.m. already.'

They left the Garden Party and walked quickly down to the Clarendon Building at the bottom of the Broad, Stephen explaining en route that the Clarendon was a sort of Oxford White House where all the officers and officials of the university had their rooms.

The Clarendon is a large, imposing eighteenth-century building which could be mistaken by a visitor for another college. A few steps lead up to an impressive hallway, and on entering you realize you are in a magnificent old building which has been converted, with as few changes as possible, for use as offices.

When they arrived the porter greeted them.

'The Vice-Chancellor is expecting us,' said Stephen.

The porter had been somewhat surprised when Adrian had arrived fifteen minutes earlier and told him Mr Habakkuk had asked him to wait in his room, and even though Adrian was in full academic dress the porter kept a beady eye on him, as he did not expect the Vice-Chancellor or any of his staff to return from the Garden Party for at least an hour. The arrival of Stephen gave him a little more confidence. He well remembered the pound he had received for his guided tour of the building.

The porter ushered Stephen and Harvey through to the Vice-Chancellor's rooms and left them.

The Vice-Chancellor's room was in no way pretentious and its beige carpet and pale walls would have made it look like the office of any middle-ranking civil servant, had it not been for the magnificent picture of a village square in France by P. Wilson Steer over the marble fireplace.

Adrian was staring out of the vast windows overlooking the Bodleian Library.

'Good afternoon, Vice-Chancellor.'

'Good afternoon again, Professor.'

'You remember Mr Metcalfe?'

173

'Yes, indeed. How nice to see you again,' Adrian shuddered. All he wanted to do was to go home. They chatted for a few minutes. Another knock and Jean-Pierre entered.

'Good afternoon, Registrar.'

'Good afternoon, Vice-Chancellor, Professor Porter.'

'May I introduce Mr Harvey Metcalfe.'

'Good afternoon, sir.'

'Registrar, would you like some . . .'

'Where's this man Metcalfe?'

The others stood stunned as a man looking ninety entered the room on sticks. He hobbled over to Adrian, winked, bowed and respectfully said:

'Good afternoon, Vice-Chancellor,' in a loud, crotchety voice.

'Good afternoon, Horsley.'

James went over to Harvey and prodded him with his sticks as if to make sure he was real.

'I have read about you, young man.'

Harvey had not been called a young man for thirty years. The others stared at James in admiration. None of them knew that in his last year at university James had played L'Avare to great acclaim. His Secretary of the Chest was simply a repeat performance—even Molière would have been pleased with it. James continued:

'You have been most generous to Harvard.'

'That's very kind of you, sir,' said Harvey respectfully.

'Don't call me sir, young man. I like the look of you—call me Horsley.'

'Yes, Horsley, sir,' blurted Harvey.

The others were only just able to keep straight faces.

'Well, Vice-Chancellor,' continued James. 'You can't have dragged me halfway across the city for my health. What's going on? Where's my sherry?'

Stephen wondered if James was going too far and looked at Harvey, but he was evidently captivated by the scene. How could a man so mature in one field be so immature in another, he thought. He was beginning to see how Westminster Bridge had been sold to at least four Americans in the past.

'Well, we were hoping to interest Mr Metcalfe in the work of the university and I felt that the Secretary of the University Chest should be present.'

'What's this Chest?' asked Harvey.

174

'Sort of treasury for the university,' replied James, his voice loud, old and very convincing. 'Why don't you read this?' and he thrust into Harvey's hand an Oxford University Calendar, which Harvey could have obtained at Blackwell's bookshop for £2, as indeed James had.

Stephen was not sure what move to make next when, happily for him, Harvey took over.

'Gentleman, I would like to say how proud I am to be here today. This has been a wonderful year for me. I was present when an American won Wimbledon. I finally bought a Van Gogh. My life was saved by a wonderful, wonderful surgeon in Monte Carlo and now here I am in Oxford surrounded by all this history. Gentlemen, it would give me a great deal of pleasure to be associated with this wonderful university.'

James took the lead again:

'What have you in mind?' he shouted at Harvey, adjusting his hearing-aid.

'Well, gentlemen, I achieved my life's ambition when I received the King George and Elizabeth trophy from your Queen, but the prize money, well, I would like to use that to make a benefaction to your university.'

'But that's over £80,000,' gasped Stephen.

'£81,240 to be exact, sir. But why don't I call it $250,000.'

Stephen, Adrian and Jean-Pierre were speechless. James was left to command the day. This was the opportunity he'd needed to show why his great-grandfather had been one of Wellington's most respected generals.

'We accept. But it would have to be anonymous,' said James. 'Only I think I can safely say that the Vice-Chancellor would inform Mr Harold Macmillan and Hebdomadal Council, but we would not want a fuss made of it. Of course, Vice-Chancellor, I would ask you to consider an honorary degree.'

Adrian was so conscious of James's obvious control that he could only say,

'How would you recommend we go about it, Horsley?'

'Cash cheque so nobody can trace it back to Mr Metcalfe. We can't have those bloody men from Cambridge chasing him for the rest of his life. Same way as we did for Sir David—no fuss.'

'I agree,' said Jean-Pierre, not having the vaguest idea what James was talking about. Neither, for that matter, had Harvey.

James nodded to Stephen, who left the Vice-Chancellor's office and made his way to the porter's room to inquire if a parcel had been left for Sir John Betjeman.

'Yes, sir. I don't know why they left it here.'

'Don't worry,' said Stephen. 'He's asked me to pick it up.'

Stephen returned to find James holding forth to Harvey on the importance of keeping his donation as a bond between himself and the university.

Stephen undid the box and took out the magnificent gown of a Doctor of Letters. Harvey turned red with embarrassment and pride as Adrian placed it on his shoulders, chanting some Latin, which was nothing more than his old school motto. The ceremony was completed in a few moments.

'Many congratulations,' bellowed James. 'What a pity we could not have organized this to be part of today's ceremony, but for such a munificent gesture as yours we could hardly wait another year.'

Brilliant, thought Stephen, Laurence Olivier could not have done better.

'That's fine by me,' said Harvey, as he sat down and made out a cheque to cash. 'You have my word that this matter will never be mentioned again.'

None of them believed that.

They stood in silence as Harvey rose and passed the cheque to James.

'No, sir.' James transfixed him with a glare.

The others looked dumbfounded.

'The Vice-Chancellor.'

'Of course. Excuse me, sir.'

'Thank you,' said Adrian, his hand trembling as he received the cheque. 'A most gracious gift, and you may be sure we shall put it to good use.'

There was a loud knock on the door. They all looked round startled except for James, who was now ready for anything. It was Harvey's chauffeur. James had always hated the pretentious white uniform with the white hat.

'Ah, the efficient Mr Mellor,' said Harvey. 'Gentlemen, I guarantee he's been watching every move we've made today.'

The four froze, but the chauffeur had clearly made no sinister deductions from his observations.

'Your car is ready, sir. You wanted to be back at Claridge's by

7 p.m. to be in good time for your dinner appointment.'

'Young man,' bellowed James.

'Yes, sir,' whimpered the chauffeur.

'Do you know you are in the presence of the Vice-Chancellor of this university?'

'No, sir. I'm very sorry, sir.'

'Take your hat off immediately.'

'Yes, sir.'

The chauffeur removed his hat and retreated to the car, swearing under his breath.

'Vice-Chancellor, I sure hate to break up our party, but as you've heard I do have an appointment . . .'

'Of course, of course, and may I once again officially thank you for your most generous donation, which will be used to benefit many deserving people. We all hope you have a safe journey back to the States and will remember us as warmly as we shall remember you.'

Harvey moved towards the door.

'I will take my leave of you now, sir,' shouted James. 'It will take me twenty minutes to get down those damned steps. You are a fine man and you have been most generous.'

'It was nothing,' said Harvey expansively.

True enough, thought James, nothing to you.

Stephen, Adrian and Jean-Pierre accompanied Harvey from the Clarendon to the waiting Rolls.

'Professor,' said Harvey, 'I didn't quite understand everything the old guy was saying.' As he spoke he shifted the weight of his heavy robes on his shoulders self-consciously.

'Well, he's very deaf and very old, but his heart's in the right place. He wanted you to know that this has to be an anonymous donation as far as the university is concerned, though, of course, the Oxford hierarchy will know the truth. If it were public knowledge all sorts of undesirables who have never done anything for education in the past would all come along wanting to buy an honorary degree.'

'Of course, of course. I understand. That's fine by me,' said Harvey. 'I want to thank you for a swell day and wish you all the luck for the future.'

He climbed into the Rolls Royce and waved enthusiastically to the three of them as they watched the car start effortlessly on its journey back to London.

Three down and one to go.

'James was brilliant,' said Jean-Pierre. 'When he first came in I didn't know who the hell it was.'

'I agree,' said Adrian. 'Let's go and rescue him—truly the hero of the day.'

They all three ran up the steps, forgetting that they looked somewhere between the ages of fifty and sixty, and rushed back into the Vice-Chancellor's room to congratulate James, who lay silent in the middle of the floor. He had passed out.

An hour later, in Magdalen, with the help of Adrian and two large whiskies, James was back to normal health.

'You were fantastic,' said Stephen, 'just at the point when I was beginning to lose my nerve.'

'You would have received an Academy Award if we could have put it on screen,' said Adrian. 'Your father will have to let you go on the stage after that performance.'

James basked in his first moment of glory for three months. He could not wait to tell Anne.

'Anne.' He quickly looked at his watch. '6.30 p.m.! Oh hell, I am meeting Anne at 8 p.m. and I must leave at once. See you all next Monday in Stephen's rooms for dinner. By then I will try to have my plan ready.'

James rushed out of the room.

'James.'

His face reappeared round the door. They all said in chorus:
'Fantastic!'

He grinned, ran down the stairs and leapt into his Alfa Romeo, which he now felt he would be able to keep, and headed towards London at top speed.

It took him 59 minutes from Oxford to the King's Road. The new motorway had made a considerable difference since the days when he was an undergraduate. Then the journey had taken anything from an hour and a half to two hours through High Wycombe or Henley.

The reason for the rush was that the meeting with Anne was most important and under no circumstances must he be late, for tonight he was due to meet her father. He was determined to make a good impression, particularly after Anne's successful weekend at Tathwell Hall. The old man had taken to her at once and never left her side.

178

They had even managed to agree on a wedding date, subject, of course, to the approval of Anne's parents.

James had a quick cold shower and removed all his make-up, losing some sixty years in the process. He had arranged to meet Anne for a drink at Les Ambassadeurs in Mayfair before dinner, and as he put on his dinner-jacket he wondered if he could make it from the King's Road to Hyde Park Corner in 12 minutes. He leapt into his car, revving it quickly through the gears, shot along to Sloane Square, through Eaton Square, up past St George's Hospital, round Hyde Park Corner into Park Lane, and arrived at 7.58 p.m.

'Good evening, my lord,' said Mr Mills, the club owner.

'Good evening. I'm dining with Miss Summerton and I have had to leave my car double-parked. Can you take care of it?' said James, dropping the keys and a pound note into the doorman's white-gloved hand.

'Delighted, my lord. Show Lord Brigsley to the private rooms.'

James followed the head porter up the red staircase and into a small Regency room where dinner had been laid for three. He could hear Anne's voice in the next room. She came through, looking even more beautiful than usual in a floating mint-green dress.

'Hello, darling. Come on through and meet Daddy.'

James followed Anne into the next room.

'Daddy, this is James. James, this is my father.'

James went red and then white, and then he felt green.

'How are you, my boy. I have heard so much about you from Rosalie that I can't wait to get acquainted.'

SEVENTEEN

'Call me Harvey,' said Anne's father.

James stood aghast and speechless. Anne jumped into the silence.

'Shall I get your usual whisky, James?'

James found his voice with difficulty.

'Thank you.'

'I want to know all about you,' continued Harvey, 'what you get up to and why I have seen so little of my daughter in the last few weeks, though I think I know the answer to that.'

James drank the whisky in one gulp and Anne quickly refilled his glass.

'You see so little of your daughter because I am modelling and I am very rarely in London.'

'I know, Rosalie . . .'

'James knows me as Anne, Daddy.'

'We christened you Rosalie. It was good enough for your mother and me and it ought to be good enough for you.'

'Daddy, whoever heard of a top European model calling herself Rosalie Metcalfe? All my friends know me as Anne Summerton.'

'What do you think, James?'

'I was beginning to think I didn't know her at all,' replied James, recovering slowly. It was obvious that Harvey did not suspect anything. He had not seen James face to face at the gallery, he did not see him at Monte Carlo or Ascot, and James had been looking ninety years of age at Oxford earlier in the day. James supposed he had got away with it. But how the hell could he tell the others at the Monday meeting that the final plan would be to outwit not Harvey Metcalfe, but his future father-in-law?

'Shall we go through for dinner?'

Harvey did not wait for a reply. He marched in to the dining-room.

'You just wait, young woman,' whispered James fiercely. 'You've got some explaining to do.'

Anne kissed him gently on the cheek.

'You are the first person who's given me the chance to beat my father at anything. Can you forgive me . . . I love you . . .'

'Come on, you two. You'll have time enough for that when you're married.'

Anne and James went through to join Harvey for dinner. James was amused by the sight of the shrimp cocktail and remembered how Stephen had regretted that touch at Harvey's Magdalen dinner.

'Well, James, I understand you and Anne have fixed the date for the wedding.'

'Yes, sir, if you approve.'

'Of course I approve. I was hoping Anne would marry Prince Charles after winning the King George and Elizabeth Stakes, but an earl will do for my only daughter.'

They both laughed, neither of them thinking it was remotely funny.

'I wish you could have come to Wimbledon this year, Rosalie. Imagine, there on Ladies' Day and the only company I have is a boring old Swiss banker.'

Anne looked at James and grinned.

The waiters cleared the table and wheeled in a trolley bearing a crown of lamb in immaculate cutlet frills, which Harvey studied with great interest.

'Still, it was kind of you to ring me at Monte Carlo, dear. I really thought I was going to die, you know. James, you wouldn't have believed it. They removed from my stomach a gall-stone the size of a baseball. Thank God it was done by one of the greatest surgeons in the world. Wiley Barker saved my life.'

Harvey promptly undid his shirt and revealed to James a 4 in. scar across his vast stomach.

'What do you think of that, James?'

'Remarkable.'

'Daddy, really. We're having dinner.'

'Stop fussing, honey. It won't be the first time James has seen a man's stomach.'

It's not the first time I have seen that one, thought James.

Harvey pushed his shirt back into his trousers and continued:

'Anyway, it was really kind of you to phone me.' He leant over and patted her hand. 'I was a good boy too. I did just what you told me and kept on that nice Doctor Barker for another week in case any complications arose. Mind you, the price these doctors . . .'

James dropped his wine glass. The claret covered the tablecloth with a red stain.

'I am so sorry.'

'You all right, James?'

'Yes, sir.'

James looked at Anne in silent outrage. Harvey was quite unperturbed.

'Bring a fresh tablecloth and some more wine for Lord Brigsley.'

The waiter poured a new glass and James decided it was his turn to have a little fun. Anne had been laughing at him for three months. Why shouldn't he tease her a little, if Harvey gave him the chance? Harvey chatted on.

'You a racing man, James?'

'Yes, sir, and I was delighted by your victory in the King George VI and Queen Elizabeth Stakes for more reasons than you realize.'

In the diversion caused by the waiters clearing the table, Anne whispered *sotto voce*,

'Don't try to be clever, darling—he's not as stupid as he sounds.'

'Well, what do you think of her?'

'I beg your pardon, sir?'

'Rosalie.'

'Magnificent. I put £5 each way on her.'

'Yes, it was a great occasion for me and I was sorry you missed it, Rosalie, because you would have met the Queen and a nice guy called Professor Porter.'

'Professor Porter?' inquired James, burying his face in his wine glass.

'Yes, Professor Porter, James. Do you know him?'

'No, sir, I can't say I know him, but didn't he win a Nobel Prize?'

'He sure did and he gave me a wonderful time at Oxford. I enjoyed myself so much that I ended up giving him a cheque for $250,000 for research of some kind, so he should be happy.'

'Daddy, you know you're not meant to tell anybody that.'

'I know, but James is family now.'

James was still not going to let Anne get away with her duplicity.

'Why can't you tell anyone else, sir?'

'Well, it's a long story, James, but it was quite an honour for me. You do understand this is highly confidential, but I was Professor Porter's guest at Encaenia. I lunched at All Souls with Mr Harry Macmillan, your dear old Prime Minister, and then I attended the Garden Party, and afterwards I had a meeting with the Vice Chancellor in his private rooms along with the Registrar and the

Secretary of the University Chest. Were you at Oxford, James?'

'Yes, sir. The House.'

'The House?' queried Harvey.

'Christ Church, sir.'

'I'll never understand Oxford.'

'No, sir.'

'You must call me Harvey. Well, we all met at the Clarendon and they stammered and stuttered and were lost for words, except for one funny old guy, who was ninety if he was a day. These people just don't know how to approach millionaires for money, so I put them out of their embarrassment and took over. They would have gone on all day about their beloved Oxford, so eventually I had to shut them up and I simply wrote out a cheque for $250,000.'

'That was very generous, Harvey.'

'I would have given them $500,000 if they'd asked. James, you look a bit pale, do you feel all right?'

'I am sorry. Yes, I'm fine. I was quite carried away with your description of Oxford.'

Anne joined in:

'Daddy, you made a promise to the Vice-Chancellor that you would keep your gift as a bond between the university and yourself, and you must promise never to tell that story again.'

'I think I shall wear the robes for the first time when I open the new library at Harvard in the fall.'

'Oh, no sir,' said James hastily, 'that wouldn't be quite the thing. You should only wear those robes in Oxford on ceremonial occasions.'

'Gee, what a shame. Still, I know what sticklers you English are for etiquette. Which reminds me, we ought to discuss your wedding. I suppose you two will want to live in England?'

'Yes, Daddy, but we will visit you every year and when you make your annual trip to Europe you must come and stay with us.'

The waiters cleared the table again and reappeared with Harvey's favourite strawberries. Anne tried to keep the conversation on domestic issues and stop her father returning to what he'd been up to during the past two months, while James spent his time trying to get him back on the subject.

'Coffee or liqueur, sir?'

'No, thank you,' said Harvey. 'Just the check. I thought we'd have a drink in my suite at Claridge's. Rosalie. I have something I want to show you both. It's a bit of a surprise.'

'I can't wait, Daddy. I love surprises. Come on, James.'

James left them and drove the Alfa Romeo to Claridge's garage so that Anne could have a few moments alone with her father. They strolled along Curzon Street, arm in arm.

'Isn't he wonderful, Daddy?'

'Yeah, great guy. Didn't seem too bright to begin with, but he cheered up as the meal went on. And fancy my little girl turning out to be a genuine English lady. Your Momma's tickled pink and I'm happy that we have patched up our quarrel.'

'Oh, I've got things back into perspective in the last few weeks. Now tell me, what is your little surprise, Daddy?'

'Wait and see, honey. It's your wedding present.'

James joined them again at the entrance to Claridge's. He could tell from Anne's look that Harvey had given him the seal of parental approval.

'Good evening, sir. Good evening, my lord.'

'Hi there, Albert. Could you fix for coffee and a bottle of Remy Martin to be sent up to my suite?'

'Immediately, sir.'

The Royal Suite is on the first floor of Claridge's—James had never seen it before. Off the small entrance room, there is the master bedroom on the right and a sitting-room on the left. Harvey took them straight to the sitting-room.

'Children, you are about to see your wedding present.'

He threw the door open in dramatic style and there on the far wall was the Van Gogh. They both stared, quite unable to speak.

'That's exactly how it left me,' said Harvey. 'Speechless.'

'Daddy,' Anne swallowed. 'A Van Gogh. But you always wanted a Van Gogh. You always dreamed of possessing such a picture, and anyway I can't possibly have anything so valuable in my house. Think of the security risk, we don't have the protection you have. We can't let you give us the pride of your collection, can we, James?'

'Absolutely not,' said James with great feeling. 'I wouldn't have a moment's peace with that on the premises.'

'Keep it in Boston, Daddy, in a setting worthy of it.'

'But I thought you would love it, Rosalie.'

'I do, I do, Daddy, I just don't want the responsibility, and in any case Mother must have the chance to enjoy it. You can always leave it to James and me if you like.'

'What a great idea, Rosalie. That way we can both enjoy it. Now I shall have to think of another wedding present. She nearly got the better of me then, James, and she hasn't done that in twenty-four years.'

'Well, I've managed it two or three times, Daddy, and I am hoping for just once more.'

Harvey ignored Anne's remark and went on talking.

'That's the King George and Elizabeth trophy,' he said, pointing to a magnificent bronze sculpture of a horse and jockey with his hoop and quartered cap studded in diamonds. 'They give a new trophy every year because of the importance of the race, so it's mine for life.'

James was thankful that the trophy at least was genuine.

The coffee and brandy arrived and they settled down to discuss the wedding in detail.

'Now, Rosalie, you must fly over to Lincoln next week and help your mother with the arrangements, otherwise she'll panic and nothing will get done. And, James, you let me know how many people you will have coming over and we'll put them up in the Statler Hilton. The wedding will be in Trinity Church, Copley Square, and we'll have a real English-style reception back in my home in Lincoln. Does all that make sense, James?'

'Sounds wonderful. You are a very well organized man, Harvey.'

'Always have been, James. Find it pays in the long run. Now, you and Rosalie must get the details sewn up before she comes over next week because I'm flying to America tomorrow.'

James and Anne spent another hour chatting about the wedding arrangements and left Harvey just before midnight.

'I'll see you first thing in the morning, Daddy.'

'Goodnight, sir.'

James shook hands and left.

'I told you he was super.'

'He's a fine young man and your mother will be very pleased.'

James said nothing in the lift on the way down because two other men stood behind them in silence, also waiting to reach the ground floor. But once they were in the Alfa Romeo he took Anne by the scruff of the neck and spanked her on her bottom so hard that she didn't know whether to laugh or cry.

'What's that for?'

'Just in case you ever forget after we're married who's the head of this household.'

'You male chauvinist pig, I was only trying to help.'

James drove at furious speed to Anne's flat.

'What about all your so-called background—"My parents live in Washington and Daddy's in the Diplomatic Corps",' James mimicked. 'Some diplomat.'

'I know, darling, but I had to think of something once I'd realized who it was.'

'What in hell's name am I going to tell the others?'

'Nothing. You invite them to the wedding, explaining that my mother is American and that's the reason we are getting married in Boston. I'd give the earth to see their faces when they finally discover who your father-in-law is. In any case, you still have a plan to think of and under no circumstances can you let them down.'

'But the circumstances have changed.'

'No, they haven't. The truth of the matter is that they have all succeeded, and you have not, so you must be sure you have a plan by the time you reach America.'

'It's obvious we wouldn't have succeeded without your help.'

'Nonsense, darling. I had nothing to do with Jean-Pierre. I just added some background colour here and there—promise you'll never spank me again?'

'Certainly I will, every time I think of that picture, but now, darling . . .'

'James, you are a sex maniac.'

'I know, darling. How do you think we Brigsleys have reared tribes of little lords for generations?'

Anne left James early the next morning to spend some time with her father and they both saw him off at the airport on the midday flight to Boston. Anne could not resist asking in the car on the way back what James had decided to tell the others. She could get no response other than:

'Wait and see, I'm not having it all changed behind my back. I am only too glad you're off to America on Monday!'

EIGHTEEN

Monday was a double hell for James. First, he had to see Anne off on the morning TWA flight for Boston, and then he spent the rest of the day preparing for the Team meeting in the evening. The other three had now completed their operations and would be waiting to hear what he had come up with. It was twice as hard now he knew that his victim was to become his father-in-law, but he accepted that Anne was right and that he could not make that an excuse. It meant that he still had to relieve Harvey of $250,000. To think he could have done it with one sentence at Oxford; that was something he could not tell the rest of the Team either.

As Oxford had been Stephen's victory, the Team dinner was at Madgalen College and James travelled out of London just after the rush hour, past the White City Stadium and on down the M40 to Oxford.

'You're always last, James,' said Stephen.

'Sorry, I have been up to my eyes . . .'

'In a good plan, I hope,' said Jean-Pierre.

James didn't answer. How well they all knew each other now, he thought. In twelve weeks James felt he had got to know more about these three men than any of the so-called friends he'd known for twenty years. For the first time he understood why his father always referred back to friendships formed during the war. He began to realize how much he was going to miss Stephen when he returned to America. Success was, in fact, going to split them up. James would have been the first to admit that he didn't want to go through the agony of another Prospecta Oil, but it had certainly had its compensations.

Stephen could never treat any occasion as a celebration, and when the servants had brought in the first course and left, he banged the table and declared that the meeting was in progress.

'Make me a promise,' said Jean-Pierre.

'What's that?' asked Stephen.

'When we have every last penny back, I can sit at the top of the table and you won't speak until you are spoken to.'

'Agreed,' said Stephen, 'but not until we do have every last penny. The position at the moment is that we have received $777,560. Expenses on this operation have totalled $5,178 making a grand total of $27,661.24. Therefore, Metcalfe still owes us $250,101.24.'

Stephen handed round a copy of the current balance sheet.

'Three sheets to be added to your own folders. Any questions?'

'Yes, why are expenses so high for this operation?' asked Adrian.

'Well, over and above the obvious things,' said Stephen, 'the truth is that the floating exchange rate of sterling against the dollar has hit us. At the beginning of this operation you could get $2.44 to the pound. This morning I could only get $2.32. I am spending in pounds but charging Metcalfe in dollars at the going rate.'

'Not going to let him off with one penny, are you?' said James.

'Not one penny. Now, before we go on I should like to place on record . . .'

'This gets more like a meeting of the House of Representatives every time,' said Jean-Pierre.

'Quiet, frog,' said Adrian.

'Listen, you Harley Street pimp.'

Uproar broke out. The college scouts, who had seen some rowdy gatherings in their time, wondered if they would be called to help before the evening was out.

'Quiet!' the sharp, senatorial voice of Stephen brought them back to order. 'I know you are in high spirits, but we still have to get $250,101.24.'

'We must not on any account forget the 24 cents, Stephen.'

'You weren't as noisy the first time you had dinner here, Jean-Pierre:

> The man that once did sell the lion's skin
> While the beast liv'd, was killed with hunting him.'

The table went silent.

'Harvey still owes the team money and it will be just as hard to acquire the last quarter as it has been the first three-quarters. Before I hand over to James, though, I would like to place on record that his performance at the Clarendon was nothing less than brilliant.'

Adrian and Jean-Pierre banged the table in appreciation and agreement.

'Now, James, we are at your command.'

Once again the room fell into silence.

'My plan is nearly complete,' began James.

The others looked disbelieving.

'But I have something to tell you, which I hope will allow me a short respite before we carry it out.'

'You're going to get married.'

'Quite right, Jean-Pierre, as usual.'

'I could tell the moment you walked in. When can we meet her, James?'

'Not until it's too late for her to change her mind, Jean-Pierre.'

Stephen consulted his diary.

'How much reprieve are you asking for?'

'Well, Anne and I are getting married on August 3rd in Boston. Anne's mother is American,' explained James, 'and although Anne lives in England, it would please her mother if she was married at home. Then there will be a honeymoon and we anticipate being back in England on August 25th. My plan for Mr Metcalfe ought to be carried out on September 13th on the closing day of the Stock Exchange account.'

'I'm sure that is acceptable, James. All agreed?'

Adrian and Jean-Pierre nodded.

James launched into his plan.

'I shall require a telex and telephone. They will be installed in my flat. Jean-Pierre will have to be in Paris at the Bourse, Stephen in Chicago on the commodity market and Adrian in London at Lloyds. I will present a full blue dossier as soon as I return from my honeymoon.'

They were all struck dumb with admiration and James paused for dramatic effect.

'Very good, James,' said Stephen. 'We wait with interest—what further instructions do you have?'

'First, Stephen, you must know the opening and closing price of gold in Johannesburg, Zürich, New York and London each day for the next month. Jean-Pierre, you must know the price of the Deutschmark, the French franc and the pound against the dollar every day over the same period, and Adrian must master a telex machine and PBX 8-line switchboard by September 2nd. You must be as good as any international operator.'

'Always get the easy job, Adrian, don't you?' said Jean-Pierre.

'You can . . .'

'Shut up, both of you,' said James.

Their faces registered surprise and respect.

'I have made notes for all of you.'

James handed two typewritten sheets to each member of the team. 'That should keep you occupied for at least a month. Finally, you are all invited to the wedding of Miss Anne Summerton to James Brigsley. I shan't bother issuing you with formal invitations at such short notice, but I have reserved seats for us on a 747 on the afternoon of August 2nd and we are all booked in at the Statler Hilton in Boston. I hope you will honour me by being ushers.'

Even James was impressed by his own efficiency. The others received the plane tickets and instructions with astonishment.

'We will meet at the airport at 3 p.m. and during the flight I shall test you on your dossier notes.'

'Yes, sir,' said Jean-Pierre.

'Your test, Jean-Pierre, will be both in French and English as you are required to converse in two languages over a trans-atlantic telephone, and to appear an expert on foreign currency exchange.'

There were no more jokes about James that evening and as he travelled back up the motorway he felt a new man. Not only had he been the star of the Oxford plan, he now had the other three on the run. He would come out on top and do his old pa yet.

NINETEEN

For a change James was the first to arrive for a meeting and the others joined him at Heathrow. He had obtained the upper hand and he was not going to lose it. Adrian arrived last, clutching an armful of newspapers.

'We're only going for two days,' said Stephen.

'I know, but I always miss the English papers, so I have to take enough for tomorrow as well.'

Jean-Pierre threw his arms up in Gallic despair.

They checked their luggage through the no. 3 terminal and boarded the British Airways 747 flight to Logan International Airport.

'It's more like a football ground,' said Adrian on his first encounter with the inside of a jumbo.

'It holds 350 people. About the size of the crowds your English clubs deserve,' said Jean-Pierre.

'Cut it out,' said James sternly, not realizing that they were both nervous passengers and were only trying to relieve the tension. Later, during take-off, they both pretended to read, but as soon as the plane reached 3,000 ft and the little red light that says 'fasten seat-belts' clicked off, they were back in top form.

The team chewed its way stolidly through a plastic dinner of cold chicken and Algerian red wine.

'I do hope, James,' said Jean-Pierre, 'that your father-in-law will do a little better.'

After the meal James allowed them to watch the film, but insisted that as soon as it was over they must prepare to be tested one by one. Adrian and Jean-Pierre moved back fifteen rows to watch *The Sting*. Stephen stayed in his seat to be grilled by James.

James handed Stephen a typewritten sheet of forty questions on the price of gold all over the world, and the market movements in the past four weeks. Stephen completed it in twenty-two minutes, and it came as no surprise to James to find that every answer was accurate:

191

Stephen had always been the backbone of the team, and it was his logical brain that had really defeated Harvey Metcalfe.

Stephen and James dozed intermittently until Adrian and Jean-Pierre returned, when they were given their forty questions. Adrian took thirty minutes over his and scored 38 out of 40. Jean-Pierre took twenty-seven minutes and scored 37.

'Stephen got 40 out of 40,' said James.

'He would,' said Jean-Pierre.

Adrian looked a little sheepish.

'And so will you by September 2nd. Understood?'

They both nodded.

'Have you seen *The Sting*?' asked Adrian.

'No,' replied Stephen. 'I rarely go to the cinema.'

'They're not in our league. One big operation and they don't even keep the money.'

'Go to sleep, Adrian.'

The meal, the film and James's quizzes had taken up most of the six-hour flight. They all nodded off in the last hour, to be woken up suddenly by:

'This is your captain speaking. We are approaching Logan International Airport and our flight schedule is running twenty minutes late. We expect to land at 7.15 in approximately ten minutes. We hope you have enjoyed your flight and will travel again with British Airways.'

Customs took a little longer than usual as they had all brought presents for the wedding and the other three did not want James to know what they had bought for him. They had considerable trouble in explaining to the customs officer why one of the two Piaget watches had inscribed on the back: 'The illicit profits from Prospecta Oil—The three who had plans.'

When they finally escaped the terminal, they found Anne waiting at the entrance with a large Cadillac to chauffeur them to the hotel.

'Now we know why it took you so long to come up with something. Congratulations, James, you are entirely excused,' said Jean-Pierre, and threw his arms round Anne as only a Frenchman could. Adrian introduced himself and kissed her gently on the cheek. Stephen shook hands with her rather formally. They bustled into the car, Jean-Pierre sitting next to Anne.

'Miss Summerton,' stuttered Stephen.

'Do call me Anne.'

'Will the reception be at the hotel?'

'No,' replied Anne, 'at my parents' house, but there will be a car to pick you up and take you there after the wedding. Your only job is to see that James gets to the church by 3.30 p.m. Other than that you have nothing to worry about. While I think of it, James, your father and mother arrived yesterday and they are staying with my parents. We thought it would not be a good idea for you to spend this evening at home because Mother is flapping about everything.'

'Anything you say, darling.'

'If you should change your mind between now and tomorrow,' said Jean-Pierre, 'I find myself available, and although I am not blessed with noble blood, there are one or two compensations we French can offer.'

Anne smiled to herself, 'You're a little late, Jean-Pierre. In any case, I don't like beards.'

'But I only . . .' began Jean-Pierre.

The others glared at him.

At the hotel they left Anne and James alone while they went to unpack.

'Do they know, darling?'

'They haven't the slightest idea,' replied James. 'They are going to get the surprise of their lives tomorrow.'

'Is your plan prepared at last?'

'Wait and see.'

'Well, I have one,' said Anne. 'When is yours scheduled for?'

'September 13th.'

'I win then—mine's for tomorrow.'

'What, you weren't meant to . . .'

'Don't worry. You just concentrate on getting married . . . to me.'

'Can't we go somewhere?'

'No, you terrible man. You can wait until tomorrow.'

'I do love you.'

'Go to bed, you silly thing. I love you too, but I must go home, otherwise nothing will be ready.'

James took the lift to the seventh floor and joined the others for coffee.

'Anyone for blackjack?' said Jean-Pierre.

'Not with you, you pirate,' said Adrian. 'You have been tutored by the biggest crook alive.'

The Team were in top form and looking forward to the wedding. They didn't depart for their separate rooms until after midnight, despite the transatlantic time dislocation. Even then, James lay awake for some time, turning the same question over in his mind:

'I wonder what she's up to.'

TWENTY

Boston in August is as beautiful a city as any in America, and the team enjoyed a large breakfast in James's room overlooking the Charles River.

'I don't think he looks up to it,' said Jean-Pierre. 'You're the captain of the Team, Stephen. I volunteer to take his place.'

'It will cost you $250,000.'

'Agreed,' said Jean-Pierre.

'You don't have $250,000,' said Stephen. 'You have $187,474.69 one quarter of what we have so far raised, so my decision is that James must be the bridegroom.'

'It's an Anglo-Saxon plot,' said Jean-Pierre, 'and when James has successfully completed his plan and we have the full amount, I shall re-open negotiations.'

They sat talking and laughing for a long time over the toast and coffee. Stephen regarded them fondly, regretting how rarely they would meet once (if, he corrected himself sternly) James's operation were accomplished. If Harvey Metcalfe had ever had a team like this on his side instead of against him, he would have been the richest man in the world, and not just in financial terms.

'You're dreaming, Stephen.'

'Yes, I'm sorry. I mustn't forget that Anne has put me in charge.'

'Here we go again,' said Jean-Pierre. 'What time shall we report, Professor?'

'One hour from now, fully dressed to inspect James and take him to the church. Jean-Pierre, you will go and buy four carnations— three red ones and one white. Adrian, you will arrange the taxi and I shall take care of James.'

Adrian and Jean-Pierre left, singing the Marseillaise lustily in two different keys. James and Stephen watched them depart.

'How are you feeling, James?'

'Great. I'm only sorry that I did not complete my plan before today.'

195

'Doesn't matter at all. September 13th will be just as good. In any case, the break will do us no harm.'

'We would never have managed it without you. You know that, don't you, Stephen. We would all be facing ruin and I wouldn't even have met Anne but for you. We all owe you so much.'

Stephen stared fixedly out of the window, unable to reply.

'Three red and one white,' said Jean-Pierre, 'as instructed, and I presume the white one is for me.'

'Pin it on James. Not behind his ear, Jean-Pierre.'

'You look fantastic, but I still haven't been able to work out what she sees in you,' said Jean-Pierre, fixing the white carnation in James's buttonhole. The four of them were ready to leave, but still had half an hour to kill before the taxi was due. Jean-Pierre opened a bottle of champagne. They toasted James's health, then the Team's health, then Her Majesty the Queen, then the President of the United States, and finally, with simulated reluctance, the President of France. Having finished the bottle, Stephen thought it wise to leave immediately and dragged the other three down to the waiting taxi.

'Keep smiling, James. We're with you.'

And they bundled him into the back.

The taxi took twenty minutes to reach Trinity Church, Copley Square, and the driver was not unhappy to be rid of the four of them.

'3.15 p.m. Anne will be very pleased with me,' said Stephen.

He escorted the bridegroom to the front pew on the right-hand side of the church, while Jean-Pierre made eyes at the prettiest of the girls. Adrian helped hand out the wedding sheets. One thousand over-dressed guests waited for the bride.

Stephen had just come to Adrian's aid on the steps of the church and Jean-Pierre had joined them, suggesting they took their seats, when the Rolls Royce arrived. They were riveted to the steps by the beauty of Anne in her Balenciaga wedding gown. Her father stepped out behind her. She took his arm and proceeded to mount the steps.

The three stood motionless, like sheep in the stare of a python.

'The bastard!'

'Who is conning who?'

'She must have known all along!'

Harvey beamed vaguely at them as he walked past with Anne on his arm.

'Good God!' thought Stephen. 'He didn't recognize any of us.'

They took their places at the back of the church, out of earshot of the vast congregation. The organist stopped playing when Anne reached the altar.

'Harvey can't know,' said Stephen.

'How do you work that out?' inquired Jean-Pierre.

'Because James would never have let us go through this unless he had passed the test himself at some earlier date.'

'Clever,' whispered Adrian.

'I require and charge you both, as ye will answer at the dreadful day of judgment when the secrets of all hearts shall be disclosed . . .'

'I should like to know some secrets now,' said Jean-Pierre. 'To start with, how long has she known?'

'James Clarence Spencer, wilt thou have this woman to thy wedded wife, to live together after God's ordinance in the Holy estate of Matrimony? Wilt thou love her, comfort her, honour and keep her in sickness and in health and, forsaking all other, keep thee only unto her, so long as ye both shall live?'

'I will.'

'Rosalie Arlene, wilt thou have this man to thy wedded husband, to live . . .'

'I think,' said Stephen, 'we can be sure that she is a fully fledged member of the Team, otherwise we would never have succeeded at Monte Carlo or Oxford.'

'. . . so long as ye both shall live?'

'I will.'

'Who giveth this woman to be married to this man?'

Harvey bustled forward and took Anne's hand and gave it to the priest.

'I, James Clarence Spencer, take thee, Rosalie Arlene, to my wedded wife . . .'

'And what's more, he didn't recognize us because he's only seen each of us once, and not as we really are,' continued Stephen.

'And thereto I plight thee my troth.'

197

'I, Rosalie Arlene, take thee, James Clarence Spencer, to my wedded husband.'

'But he must have a chance of working it out if we hang around,' said Adrian.

'Not true,' said Stephen. 'Now don't panic. Our secret has always been to catch him off his own ground.'

'But he is on his own ground,' said Jean-Pierre.

'No, he isn't. It's his daughter's wedding day and it's totally strange to him. Naturally, we avoid him at the reception, but we don't make it obvious.'

'You'll have to hold my hand,' said Adrian.

'I will,' volunteered Jean-Pierre.

'Just remember to act naturally.'

'. . . and thereto I give thee my troth.'

Anne was quiet and shy, her voice only just reaching the astonished three at the back. James's was clear and firm:

'With this ring I thee wed, with my body I thee worship, and with all my worldly goods I thee endow . . .'

'And with some of ours, too,' said Jean-Pierre.

'In the name of the Father, and of the Son and of the Holy Spirit. Amen.'

'Let us pray,' intoned the priest.

'I know what I'm going to pray,' said Adrian. 'To be delivered out of the power of our enemy and from the hands of all that hate us.'

'O Eternal God, Creator and Preserver of all mankind . . .'

'We're near the end now,' said Stephen.

'An unfortunate turn of phrase,' replied Adrian.

'Silence,' said Jean-Pierre. 'I agree with Stephen. We've got the measure of Metcalfe, just relax.'

'Those whom God hath joined together let no man put asunder.'

Jean-Pierre continued mumbling to himself, but it didn't sound like a prayer.

The blast of Handel's Wedding March from the organ brought them back to the occasion. The ceremony was over and Lord and Lady Brigsley walked down the aisle to two thousand smiling eyes. Stephen looked amused, Jean-Pierre envious, and Adrian nervous. James smiled beatifically as he passed them.

After a ten-minute photographic session on the steps of the church, the Rolls Royce carried the newly married couple back to the Metcalfes' house in Lincoln. Harvey and the Countess of Louth took the second car, and the earl and Arlene, Anne's mother, took the third. Stephen, Adrian and Jean-Pierre followed some twenty minutes later, still arguing the pros and cons of bearding the lion in his own den.

Harvey Metcalfe's Georgian house was magnificent, with an oriental garden leading down to the lake, great beds of roses and in the conservatory his pride and joy, a rare orchid collection.

'I never thought I'd see this,' said Jean-Pierre.

'Nor me,' said Adrian, 'and now that I have, I'm not too happy.'

'Now we run the gauntlet,' said Stephen. 'I suggest that we join the receiving line at well-separated intervals. I'll go first. Adrian, you come second at least twenty places behind, and Jean-Pierre, you come third at least twenty places behind Adrian, and act naturally. We're just friends of James's from England. Now, when you take your places in the queue, listen to the conversation. Try and find someone who's a close friend of Harvey's and jump immediately in front of them. When it comes to your turn to shake hands, Harvey's eyes will already be on the next person because he won't know you and will know them. That way we should escape.'

'Brilliant, Professor,' said Jean-Pierre.

The queue seemed interminably long. A thousand people shuffled past the outstretched hands of Mr and Mrs Metcalfe, the Earl and Countess of Louth, and Anne and James. Stephen eventually made it and passed with flying colours.

'So glad you could come,' said Anne.

Stephen did not reply.

'Good to see you, Stephen.'

'We all admire your plan, James.'

Stephen slipped into the main ballroom and hid behind a pillar on the far side of the room, as far as he could be from the multi-storey wedding cake in the centre.

Adrian was next and avoided looking Harvey in the eyes.

199

'How kind of you come all this way,' said Anne.

Adrian mumbled something under his breath.

'Hope you have enjoyed yourself today, Adrian?'

James was obviously having the time of his life. He'd been put through it by Anne and was relishing the Team's having to go through the same discomfiture.

'You're a bastard, James.'

'Not too loud, old fellow. My mother and father might hear you.'

Adrian slipped through to the ballroom and, after a search behind all the pillars, found Stephen.

'Did you get through all right?'

'I think so, but I don't want to see him ever again. What time is the plane back?'

'8 p.m. Now don't panic. Keep your eye out for Jean-Pierre.'

'Bloody good thing he kept his beard,' said Adrian.

Jean-Pierre shook hands with Harvey, who was already intent on the next guest as Jean-Pierre had, by shameless queue-barging, managed to secure a place in front of a Boston banker who was obviously a close friend of Harvey's.

'Good to see you, Marvin.'

Jean-Pierre had escaped. He kissed Anne on both cheeks, whispered in her ear, 'Game, set and match to James,' and went off in search of Stephen and Adrian, but forgot his original instructions when he found himself face to face with the chief bridesmaid.

'Did you enjoy the wedding?' she inquired.

'Of course. I always judge weddings by the bridesmaids, not the bride.'

She blushed with pleasure.

'This must have cost a fortune,' she continued.

'Yes, my dear, and I know whose,' said Jean-Pierre, slipping his arm round her waist.

Four arms grabbed a protesting Jean-Pierre and unceremoniously dragged him behind the pillar.

'For God's sake, Jean-Pierre. She's not a day over seventeen. We don't want to go to jail for rape of a juvenile as well as theft. Drink this and behave yourself.' Adrian thrust a glass into his hand.

The champagne flowed and even Stephen had a little too much. They were clinging to their pillar for support by the time the toast-master called for silence.

'My lords, ladies and gentlemen. Pray silence for the Viscount Brigsley, the bridegroom.'

James made an impressive speech. The actor in him took over and the Americans adored it. Even his father had a look of admiration on his face. The toast-master then introduced Harvey, who spoke long and loud. He cracked his favourite joke about marrying his daughter off to Prince Charles, at which the assembled guests roared heartily as they always will, even for the weakest joke, at a wedding, and he ended by calling the toast for the bride and groom.

When the applause had died down, and the hubbub of chatter had struck up again, Harvey took an envelope from his pocket and kissed his daughter's cheek.

'Rosalie, here is a little wedding present for you, to make up for letting me keep the Van Gogh. I know you will put it to good use.'

Harvey passed her the white envelope. Inside there was a cheque for $250,000. Anne kissed her father with genuine affection.

'Thank you, Daddy, I promise you it will be wisely used.'

She hurried in pursuit of James, whom she found besieged by a group of American matrons:

'Is it true you are related to the Queen . . .?'

'I never met a real live lord . . .'

'I do hope you will invite us over to see your castle . . .?'

'There are no castles in the King's Road.' James was more than relieved to see Anne.

'Darling, can you spare me a minute?'

James excused himself and followed Anne, but they found it almost impossible to escape the crowd.

'Look,' she said. 'Quickly.'

James took the cheque.

'Good God—$250,000!'

'You know what I'm going to do with it, don't you?'

'Yes, darling.'

Anne hunted for Stephen, Adrian and Jean-Pierre, which was not easy as they were still hidden behind a pillar in the far corner. She was eventually guided to the spot by the subdued but spirited rendering of 'Who wants to be a millionaire?' issuing from it.

'Can you lend me a pen, Stephen?'

Three pens shot out for her use.

She took the cheque from the middle of her bouquet and wrote on

201

its back, 'Rosalie Brigsley—pay Stephen Bradley'. She handed it to him.

'Yours, I believe.'

The three of them stared at the cheque. She was gone before they could even comment.

'What a girl our James has gone and married,' said Jean-Pierre.

'You're drunk, you frog,' said Adrian.

'How dare you, sir, suggest that a Frenchman could get drunk on champagne. I demand satisfaction. Choose your weapons.'

'Champagne corks.'

'Quiet,' said Stephen. 'You'll give yourselves away.'

'Well now, tell me, Professor, what is the latest financial position?'

'I'm just working it out now,' said Stephen.

'What?' said Adrian and Jean-Pierre together, but they were too happy to argue.

'He still owes us $101 and 24 cents.'

'DISGRACEFUL,' said Jean-Pierre. 'Burn the place down!'

Anne and James left to change, while Stephen, Adrian and Jean-Pierre forced down more champagne. The toast-master announced that the bride and groom would be leaving in approximately fifteen minutes and requested the guests to gather in the main hall and courtyard.

'Come on, we'll watch them go,' said Stephen. The drink had given them new confidence and they took their places near the car.

It was Stephen who heard Harvey say, 'God damn it. Do I have to do everything?' and watched him look round until his eyes fell on the trio. Stephen's legs turned to jelly as Harvey's finger beckoned him.

'Hey you, weren't you an usher?'

'Yes, sir.'

'My only daughter is going to leave at any moment and there are no flowers. God knows what's happened to them, but there are no flowers. Grab a car. There's a florist half a mile down the road, but hurry.'

'Yes, sir.'

'Say, don't I know you from somewhere?'

'Yes, sir—I mean, no, sir, I'll go and get the flowers.'

Stephen turned and fled. Adrian and Jean-Pierre, who had been watching horrified, thinking that Harvey had at last rumbled them, ran after him. When he reached the back of the house, Stephen stopped by the most beautiful bed of roses. Adrian and Jean-Pierre

202

shot straight past him, stopped, turned round and staggered back.

'What the hell are you up to—picking flowers for your own funeral?'

'It's Metcalfe. Somebody forgot the flowers for Anne and I have five minutes to get them, so start picking.'

'Mes enfants, do you see what I see?'

The others looked up. Jean-Pierre was staring rapturously at the conservatory.

Stephen rushed back to the front of the house, the prize orchids in his arms, followed by Adrian and Jean-Pierre. He was just in time to pass them over to Harvey before James and Anne came out of the house.

'Magnificent. They're my favourite flowers. How much were they?'

'$100,' replied Stephen, without thinking.

Harvey handed over two $50 bills. Stephen retreated, sweating, to join Adrian and Jean-Pierre.

James and Anne fought their way through the crowd. No man in the gathering could take his eyes off her.

'Oh Daddy, orchids, how beautiful.' Anne kissed Harvey. 'You have made this the most wonderful day in my life . . .'

The Rolls Royce moved slowly away from the large crowd, down the drive on its way to the airport for James and Anne to catch the flight to San Francisco, the first stop on the way to Hawaii. As the car glided round the house, Anne stared at the empty conservatory and then at the flowers in her arms. James did not notice. He was thinking of other things.

'Do you think they will ever forgive me?'

'I'm sure they will find a way, darling, but let me into a secret. Did you really have a plan?'

'I knew you would eventually ask and . . .'

The car purred effortlessly along the highway and only the chauffeur heard his reply.

Stephen, Adrian and Jean-Pierre watched the guests dispersing, most of them saying their goodbyes to the Metcalfes.

'Don't let's risk it,' said Adrian.

'Agreed,' said Stephen.

'Let's invite him out to dinner,' said Jean-Pierre.

The other two grabbed him and threw him into a taxi.

'What's that you have under your morning coat, Jean-Pierre?'

203

'Two bottles of Krug dix-neuf cent soixant-quatre. It seemed such a shame to leave them there on their own. I thought they would get lonely.'

Stephen instructed the driver to take them back to the hotel.

'What a wedding. Do you think James ever had a plan?' asked Adrian.

'I don't know, but if he has it will only have to bring in $1.24.'

'We should have retrieved the money he made from his win on Rosalie at Ascot,' mused Jean-Pierre.

After packing and signing out of the hotel, they took another taxi to Logan International Airport and, with considerable help from the British Airways staff, managed to board the plane.

'Damn,' said Stephen. 'I wish we hadn't left without the $1.24.'

TWENTY-ONE

Once on board, they drank the champagne Jean-Pierre had captured at the wedding. Even Stephen seemed content, although he did occasionally revert to the missing $1.24.

'How much do you imagine this champagne cost?' teased Jean-Pierre.

'That's not the point. Not a penny more, not a penny less.'

Jean-Pierre decided he would never understand academics.

'Don't worry, Stephen. I have every confidence that James's plan will bring in $1.24.'

Stephen would have laughed, but it gave him a headache.

'To think that girl knew everything.'

On arrival at Heathrow, they had little trouble in clearing customs. The purpose of the trip had never been to bring back gifts. Adrian made a detour to W. H. Smiths and picked up *The Times* and the *Evening Standard*. Jean-Pierre bargained with a taxi-driver about the fare to central London.

'We're not some bloody Americans who don't know the fare or the route and can be easily fleeced,' he was saying, not yet sober.

The taxi-driver grumbled to himself as he nosed his black Austin towards the motorway. It was not going to be his day.

Adrian read the papers happily. He was one of those rare people who can read in a moving car. Stephen and Jean-Pierre satisfied themselves with watching the passing traffic.

'Jesus Christ.'

Stephen and Jean-Pierre were startled. They had rarely heard Adrian swear. It seemed out of character, as indeed it was.

'God Almighty.'

This was too much for them, but before they could inquire, he began to read out loud:

' "British Petroleum announced a strike in the North Sea which is likely to produce 200,000 barrels of oil a day. It is described by their

Chairman, Sir Eric Drake, as a major find. The British Petroleum Forties Field is one mile from the so far unexplored Prospecta Oil field and rumours of a bid by B.P. have sent Prospecta Oil shares to a record high of $12.25 at the close of business".'

'Nom de Dieu,' said Jean-Pierre. 'What do we do now?'

'Oh well,' said Stephen. 'I suppose we'll have to work out how to give it all back.'